KYSERAN

MARCH OF THE MADLANDERS

JOSEPH DAVIES & NICK BROWN

Copyright © Joseph Davies & Nick Brown 2025
All rights reserved.

The rights of Joseph Davies and Nick Brown to be identified as the Authors has been asserted by him in accordance with the Copyright, Designs and Patents Act 1988.

All rights reserved. No part of this publication may be reproduced, stored in a retrieval system, or transmitted, in any form or by any means without the prior written permission of the author, not be otherwise circulated in any form of binding or cover other than that in which it is published and without similar condition being imposed on the subsequent purchaser.

All characters in this publication are fictitious and any resemblance to real persons, living or dead, is purely coincidental.

Illustrations by stellacheyne.arts

Paperback ISBN: 9798306248707

CONTENTS

PROLOGUE 1
CHAPTER 1 9
CHAPTER 2 21
CHAPTER 3 37
CHAPTER 4 53
CHAPTER 5 61
CHAPTER 6 73
CHAPTER 7 83
CHAPTER 8 95
CHAPTER 9 107
CHAPTER 10 123
CHAPTER 11 133
CHAPTER 12 149
CHAPTER 13 163
CHAPTER 14 171
CHAPTER 15 183
CHAPTER 16 193
CHAPTER 17 203
CHAPTER 18 215
CHAPTER 19 231
CHAPTER 20 245

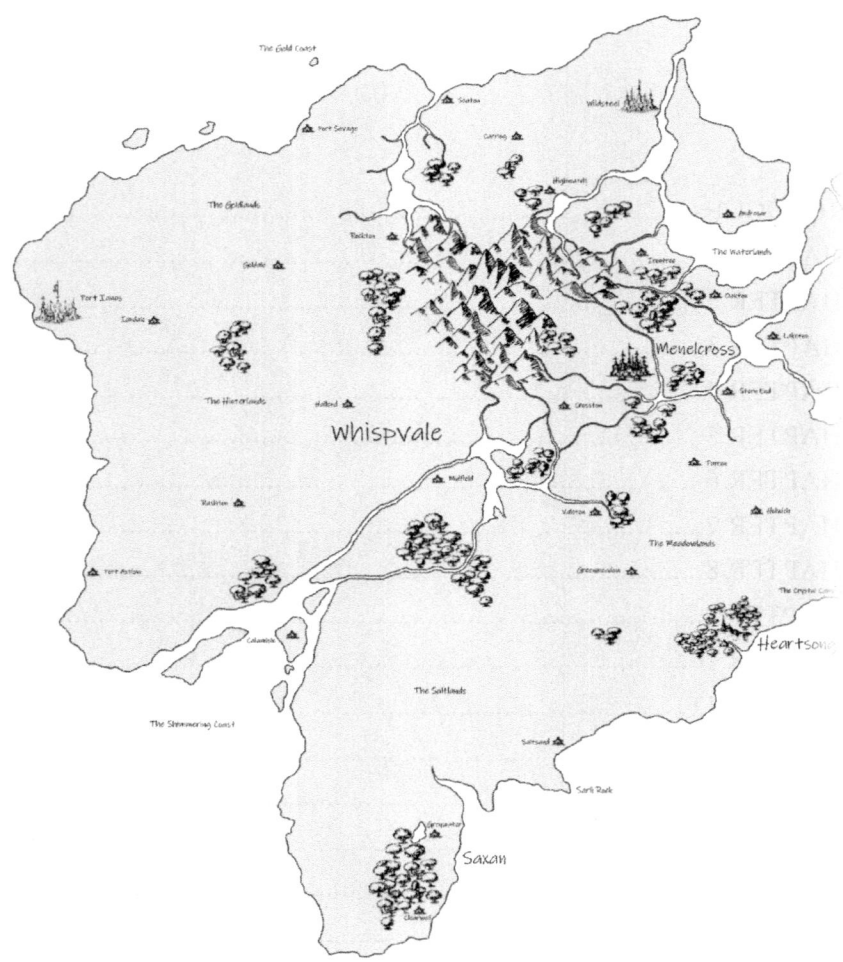

PROLOGUE

With the last of the great desert dunes far behind them, the army at last reached the walled city of Shya. Those walls were old but intact; a mile wide, eighty feet high and constructed of great stone blocks. The usual surrounding camps and markets had withdrawn behind the immense iron gate, each bar of which was wider than a man's head. Knowing the Shyan archers would be ready behind the battlements, Xalius called a halt at a quarter-mile. He had only five hours of daylight to work with and was determined to be inside before dusk. The pace had been hard and water was short. More importantly than that, the Imperator expected; and Xalius could not disappoint.

Shya was the key. To the north were the lands the Haar Dari aimed to conquer. Within the walls lay thousands of inhabitants to be taxed and enslaved; valuable wells, provisions, animals and treasure to be claimed. Xalius had been very careful to ensure that he had amassed sufficient force to guarantee victory. Everyone else had wanted to attack sooner; he had staked his reputation on a single overwhelming strike that would win much with minimal cost. This had to work.

One attendant took the reins of his camel, another placed some steps below and Xalius dismounted. His aged bones ached from the many days of riding and he took the hand offered by his assistant, Darian. He too was old, but nothing like as ancient as his master. A small awning had been hastily erected nearby and the two made their way under the shelter. More attendants rushed in with furniture and Xalius was soon lowering himself onto a chair, glad to be out of the sun. A table was placed in front of him and Darian placed the correct tome upon it, then opened it at the appropriate page. Xalius had spent months memorising and perfecting the chant, but some last-minute practice never hurt.

He let out a long breath and gazed at the walls. Wind whipped sand off the battlements and pulled at a single high banner bearing the city's red and white emblem. The area around the imposing gatehouse had also been adorned with red triangles, which Xalius knew to be a Shyan symbol of fortune. Not a single soldier had shown themselves. He wondered how well prepared they were; how hard they would fight.

Dust rolled into the tent as Marshal Siad Borshan reined in his horse and dismounted. Immensely tall, broad and muscular, the veteran warrior had not yet donned his armour, though he was already wielding his double-bladed axe.

'You're sitting down?' Siad's considerable brow furrowed.

'Not for long.'

'When do we hit the gate?'

'When I've done my part. I believe we discussed this.'

The issue of superiority never really went away. Siad commanded the Imperator's armed forces but Xalius was his deputy and had served him for longer. Xalius generally deferred to the younger man in military matters but, on this occasion, he believed his contribution would be crucial. He also didn't want Siad to take *all* the glory.

'The men are ready. Their blood's up.' The marshal smacked the head of his axe into the sandy ground. 'When?'

'You'll see.'

Siad gave an almost imperceptible nod and turned to the city. 'I'll tear that standard down myself – and burn it to ash.'

Xalius rolled his eyes. War was necessary, of course, but he could never understand such zeal. So exhausting.

'You'll keep your Ironhands back?' This had also been discussed.

Siad ran a large, hairy hand across his large, hairless head. 'Unless they're needed.'

'No sense in risking our best. Sand Lions first, then the Irregulars.'

Siad gestured to the book. 'I'll leave you to your tricks. I hope it will be worth the wait.'

Once the marshal had left, Darian brought a glass of water. Xalius enjoyed a long drink then removed his gloves; neither a swift nor painless process. After years of Waymaking, his hands were thin, dark and gnarled. Several fingers had curled inward and two were fused together. These were not afflictions that could be mended by medicine or surgery.

Grim though it was to look upon his hands, they reminded him of many great moments and achievements. But the pain was always there, and it would surge within him again soon. Such was the cost of greatness. Such was the cost of the Way.

***

Xalius stood alone, directly opposite the gate, with three warlocks some way behind him. Two male, one female: three experienced and reliable. Xalius raised a hand to signal them to begin their own preparations. Then he began his chant: two hundred and eleven words that had to be recited precisely and with utter conviction and power. And if – when he spoke the last of those words – he had not simultaneously channelled every last fraction of his energy, the result would be failure. Such thoughts left him as he said the words and ignited the fires within. Soon he could feel it: a warm glow that began in his core and radiated outwards. At the last word, the power reached his fingers. Xalius kept his eyes open and raised his arms, willing the elements to obey.

He drew the sand in from all around, shaping it onto a vertical formation that grew and grew, and soon dwarfed even the walls of Shya. He saw the spinning tower grow in breadth as the three warlocks added their efforts to his. When he could add no more, his gaze switched to the gate. The sand soon followed and was sent speeding through the gaps in the iron gate. Under the wooden door beyond into the city, along every street, into every building – and the eyes of every man, woman and child.

He could sustain it for only a minute. Once he lost focus, he lost control. When his vision cleared and the sand settled, he saw great banks of it piled up against the gatehouse. So much had been lifted and thrown into the city that the ground in front of him was a different colour. Exhausted, he summoned the strength to turn. Behind him, two of the warlocks were on their knees, also recovering.

Siad rode past them, waving dust away from his face. He stopped his horse beside Xalius, towering over him.

'Not bad. Not bad at all.'

The marshal waved his army forward.

***

The Sand Lions were a dark-skinned people from the harsh western coasts of the Madlands. Tough, lean and fearless, it was their custom to keep their black hair cropped short and they wore only the minimum of clothing. On this day they would be employed to dig under the iron gate so half of the hundred warriors were equipped with shovels and picks. Once they had cleared space, a second crew would go in and set fire to the wooden doors. Looking on from his tent, Xalius hoped that there were now few within the walls who could see well enough to fight back. He had made a study of the four previous sieges of Shya attempted in the last century. The one that had come closest to victory had employed the digging and burning technique. None of the previous attacking armies had possessed the numbers of the Haar Dari; nor had they possessed any Waymakers.

Siad sat on his mount, a hundred archers either side of him. These were his best marksmen, men drawn from various units. The Sand Lions stood in formation ahead of them, faces turned towards their marshal, awaiting the order. Siad did not look to Xalius before giving it. Every one of the Sand Lions unleashed a battle-cry as they sprinted across the sand. Waving Darian away, Xalius used his staff to help himself stand and looked on.

Archers appeared immediately at the battlements, helmets gleaming. Xalius had expected that and so most of the Sand Lions had hand-shields. What he had not expected was the sheer volume or accuracy of the enemy fire. And he had definitely not anticipated the hatches that opened up below the battlements, apparently in the middle of solid stone blocks. The result was a hail of arrows that struck at least half of the Sand Lions before they had taken twenty steps. The brave warriors ran on but a second volley claimed dozens more. One man threw his hands skyward as he fell, an arrow lodged between his eyes.

Siad ordered his archers to return fire. Xalius heard the bows snap but he did not see a single enemy struck. The protection of the hatches and well-designed battlements meant that nothing other than an inch-perfect shot would find a living target.

Half of the remaining Sand Lions fled back to the lines and were spared by the enemy archers. The hardier souls ran on but most were struck by more than one bolt and only five actually reached the gate. To their great credit, they set to digging immediately.

'Quite ingenious, sir,' observed Darian as he shook sand out of his beard. 'They appear to have hollowed holes in the stones, and disguised them with painted wood.'

Most of the archers had now withdrawn though Xalius could still see a few helmets. One of the senior Sand Lions – an elderly warrior who carried a spear decorated with bones – approached Siad. The marshal nodded and the second line went forward. Siad gave a brief, stern glance at Xalius then bellowed at his archers.

They marched forward until they were thirty feet behind the Sand Lions and this time they opened up before the warriors charged. The Shyans made no attempt to fire back at the opposing archers but instead targeted the Sand Lions again. These unfortunate warriors had to pass their injured and dead compatriots but not one took a backwards step. The result of such blind courage was a bloody scene.

Xalius counted eleven who reached the gate. A cry went up from the battlements as a defender was at last struck but there was precious little else to celebrate. The Shyans did not bother to shoot at the dozens of wounded Sand Lions limping back or trying to pull bolts out of their flesh. They simply hid themselves and withdrew, no doubt readying their bows once more. The efforts of the tiny group at the gate seemed rather pathetic; at this rate it would take them months to dig under the gate.

Marshal Siad ignored Xalius but dismounted from his great horse and collared another of his deputies. Xalius was too drained to intervene himself but he knew his remaining warlocks would be ready to serve.

'Darian, have Neritya sent forward.'

***

The third wave was ready. Siad had replaced the Sand Lions with two hundred Irregulars. This unit was made up of a disparate collection of criminals, wanderers, vagrants and outcasts that had found a home with the Haar Dari. They were of many different races and creeds and employed every weapon imaginable. Crucially, the two hundred Siad had called forward were all equipped with larger, rectangular shields. The marshal had also reinforced his archers, ordering anyone with a bow to join their ranks.

Xalius now stood just behind Siad, propped up against his staff. With him were Darian and his longest-serving warlock. Neritya was an unexceptional-looking fellow: small, thin-featured and clad in the drabbest clothes imaginable. But he never needed much preparation time and had just informed Xalius that he was ready. It appeared the defenders of Shya were ready too. Despite his poor eyesight, Xalius could spy the multitude of arrows visible at the battlements and hatches.

Siad gave the order. As one, the Irregulars charged for the gate, shields up. Just as the first of the enemy arrows were unleashed, Neritya did his work. Channelling the bright sun, he clapped his hands together and cast a blinding wall of light at the city. The volume of fire was instantly reduced. Xalius ducked as one errant bolt hit the sand a few yards away. Only a handful of the Irregulars were downed and – despite their shields – they were covering the ground quickly.

Xalius ran his gaze across the battlements, where few bows and helmets could now be seen. 'Ha, first sand, then light – I doubt a single one of them can still see.'

The Irregulars were close to the gate. The first of them had just reached the small group of Sand Lions when the banks of sand began to shift and acquire form, clearly guided by some unseen hand. In seconds, tongues of sand were whipping straight into the faces of the onrushing Irregulars. Most fell to the ground, pawing at their eyes. The sand became a churning maelstrom that struck every last man at the gate, sending them stumbling away, dropping their shields, clearly unable to see a thing. As a fighting force, they were now useless.

'It would appear the Shyan Council of Mages is still active,' observed Darian.

Xalius would have admonished him but he was preoccupied by Siad. The marshal was watching the third attack fail with clenched fists, his mouth set in an enraged sneer. Moments later, he was forced to grab his mount as the great horse began to whinny and stamp its feet. The many hundreds of mounts and pack-animals to the rear also began to panic and only when he looked up did Xalius understand why.

The sky had grown dark. Wispy white cloud became grey and formed a single bulbous shape, shadowing the city and the attacking army. Thunder rumbled; not yet loud but ominous. At its heart, the cloud became a hellish, broiling black. The thunder came again; a shuddering crack that seemed to reach into the very earth itself. Lightning flashed and time seemed to slow as an immense shard of blue leapt from the heavens. Xalius could barely believe what he saw as the bolt stopped somewhere over his army and became a spinning ball of blue flame. Even the hardened ranks of the Haar Dari scattered.

The ball of flame then leaped towards Xalius – at least that was how it seemed to him. He ducked as it flew overhead and turned just in time to see it strike the walls to the right of the gatehouse. Upon impact the ball seemed to explode, unleashing a nerve-splitting shockwave that almost knocked Xalius off his feet. Gripping his staff with both hands, he looked on as great ragged sections of stone were sent flying hundreds of feet into the air. One of them landed not far from Siad, who was still fighting to control his horse.

When the ensuing dust cloud began to lift, a most welcome sight was revealed. The attack had torn a hole through the walls, leaving a twenty-foot gash from the battlements almost to the ground. At the bottom of this hole was a pile of rubble and dead soldiers, bodies bloodied and crushed. Beyond lay a street filled with dumbfounded soldiers still gazing at their shattered defences.

Siad bellowed orders for his archers to target the gap. As bolts began to strike the defenders, the marshal quickly gathered the Ironhands, an elite force equipped with heavy armour and broadswords. Siad donned his helmet, lifted his axe high and gave a great battle-cry as he charged towards the ruined wall.

'Sir.' Darian pointed behind them.

Xalius turned around and saw the remaining troops parting to clear a path. As they did so, they fell to their knees and bowed their heads. It could only have been the Imperator.

He strode towards Xalius, hooded black robe trailing in the sand. Xalius felt a tremor of unease. Such feelings only seemed to worsen during his increasingly rare meetings with the Imperator. They had been equals once – friends, in fact – but so much had changed since then. Atavius showed no sign of discomfort, despite the tremendous effort – unthinkable even – necessary for the power he had unleashed. Above, the sky was already clearing, the cloud turning white and breaking up.

The ruination of his body, however, was beyond even the Imperator's power to repair. Though he stood tall and walked quickly, the right side of his face was a mess of scars and dead flesh, the marks of battles with beings beyond the comprehension of most men. As he halted, Darian stepped back and knelt down.

Xalius bowed his head. 'Good day, Imperator.'

His eyes more red than white, Atavius looked on as Siad led the charge. From the corner of his wrinkled mouth, the slightest of smiles.

'Yes,' said the Imperator in his gentle, inhuman tone. 'I think it will be.'

CHAPTER 1

Elaria Rose Carlen flew backwards, tripped on a tree root and landed face down in a pile of leaves. Wiping dirt off her cheek, she stood and placed both hands back on her fighting stave.

Garrett smirked as he twirled his stave one-handed, 'Don't lose heart, Rosie – you managed to stay on your feet for at least a minute. Not exactly impressive, but still better than last time.'

She hated him. She really did hate him.

Elaria walked across the clearing and drew in some deep breaths, trying to clear her mind and settle again. The trouble was, you never knew what he was going to do next. Garrett was quickfooted in deed but even quicker in thought. He never attacked the same way twice, and always found a way to evade any intended blow with infuriating ease.

'Ah, a bit of colour in your cheeks. That usually means you're getting angry. Don't get angry, Rosie. Stay calm.'

As she approached, he deployed the stave lengthways, the tip angled towards Elaria's face. The staves were hollow and made of palewood but each blow was still painful; and Elaria carried several bruises from their last encounter. She didn't have to fight, of course – her mother had expressly forbidden it – but she was desperate to improve. When fighting the boys in the village with a stave, wooden sword or wooden mace, she generally won most contests. But Garrett was a level above them all.

As they circled each other, he made an adjustment to his hair. He was as fair as Elaria; tall and undeniably handsome too. And as a respected member of the Mayor's Guard, he was never short of female attention. He seemed unable to make a trip to Clearwell without several approaches from local girls. The men of the Guard could often be heard complaining about his arrogant attitude but even they had a begrudging respect for his skill. Many a conversation had considered who would win in a "proper fight" between Garrett and Captain Thorrsen, the local Guard commander. At twenty-two, Garrett was only six years younger than Thorrsen, if far less mature.

Elaria was just seventeen but also broad-shouldered and tall. Her mother and aunts had often made remarks about how her impressive build might put men off but Elaria didn't care. She knew her height and reach gave her an advantage; an advantage she was determined to use. Her mother – and "the old crows" as she called her aunts – might be behind the times but the Pathfinders weren't; they selected on ability. Of course, there were more male soldiers than female, but Elaria reckoned she stood a decent chance of getting in at the next Tournament. She knew she was a good fighter, but she would have to be at her best; and that meant fighting Garrett.

'It's a shame you tie your hair up,' he said.' I do like to see your locks fly through the air. Quite lovely. Oh-'

Garrett stepped backwards, deftly evading a lunge from Elaria without even raising his stave. He countered with a flurry of attacks, testing her defences and occasionally using a one-handed grip to swing at her, tucking his other arm nonchalantly behind his back.

Elaria ducked and weaved and blocked as the pace of the duel quickened. Boots shuffled and leaves flew as the staves clattered against each other. Elaria stifled a yelp as she was caught on the knuckles.

Now Garrett had that grin planted on his face; the one that meant he'd had enough and was about to pick his moment. He drove his stave at her head. Elaria batted the attack away and jabbed back at him. Either she was quicker than usual or Garrett was slower because the weapon got close enough to ruffle his hair. Shock registered on his face and Elaria told herself not to get carried away.

The inevitable counter-attack came from her right. She scuttled left and leaped the foot put out to trip her. His flank was open. She swung hard, already anticipating the joy of hurting him. Somehow, he contorted his body, arms and weapon into a parry, his stave suddenly vertical. And in a flash, he had moved one hand from his stave to hers and shoved it upward. The palewood struck her chin with a solid crack. Stunned, Elaria somehow kept her feet as she tottered backwards.

Until Garrett hooked his boot around her heel.

Then that familiar, dispiriting thump as she hit the ground. Then the pain from her chin. She checked with her fingers: no blood, but the blow had reverberated up through her jaw. A headache was already on its way.

'Sorry, Rosie. I've been saving that one. Remember that you never know what your opponent is going to do.'

Elaria sighed.

'You got angry again. How many times? It's all about discipline.'

She had to admit she had learned a lot from him. Painful lessons were still lessons.

Garrett threw his stave aside and squatted down in front of her. He put a hand inside his tunic to scratch his chest then smiled.

'Poor Rosie. Shall I make you feel better?'

She forced herself to stand, ignoring the pain. 'Let's fight.'

'I'd rather do something else. Come on, I know that's why you wanted to come out here – so no one will see us.'

He had a way of twisting things, Garrett. She fought here because she didn't want Mother to find out.

'I don't have long,' he added. 'Duty at the main gate tonight. I need to use my spare time wisely.'

He made a grab for her hand.

Elaria knew he wouldn't fight anymore today so she wheeled and ran. They both knew he couldn't catch her in the two hundred yards before she reached Janna's watermill.

'Goodbye, Rosie! I'll come to you tomorrow night.'

Elaria picked up the pace, fuelled by a surge of anger. She cleared the forest and struck the river path. She hated him more than anyone in the entire world. But she loved him too. How could she not? He was her brother.

***

Though it was her home, Elaria had always considered the Forest of Serenity to be poorly named. True, it contained some wonderful things: colossal blackwood trees two-hundred feet high; untouched, peaceful groves; exotic, flavoursome fruit and more varieties of insects, rodents, birds, deer, boar and wild horses than anyone could count. But many of those beasts were as dangerous to man as they were to each other; and the forest also provided a home to smugglers, robbers and the occasional wandering lunatic. There were countless stories about strange, terrible events within the forest's dark depths, some of which Elaria reckoned to be true. Even so, Clearwell was a good place to grow up and live; a relatively safe corner of Lower Saxan.

As her long stride took her swiftly past the mill, she ignored the leers of Janna's three employees. The men were unloading sacks of grain from a cart. Sometimes they would make comments but on this day the cart-owner and his wife were also present. Overall, Elaria reckoned she had been lucky with her looks: in her best dress she was still only pretty – not beautiful. There were two or three girls in Clearwell who could be classed as beautiful and from what Elaria had seen, their looks brought them as much trouble as happiness. She imagined it must be terrible to be looked at all the time. Unless you had done something, of course; better to be known for having done something.

Spying Janna, who was replacing a tile on the roof, she shouted a greeting. The old man looked over his shoulder and waved. She had known him all her life. It was a shame he wasn't so talkative and friendly these days. He had changed when his first wife had died; some incurable disease of the lungs.

Once past the mill, Elaria ran along the uneven track until she reached Market Road. Halfway to town, she passed Mellissa and Tyrie, girls from her class at Clearwell School, which they had all left the previous year. Mellissa was already engaged to a wealthy merchant in Middle Saxan and Tyrie was doing her best to emulate her friend. Elaria thought that rather sad. Mellissa had a good mind for mathematics and Tyrie was a fast runner. There weren't many opportunities for young women in Clearwell but Elaria thought they could at least have tried to follow their own path. In any case, she was sure they couldn't have cared less what she thought. She had been close to Tyrie when they were younger and they often raced one another, but they moved in very different circles now. Tyrie returned her wave but neither girl said anything.

Elaria almost laughed at herself. She was so contemptuous of others but what of *her* plans? Her mother was determined that she follow her and become a seamstress: "honest, proper, reliable work". Elaria did not hate sewing; in fact, she enjoyed it. But only for a few hours, not for the long days that her mother insisted upon – it made her hands ache and she could not bear to sit for so long. Most others worked a good deal harder, of course; her family was comparatively fortunate.

Before his death, her father had amassed considerable wealth as a trader in gems, much of which he had put into the house. On Elaria's tenth birthday, he had given his daughter a rare stone – the 'Night's Eye'. It was barely an inch across but sparkled with kaleidoscopic colour and remained her most prized possession. Without her father's expertise, the family had been unable to continue trading and tough times had ensued. Now though, a share of Garrett's wage and the earnings of their tailoring was sufficient to keep them going. And with a day and a half free every week, perhaps Elaria was the 'lucky girl' her mother often told her she was.

Yet she admired the Pathfinder patrols that marched through Clearwell since her earliest days. For hundreds of years, they had guarded all of Whispvale from men and creatures bent on its destruction. They had led by example and lit a path in the darkness for others to follow. Elaria could imagine no greater honour than to walk in their ranks, wear the coveted blue and white. The next Tournament was scheduled for autumn, which gave her only a few months. In every spare moment she would practice fighting, running, climbing and swimming. When the time came, she would be ready.

***

Six apples, two loaves of berry-bread and a pound of cheese. Once she'd purchased the items with the coins her mother had given her that morning, Elaria left the market and set off for home. Passing a row of six low, ramshackle dwellings, she looked at the fourth house along. But Mrs Spirling was not in her garden, nor sitting by the window. Elaria knew this meant she was probably not back from visiting her sister over in Fieldhaven, a town on the outskirts of Saxan.

It was a shame, because Elaria always liked to hear news of Mrs. Spirling's niece, Tamia. Three years older, she had been part of a group of wilful local women who had trained together and tried their hands at the Tournament two years earlier. Three had succeeded and been admitted but the two others had been cast aside during probation. Tamia, however, had completed her first year's training and spent the last year as a fully-fledged Pathfinder.

Elaria sighed again as she continued along the street. Her free time was almost over. From tomorrow she faced five and a half days with her mother. Thinking of the pile of cotton in the storeroom and the complicated dress design hanging from the wooden mannequin, her head dropped and she muttered a curse. At least she could go for a run afterwards. Janna had told her that the white orchids were in bloom near Deep Grove. Five miles there and back. Something to look forward to, at least.

'Lari!'

Elaria spun around and was delighted to see the plump Mrs. Spirling coming up the street on a pony. She hurried back to her.

'I thought that was you,' said Mrs. Spirling, flushed from her ride. 'How are you, my dear?'

'Fine, thank you.' Elaria held the reins of the pony and stroked its nose. It looked grateful for a rest. 'Any news of Tamia?'

'Better than that. I've just spent the day with her. She's on leave.'

'Oh, if only I'd have known – I'd have come to Fieldhaven.'

Elaria couldn't help feeling angry; why hadn't the silly woman told her?

'Actually, she rode back with me. She says no one can shoe a horse like Merrick.'

'She's *here*? Now?'

'She is.' The fat woman nodded merrily. 'Merrick's good but he's not quick so she'll probably have some time to–'

Elaria didn't hear the rest. She was some distance away when she realised how rude she'd been.

'Sorry, Mrs. Spirling!' she shouted over her shoulder. 'And thank you!'

***

She found Tamia sitting on a stone bench outside Merrick's while the blacksmith worked. Next to the workshop was a huge stack of wood for the forge. Merrick's muscular apprentice – Elaria didn't know his name – was loading a large barrow. Thick smoke was issuing from the workshop's chimney and an orange glow could be seen through the open door.

Tamia grinned as she stood. 'Well, well.'

'It's so good to see you!'

The two young women gripped wrists in the Saxan style but Elaria felt like kissing her old friend.

Tamia was stoutly-built; short but broad and Elaria noted that her forearms were even more knotted with muscle than before. Her dark brown hair had been cut straight at the neck and across her brow. But what made most of an impression on Elaria was the uniform. Tamia wore brown leather riding boots and the white trousers and tunic of the Pathfinders, both striped with dark blue. Hanging over her saddlebags nearby was the matching blue cloak, edged with silver. Elaria was both proud of her friend yet fiercely jealous.

'Sorry,' said Tamia.

'What for?'

'Not coming to the house. I really am only here for Merrick. Have to be gone within the hour.'

'Oh, don't worry, I'm just glad to see you.'

Only when Tamia withdrew her arm did Elaria realise she was still holding it.

'Are you ... how's work?'

'Oh, you know – boring. What about you? Where have you been?'

Tamia exhaled loudly. 'A few places.'

'Hello, Elaria!' Merrick hailed her from the doorway then wiped his hands on his leather apron and returned to work.

Elaria waved back as Tamia sat down. 'We can talk here.'

Elaria placed her bag of shopping under the bench and sat down. She could hardly take her eyes off the uniform. She knew good clothing when she saw it; these were made in the prestigious workshops of Upper Saxan. 'So where exactly?'

'When did I last see you?'

'Six months ago, or thereabouts. You were hoping to join that patrol with a captain, Shay something?'

'Captain Kano. Shai Kano. Yes, in the end they took just about everybody. We were supposed to split up and monitor the area around Riverton for Beastkin but it turned into something else.'

'Did you see any?'

'We thought we did, once.'

'Oh.' Elaria could not hide her disappointment.

'From a lookout post. A raiding party – possibly. But it was night. We couldn't be sure. We spent most of our time on the border with the Skornlands, hunting down sellswords.'

Elaria sat angled towards Tamia, hands clasped together, listening intently.

'Because of the Beastkin activity further north, there are bands of men offering their services to the villages and towns in danger. Except they're not really offering. They charge a fortune and if the coins don't come, buildings mysteriously go up in flames or livestock are killed or wells are poisoned. It's almost out of control. Captain Kano did well though; gave speeches in all the town squares, told the people they didn't have to be afraid. We got information on the gangs and we used it. Forty odd we captured in the end. They're all breaking stone in Boughbend Prison now. Eight executions too. There was a leader called One Eye – the very worst of them. Captain Kano made sure he had plenty of witnesses and that the court charges were all done properly. He told us we had to win their hearts and minds. He's very sharp, Captain Kano.'

'Was there any fighting?'

'A little,' said Tamia as she smoothed out her tunic. 'But when we caught up with them there was usually a lot more of us so in the end they surrendered. I clobbered one fellow with the hilt of my sword. He had a helmet on but I still put him down! And another time, they were shooting arrows at us from a cave. Do you know, Lari, I heard one whistle right past my ear!'

Elaria could hardly take all this in. It was like something from a book of adventure tales. 'Were you scared?'

Tamia gave this some thought. 'I was. I was. But when you've got your mates with you, it's different. We eat together, march together, sing together. You never feel alone. It ...' Tamia gulped loudly and looked up at the sky for a moment, clearly gripped by her emotions. Then she smiled and turned to her friend. 'It's good. It's going well.'

She put her hand on Elaria's wrist. 'No reason why you can't try next year. If I'm back for long enough I'll do everything I can to help in the autumn.'

'Next year? No, Tami, it's *this* year. I've been training. I'll be ready.'

'But the Tournament's in three days – when I leave here, I'm meeting up with two others then riding for Greylake. They brought it forward because of the Beastkin and the sellswords; we need numbers, and quickly. Didn't you know? There's a notice on the town hall. I rode past today; it must have been up for a while.'

Elaria felt a hollow forming in her stomach and stared blankly at her friend. She couldn't summon a reply. She checked the town hall notices every now and again but no one had mentioned this to her. Then again, who would? Other than Tamia, there wasn't a single person who'd responded to her aim of joining the Pathfinders with anything other than derision.

Tamia kept her hand on her arm and gripped it tighter. 'Lari, are you all right?'

***

She walked home in a daze. In fact, she got halfway there before realising she had left the shopping under the bench. By the time she returned to the blacksmith to reclaim it, Tamia had already left. There was no chance of riding off with her; Elaria would not rob her mother of her pony and she didn't dare take Garrett's. Nor did she have the money to buy one. Yet as she approached the family home, the seeds of an idea were already forming.

The house was in its own grounds, the surrounding plants and trees rather overgrown. Since Father's death, they could not afford a gardener. Elaria and mother did what they could but Garrett was of course above such work. The house – two stories of solid brick and ironwork – was in good repair. Whenever Mother had spare money, she employed workmen to keep it that way. As she often told her children, they were fortunate to have it and one day it would be theirs. By her estimation, it was the fourth best house in the village of Clearwell.

Having placed the shopping in the kitchen, she found Mother in the workroom, surrounded by piles of coloured cloth. When she eventually looked up, she saw saw the welt on her daughter's chin.

'I fell.'

Marris Carlen shook her head. 'I'm too tired to argue. Did you get what I asked you to?'

Elaria nodded and took the change from her pocket and placed it on the corner of the table. For the briefest moment, she considered telling mother about Tamia but she knew that would be a mistake.

She was used to not telling her things. Once, when she was twelve, she'd summoned the courage to tell her about Garrett coming into her room. Mother had told her not to be "silly" and to "stop making things up". Elaria had never told her again but often wondered what Father might have said. Not that it mattered; by that point he was already three years dead.

'And you'll make dinner?'

'Yes.'

'It's just us. Garrett's on duty tonight.'

Elaria nodded, determined to not even think about him.

Her mother gestured at the nearest pile of cloth. 'Behind again. Glad to have you back tomorrow. Did you enjoy your day?'

Another nod.

'Why so quiet, girl?'

'No reason,' said Elaria, unable to resist chewing her lip. 'I'll get started on dinner.'

***

As she chopped potatoes and carrots, Elaria almost changed her mind. She thought of her mother's face when she found out; the fact that she would have to keep the business going on her own. Elaria kept chopping but had to wipe tears away because, for all her faults, Marris Carlen was a fine mother. She had clothed and fed her daughter; never struck her and rarely even shouted at her. There had also been some wonderful moments in recent times when they had sung together in the workshop and it had sounded as good as any choir. Mother had done her best to protect Elaria from the world, certainly from the ravages of losing Father at such a young age, but she could not protect her from the greatest danger of all – because she didn't even know of it. And the knowledge of it would, in all likelihood, ruin her life.

But she need not know; because if Elaria wasn't there then it would stop. And Elaria could finally do what she wanted to. She was old enough; now was the time. When she thought of that; and what Garrett would do the following night, the doubts evaporated, and so did her tears.

While the dinner cooked and her mother worked, she took her backpack, filled it with what she would need, then hid it under her bed. And when Marris returned to the workshop after dinner, Elaria retrieved an old, folded piece of paper from what had been her father's desk. She took this and a lantern and went upstairs. She sat by the window in her room and looked out at the sky. There was little cloud and two full moons; perhaps the gods were on her side.

She unfolded the map, confident she wouldn't need it for the night and most of the next day. She could find the Great Oak in any weather without a map. But from there to Greylake was more than thirty miles of ground that nobody willingly walked through. The road that Tamia had taken was safe but almost twice the distance. This route would take Elaria through forests where numerous shady characters were said to dwell. Yet she did not trouble herself with worry. She would reach Greylake in time for the Tournament or die trying. Nothing else mattered.

***

Knowing Mother would be exhausted from her day's labours, Elaria crept into her room three hours later. She bent over the bed and kissed her gently on her cheek. Mother did not wake. Elaria watched her for a while then left, closing the door behind her.

She was already dressed, wearing her strongest boots plus her thickest trousers and tunic; both pale green. In her pack was a change of clothes, a cloak, food, a large flask of water, a lantern, a fire-starting kit and the six gold coins she had saved from what Mother paid her. Two of these went in her boots – just in case.

Once downstairs, she placed the brief note she had written on the kitchen table. She then quietly unlocked the back door, locked it behind her and slid the key back under. She was carrying her palewood fighting stave on a string over her shoulder. She ignored the rear gate and stepped over a section of fence that had collapsed several weeks previously. She crossed the brook at the rear of the property and set off north-west along a path she knew well. She did not look back once.

CHAPTER 2

'They call it the Great Palace.' Xalius shook his head and tutted. 'The only great thing about it is the view.'

He approached the balcony and leaned upon his staff. The front of the palace was a pyramid made up of vast, rectangular stone blocks. The edifice shadowed the centre of Shya, towering three hundred feet above the ground.

'Yes, sir,' mumbled Darian as he shuffled some papers.

Xalius peered over the balcony wall and gazed down at the densely-packed streets. Pale yellow sandstone seemed to have been used for every building and most of the roofs were daubed with the distinctive red triangles. Due to the limits of the walls, Shya was a crowded city with little open space.

Directly below was the large central square where the bodies of the council of mages still hung. Apparently, they were starting to smell and even the soldiers on duty had begun to complain. Xalius was under instructions to leave the rotting corpses in place. He thought that excessive but was not about to argue with Imperator Atavius. He also felt it had been excessive to attack the mages in the first place; because they could be more useful alive. Then again, eliminating them had sent a powerful message. If they couldn't resist the Haar Dari, no one else in Shya would dare try.

Subduing them had not been simple or straightforward however; Xalius had lost twenty men and two warlocks in doing so. The council's leader – some aged hag whose name he hadn't bothered to learn – had managed to summon a death-inducing fog that had taken Xalius several minutes to dispel. He grinned as he recalled the final moments of the battle, when the bolt he'd sent her way had frazzled her decrepit form to a crisp.

Across the city there had been isolated pockets of resistance but overall the thirty thousand people of Shya seemed to have accepted their new masters; or at least accepted that they were outmatched.

'Shall we sit, sir?' suggested Darian.

Xalius walked over to the large, circular table.

Though the balcony was often too hot for him, he'd spent much of the last five weeks there. Gazing up at the cloudless sky, he found it easier to forget the onerous responsibilities of administering the city. Of course, he should have been spending time practising his Waymaking skills but the demands of this new job sapped all his energy.

Having placed Xalius in charge of the city, Atavius had then abruptly departed with barely a word. A silver eagle had arrived two weeks later, bearing a message that instructed Xalius to consolidate their position and squeeze everything he could out of the city before the campaign continued. He had no idea where they would be moving on to, nor exactly what his master was up to. Atavius was always playing a greater game.

There were rumours, of course – there always were where the Imperator was concerned. He had previously announced his intention to find the fabled Temple of Azdul – which he had tried and failed to locate before – in the far west of the Madlands. Xalius had no idea which of the many artifacts said to reside there his master was interested in. It wasn't unusual for him to go missing for months. A decade previously he had left for two entire years; Xalius had believed him dead.

Darian – who was seventy-one – had only just sat down.

'I hope you'll speak quicker than you move.'

'Sorry, sir.'

'Do you know I am eighty years older than you?'

'Yes, sir. But unfortunately, I do not have the blessings you enjoy.'

'Blessings? Is your eyesight really that bad?'

Darian didn't answer that, instead tugging on his beard as he surveyed his papers. 'The first issue, sir-'

'- is the priests. The accursed Espheral priests.'

'Well, yes, sir.'

'As it has been every day for the last week.'

Darian continued the beard-tugging.

'No more have agreed to convert?'

'No, sir.'

Xalius had a dozen of them locked up in Shya's jail. The angry city-folk had assembled outside the palace earlier that week, demanding the release of their spiritual leaders. Looking on from the balcony, Xalius had instructed Verris, his chief of guards, to arrest a few troublemakers. When some of these Shyans had proudly stated their willingness to die for their cause, Xalius realised he was simply playing their game. A few martyrs would enrage the entire population, so he had ordered that they be released.

His intention now was to recruit some of the priests and reach some form of compromise. If the holy men could persuade the people to obey their new masters and show at least a superficial commitment to the Haar Dari, then that would suffice for the moment. The strategic importance of the city was economic; there would be time to eradicate their beliefs in false deities later on. For now, Xalius just needed calm streets and everyone back at work. But it seemed the priests were not given to pragmatism.

'And what about the research I asked you to do?'

'Apparently one of them has a mistress, another an illegitimate son, and another a gambling habit.'

'Then pressure can be applied. Instruct Verris to turn those three. Once they're under our control, we'll give them a week to do what they can with the others. If there's no progress, any who have failed to see the light will be eliminated. We'll do it quietly one night – bury them out in the desert. What's next?'

'The traders, sir. We've not had a single caravan arrive in the last month.'

'That is unfortunate. We need those tax revenues.'

'A question of perception, sir. The desert people know we are in charge and have spread word to other traders. They may not realise how … reasonable we can be.'

'Not many do. The mayor is still being cooperative?'

'He is, sir. I believe the reality of his situation has finally sunk in.'

Shya's political leader had surrendered to the Haar Dari in person after the demise of the council of mages. He had at first attempted to obstruct the occupiers wherever he could but a nocturnal visit from Captain Verris and his guards had achieved the desired effect.

'Good. Ask him to identify an envoy for each of the main traders. I believe most lead tribal or familial groups. Send them an invitation with a gift of some kind, advising them that Shya is still very much open for business and that taxes will remain the same for at least two hundred days. Have Verris ensure that each envoy does precisely as he is bid.'

'Yes, sir.'

Despite his age, Darian rarely took notes. Xalius was not concerned. He knew that his instructions would be implemented to the letter. Darian was a dull but utterly reliable individual.

'Next?'

'The Ceremony of Acceptance.'

'Ah, yes. How are things coming along?'

***

The women made their way along the forest path, bent by their heavy loads. Upon their backs were great sacks mounted on roughly-made wooden frames, every one utterly full. They walked in single file, singing half-heartedly. There were eight in all: dark-skinned and difficult to age, wearing sandals and shabby robes.

Only when the last of them had rounded the bend did Elaria move from her hiding place and return to the path. As she hurried onward, she noted a few red berries on the muddy ground; this was why the women had foraged so deeply into Serenity.

She had spent the previous night at the ruined wall that marked the edge of Lesser Saxan territory, roughly six miles from home. With a makeshift bed of fern leaves, wrapped up in a cloak and blanket, she'd been just about warm enough. Having left at dawn, she reckoned she'd covered another ten miles. The path was far too narrow and rough for horses, so it was unlikely she would be caught.

Mother would have read the note by now. Elaria had not told her what she was doing; only that she wasn't to worry and that she would write soon. Of course, they would guess where she was headed but, under Whispvale law, at seventeen Elaria could not be compelled to remain within the family home.

During the morning, she had spotted only the women and a shaggy-haired man, who'd been drinking from a bottle as he walked. Elaria wasn't sure if he'd seen her or not but she would stick to her policy of hiding if she spied someone coming the other way. Even seemingly harmless folk might carry news of her back to Clearwell.

The last time she had used this route had been with an expedition from school several years ago. The path seemed far more overgrown now, though it was still easy to follow. Elaria expected to reach the Great Oak sometime that afternoon. The way north from there was notoriously difficult to navigate because no one was in charge of maintaining the paths between Lesser and Middle Saxan. This suited those who made most use of the area, as it discouraged others without expert knowledge from attempting to navigate the innards of the forest. Her old map featured two ancient paths and several landmarks; and Elaria knew there were several outlying villages south of Greylake. But even if she made good time, she would be spending two days and two nights in Serenity.

Whistling a tune of her own, she quickened her pace.

***

At first sight, the Great Oak was slightly disappointing. Elaria's school expedition had turned back due to a storm so she had in fact never seen it before. It was a quarter the height of a blackwood and actually shorter than some of the nearby pines. But as she got closer, taking in the thick, ravaged trunk – fully fifteen feet across – and the gnarled, twisting branches, she was struck by its elemental solidity; its *presence*. There was an undeniable sense that everything around it: the grass, the soil, the other plants, was transitory and insignificant. She craned her neck and looked up at the top, faintly amused by the tiny new branches sprouting leaves.

The area around the Great Oak had obviously been cleared at some point: the nearest trees were fifty feet away. The waist-high grass showed evidence of recent activity; several areas had been flattened and trampled. Elaria took off her pack and sat down in one such area. Next off were her boots. Her feet were aching but she was pleased to find no blisters when she removed her socks. She drank water from her flask then downed a strip of bacon and a corner of bread. She didn't want to eat too much; that would make her drowsy and she needed to get as far as possible before nightfall. Still munching on the bread, she took out the old map and spread it out across her pack.

Just as she did so, she heard a strange noise away to her right. She turned and sat up on her knees to better see over the grass. Had the cry come from a human or an animal? Her eyes scanned the trees and the shadows. A minute later she was satisfied that there was nothing to concern her, though she pulled the stave closer.

Lifting the wrinkled, faded map, Elaria examined the two routes that ran north: one more to the east, the other west. The north-eastern route contained several landmarks: a cluster of ancient grassy barrows after about five miles, and a lake after ten. The north-western route looked to be straighter but the first landmark was at around twelve miles; the illustration was hard to decipher but seemed to denote a spring. Elaria knew she couldn't put much trust in the distances related by the map but the barrows would at least be visible from some distance.

With the decision made, she downed some more water and packed up. Wincing as she stood, she heard a flap of wings and spied a crow high in the branches of the Great Oak. The presence of the cawing bird seemed almost disrespectful. As she passed the tree, Elaria noted some carvings on the lower trunk and a pattern of holes further up. Recalling some vague memory about how the tree had been used by mages, she watched as the crow flapped into the air then landed on the branch closest to her. Despite the manic movements of its head, she could not avoid the feeling that the dark, tiny eyes were watching her.

***

For the first three or four miles, the path was easy to follow; so Elaria was not faced with a decision until late afternoon, when the sun had long begun its descent. The path forked around a slab of rock inscribed with a language she could not decipher. There was nothing to help her choose between the paths and the forest was too dense up ahead for her to gain any view of the barrows. Worse still, she had already passed a number of hillocks that might actually have been those barrows. Though initially grateful not to have encountered other travellers, she now wished someone would appear.

As she stood there, the only noise was a light wind moving the trees. The weight of the decision grew. If she got it wrong, if she wasted hours or got lost, she might easily not reach Greylake in time. And if she did not make the Tournament, what then? Elaria tapped her stave on the path as if contact with the ground might somehow help. Reasoning that the westward path might at least take her in the direction of the map's second route, she set off.

But hours later, Elaria was lost. Fighting back tears, she squatted down on the path and looked around. She could see nothing but trees and was beginning to wonder if she would ever see anything else. Since the first fork, she had encountered two more and the paths had become increasingly indistinct. In fact, she was no longer entirely certain that this was anything more than a well-used animal trail; there were a lot of hoof prints.

Worse still, a clammy, white mist had materialised, reducing visibility to thirty feet and dampening her clothes as if to match her spirits. Elaria tried to forget the widely-held notion that the sudden appearance of a fog or mist presaged the arrival of a mage or warlock. As she glanced warily in every direction, shapes seemed to reveal themselves then disappear. *Clouds do the same*, she told herself. *It doesn't mean anything.*

But this was strange; such a mist was unusual at this time of day. Elaria had just decided to sit and wait for it to clear when she heard something behind her. She spun around, both hands on the stave. Swathes of mist drifted past. The forest was oddly silent. Another shape appeared: something twisted, something inhuman.

The antlers of a great stag, its broad back five or even six feet from the ground. The burdened head turned towards her and the unblinking eyes regarded her for a moment. Elaria sensed no aggression, only the curiosity of a fellow traveller. As it trotted away, she glimpsed spots of red and pink low on its hind legs. A spotted-heeled stag; they were said to be very rare, even within Serenity. The creature was already lost to the mist but Elaria felt her spirits rise.

She was still feeling the glow of the encounter when the mist cleared some time later. Considering whether to continue or retrace her steps, she spied a nearby pine with a thin covering of leaves. It was the rarest of trees; one with branches that almost offered themselves as natural steps. Depositing her pack, Elaria climbed swiftly until she was twenty feet from the ground and well above the remaining mist. Once there, she felt almost embarrassed by the childish sense of achievement.

With the sun now visible again, she could orientate her gaze roughly to the north. Much of the ground was hidden by the trees but through a gap she spied three grassy mounds: two nearer and one behind them. The mound to the rear also had a stone on top. Barrows.

***

Xalius would have rather been up on the balcony but he knew he had to show his face. Not that his face was a pleasant one: grey, leathery skin, one clouded eye and not a single scrap of hair. Still, the time when he'd cared about such things was long since passed.

His trip into the city was designed firstly to reinforce his authority, secondly to reassure the denizens of Shya that their new overlord was no monster. With this in mind, he stopped on the way to the square and approached a young fruit-seller. The woman appeared utterly terrified, so Xalius instructed his companions – Darian, two warlocks and nine soldiers – to stand back. He knew several hundred city-folk were watching.

'Good day to you.' It had taken him several hours to master basic Shyan. It was an unsophisticated tongue but he felt the effort worthwhile.

The woman still looked terrified. 'Good day …'

'Sir will do fine.'

'Sir. Can I get you something?' The woman clasped her hands together but this only emphasized the trembling. Xalius supposed she was rather attractive: clear skin, jet black hair, gleaming white teeth. But it had been so long – decades in fact – since he had concerned himself with pleasures of the flesh.

'Well, what do you recommend?'

'The dates are very good, sir. The dried apricots too. I'm afraid we're running a bit low on everything else.'

'Because of the caravans.'

'Er …'

She looked at his companions, then at the closest stall-holder, who was suddenly very interested in his fingernails.

'You can answer honestly,' offered Xalius.

'Well, yes, sir.'

'That situation is in hand, I can assure you. I shall take a bag of dates then. Thank you.'

Xalius waved a hand at Darian, who rummaged in his money-bag as he approached the stall. Xalius continued along the street at his usual slow pace. He could have used a mount but he thought perhaps this demonstration of 'human frailty' might ease local fears. It amused him to note the hulking soldiers of his bodyguard having to curtail their usual speedy march. This squad had been assigned to him by Siad, who was currently overseeing the deployment of scouting parties. With them was the chief of guards, Captain Verris.

'Tell me, captain, why do those local troops not wear the sign?'

Xalius aimed a clawed finger at a quartet of local soldiers standing with more of Siad's men. The Shyans had been disarmed but those who had pledged themselves to the Haar Dari were allowed to continue their duties in a limited capacity. They were not, however, wearing the sign that all Haar Dari bore: Rael's eye. Xalius wore the sigil as an emblem upon his cloak. Soldiers were expected to don a black and white tunic over their armour.

'I believe there is a supply issue, sir.'

'Then solve it. We must assimilate these men as quickly as possible. When more of them join, our forces will be enlarged and our number of potential enemies reduced.'

'Yes, sir.'

Upon reaching the square, Xalius encountered another disappointment. Twenty enormous flags now hung around the perimeter but there was insufficient wind to make them fly. Wiping sweat from his brow, he leaned on his cane. Darian had by now caught up and swiftly anticipated what his master would say.

'Of course, sir – the flags. I believe they are a heavy material, fine for windy regions where-'

'Banners. Turn them into banners – then we will not have to worry about the wind.'

Tapping his staff against the broad tiles that covered the square, Xalius surveyed the decaying bodies of the seven local mages. His sense of smell was another of his ailing faculties but even he could detect the sickly scent.

'Presumably, you'd like them taken down before the ceremony?' said Darian.

'Of course.' Surely even Atavius couldn't object to that. 'By Rael, it's hot.'

'Sir, I arranged for a litter to be standing by.'

'Not now. I'll need it to get back up those accursed steps at the palace though.'

Xalius glanced over at Shya's trading house, a large, domed structure that faced onto the square. He spied several groups behind the windows and standing outside: a mixture of his officials – all bearing the sigil – and locals wearing the traditional Shyan robes. The Ceremony of Acceptance – in which the first tranche of respected city-folk would pledge themselves to the Haar Dari – was to take place in two days' time. They were a mix of administrators, merchants and other notables. Some had volunteered; others had required a little persuasion. On the day in between, Xalius was scheduled to make a speech to the trading house; the thought of it reminded him of something.

He turned to Captain Verris. 'The envoys have left to make contact with the traders?'

'Yes, sir. I posted two men outside each of their homes. They will cooperate.'

Verris was also sweating; no surprise given his bronze chest-plate and helmet.

'Captain, you and your men may dispense with your armour. Siad's warriors too. We should not appear overly concerned by the possibility of attack. Nor should we appear as an army of occupation. We are here for the foreseeable future.'

Verris nodded vaguely. 'The threat of assassination though, sir.'

Xalius gestured at his two warlocks, both wearing dark, hooded robes. One was a middle-aged woman: rather plain, but prodigiously talented.

'You know Carvi, I believe – no one has developed the skill of premonition to such a degree. And Ogon, his ability to conjure a shield of Wayforce?'

Ogon tilted his head in acknowledgement. He was not even fifteen yet but had been with Xalius for several years: a slight, pale youth who spent most of his time reading magical tomes.

'Then of course there is yourself and your able troops, captain,' added Xalius.

'Understood, sir.'

There had been a time when Xalius had developed various defensive skills to such a degree that he could have ventured anywhere alone, confident in his ability to protect himself. But he was old and slow, and his use of the Way did not come easily these days. Having said that, with a bit of preparation and the right motivation, he could still perform as he had while incinerating that old mage during the taking of the city. The effort required, however, was immense. Practical Waymaking was for younger folk; those whose bodies it was yet to ruin.

Xalius shielded his eyes and gazed up at the four towers in each corner of the city, which were almost as tall as the palace. 'Some banners up there too, Darian – they will be seen for miles.'

'Of course, sir.'

Xalius lowered his gaze and noted a figure lurking in the shadows beside the trade house. When the figure moved, he realised he was looking at a tall, slender woman. He glimpsed a narrow face framed by red hair before she withdrew into the shadows and around a corner. Xalius felt something: a twinge that usually suggested an individual of talent.

'By Rael, it's hot,' muttered Verris.

'Indeed, it is,' replied Xalius, his mind turning to more mundane matters. 'Darian, find us some shade and something to drink.'

Verris nodded enthusiastically. 'Preferably somewhere well away from this smell.'

***

Elaria smiled whenever she thought of the stag. Momentary though its appearance had been, the encounter had signalled an upturn in her fortunes. She had not tarried long at the barrows. Uttering a prayer to assuage any lingering spirits offended by her climbing the largest of the hillocks, she had spied a small lake, roughly where the map showed it should be. Soon back on what she assumed to be the main path, she arrived before nightfall and slept close to the shore. It was a cold night and she was away by dawn, knowing she needed to reach Greylake the following day.

Supplementing the last of her rations with some small, sharp-tasting apples, she pressed onward, stopping only when she had to. Her feet were now blistered on her toes and heels but Elaria knew this was unavoidable: she had never walked so far at such a rate.

She did not spare a thought for Garrett, though the image of her mother reading her note was difficult to dispel. Mainly, she thought of the Tournament: a vision constructed from all the little pieces of information she had gleaned over the years. Yet there were still so many questions: How many candidates will there be? How many will the Pathfinders want? How many bouts do I have to win? What weapons will be used? What will the climbing test be like? The swimming test? The marching test? After this long trek, would she even be able to march?

Around midday, she reached a crest and was rewarded with a view across a bowl-like valley carpeted by trees. There seemed to be not a single path or clearing but on the other side lay the prize of an unmistakable landmark. Scarring the near side of a distant ridge was a large square of rock. Etched upon it in white were the lines of a vast head topped by a crown. Elaria had always enjoyed her history classes and she knew this to be an image of General Axa-Karr, the military commander who'd led the defence of Saxan two centuries before. The general had hailed from these forests and the local people still honoured him with as much zeal as any of the Espheral gods. The map showed Greylake to be only a few miles beyond the carving.

Elaria started down a zig-zagging path that avoided occasional outcrops of rock. She was about halfway down when she saw smoke rising from a fire in the middle of the forest. There was no chance of reaching the other side before nightfall. She would have to spend the hours of darkness within; and it seemed she would not be alone.

***

The palace library had clearly been neglected by the previous regime. Several shelves had collapsed and the floor and the walls were filthy and patched with mould. The three large, diagonal windows were at least open, but Xalius was sure he could actually feel the dust settling upon him. In one corner, Carvi and three assistants were sorting through an immense pile of books. Young Ogon, meanwhile, was at an enormous table, poring over some tomes that seemed to be salvageable.

'I do hope this is worthwhile,' said Xalius as he negotiated the last step. 'It took me half a bloody hour to get down here.'

Ogon turned and bowed; as did the others. 'My apologies, sir – I should have had the items of interest bought up to you.'

'Ah, it's probably good for me to move around a bit before I retire to bed. What do you have there?'

'A historical text, sir, summarising the possessions of the Shyan kings. I don't believe anyone has had time to examine the contents of the vault yet but there are some interesting artefacts listed.'

'Such as?'

'This, for example – a hoard apparently given as a dowry, three centuries ago.' Ogon ran his pale, slender finger down a worn page. 'Among the items is a kalka gem. They were very rare and rumoured to be-'

'The rumours were false,' replied Xalius as he finally reached the table. 'Those gems are useless, trust me.'

'Ah.' Ogon flipped the page. 'This perhaps – the Sceptre of Gerrius. Seven feet long and supposedly empowered with Wayforce after absorbing the sins of the Shyan folk to appease the gods and end a plague.'

Xalius grimaced at his aching bones as he sat. 'Nonsense. What would a king know about such artefacts or how to use them?'

Ogon set the book aside and opened the one underneath. As he searched for a specific page, Xalius glanced towards the windows. It was a clear evening. Through the central window, he could see a single, low star.

'Here it is,' said Ogon.

Leaning against the table, Xalius examined the script, which he recognised as Ilerian, an arcane language understood by few.

'I can't be sure,' added the young mage, 'but I think this refers to transformative incantations. The Ilerians were said to be experts but I believe much of that knowledge has been lost.'

'Quite so.'

Xalius soon realised that he was reading something exceptionally old, perhaps even more than a thousand years. He noted that the script was a page that had been cut and glued into the book; it might have originally come from a scroll. The content was very complicated; mostly involving chemical combinations and their effects on physiology. He gently turned the page and continued reading for several minutes. He had completely lost track of time when Ogon eventually spoke up again.

'Something of interest, sir?'

'Certainly. It seems this tome is one of a series. Have you seen the others?'

'No, sir.'

'Start searching. Ask Darian for more people to help. And check if there was a librarian or anyone else with knowledge of these books.'

'Yes, sir, of course. Now?'

Xalius nodded.

Before leaving, Ogon whispered to his superior. 'Sir, I know that you have always been interested in the limits of The Way and acquired abilities. Now we come across this long-neglected text. May I ask, could this be Rael's will at work?'

Xalius might normally have told him to hurry up but he admired the youngster's curiosity and enthusiasm.

'Rael's will is that the Haar Dari conquer all. I'm sure he would approve of anything that makes that more likely.'

Ogon nodded earnestly.

'My concerns are also strategic,' added Xalius. 'We have an army of, what, nine thousand? The people of Whispvale and the Skornlands number in the hundreds of thousands; and they possess many Waymakers of their own.'

'The odds are against us,' replied Ogon, his young eyes gleaming.

'Indeed' said Xalius, 'so we need every advantage we can get.'

***

Estimating that she was roughly a third of the way across the valley, Elaria halted while there was still some light. The path seemed well-used, and she'd noted several carvings on trees that suggested some sort of navigational code. For the last half an hour or so, she'd been able to smell smoke but had neither seen nor heard anything of whoever had made the fire.

Swiftly downing the last of her bread and one of the apples, she left the path and scouted around for somewhere to bed down. There was no fern or similar vegetation here and she did not want to make noise by snapping branches. However, she soon located a clear patch of ground beneath a broad tree. The trunk was so knobbly and misshapen that climbing up would be easy – should the need arise.

Elaria took off her boots and put them to one side. She then retrieved her cloak and wrapped it around her before pulling the blanket over the top. A puff of breath showed just how chilly it was but she was confident that her tiredness would make sleep easy.

Resting her head on her pack, she lay there, listening as her breathing slowed. When her eyes closed, she saw only paths and trees and shadows. Time seemed to have passed so slowly; the night she'd left home seemed like weeks ago. She could not believe how vast and devoid of human life the Serenity was. Whatever happened at the Tournament, she knew she would be stronger for having made this journey alone.

Sleep was near when she heard the dogs. First, a rustling of branches, then the quick-moving steps, then the sniffing. She was up in an instant, stuffing her feet into her boots and her blanket into her pack. The darkness was near total, and she had to feel the trunk to find holds before lifting herself upward. With the pack on her back, she clambered further until nestled where the trunk diverged. By now the dogs – at least two – had arrived and were scouring the ground beneath, whining. They knew she was there.

Then came a shout. A question that received an answer from another voice. Elaria scanned the darkness but could see no trace of a light. Then she heard them – behind her. Not daring to adjust her position, she winced as she turned her neck. Two orange smudges: lanterns. The men continued to talk: calmly, without alarm. Elaria at first thought they were speaking Saxan but – though the rhythm and tone was similar – it was some foreign dialect. The lanterns moved away…only to reappear directly below her. When the closest light was held up, Elaria glimpsed a sharp jawline and a thin mouth, below that a loose tunic and a necklace of pale red stones. She reckoned she was at least ten feet off the ground; the light of the lantern could not reach her. The second man said something; and again it sounded like a question. The closer man looked upwards and spoke, as if addressing Elaria directly. She closed her eyes and prayed for them to leave. One of the dogs was now growling, as if assuring its masters that their suspicions were correct.

The man took something from his shoulder. The lantern-light caught the metal head of a spear. Fingers tight on the shaft, he tapped his thumb against it. The second man said something then yawned. The thumb was still tapping against the spearhead. The second dog began to growl.

The man turned and walked away. As the two lights moved clear, the growls of the dogs turned to whines of disappointment. The spearman snapped at the animals, quietening them instantly. His compatriot chuckled as they departed.

Elaria let out a long breath and prayed that the men and their dogs would not return.

***

Eight hours later, she dropped down to the ground and stretched out her cold, aching joints. She was just finishing the last of her food, when she heard a distant cry. If the men and their dogs came in daylight, she'd have no chance. Elaria decided she had to avoid the path completely. With the decision made, she took her bearings from the newly-risen sun and set off to the west.

Occasionally the thick canopy obscured the sky but she was able to keep the sun behind her and follow what seemed a reasonably straight course. Having avoided several broad patches of undergrowth, she eventually found herself on another north-south path. She hadn't heard anything of the men or their dogs in hours and was glad to be heading in the right direction again. Around midday, she reached a faded milestone that told her Greywater was only ten miles away.

After five miles, Elaria found herself at the edge of the forest. Relief turned to fear when she realised the path turned back to the west, skirting the base of the ridge. The slope above her was steep, riven by gullies and covered in thorny bushes. Elaria guessed the only way up was to join the original path she had followed the previous day. Hoping the men and dogs were long gone, she forged onward.

At the point where the paths met, all was quiet. Beside the crossroads was a small, moss-covered shrine to one of the gods, though it was too worn to make out which one. Elaria was far more interested in the spring beside it. She tested the water on her tongue, found it to be sweet-tasting and filled her flask.

The first section of the climb was easy going but once she reached the carving she'd seen from across the valley, the path became a zig-zag and the ground uneven. This close, the image of the general could not be made out, though the immense effort required to create the carving was even more evident. Once past it, Elaria thought the top of the ridge was close but she had to negotiate a series of ledges before finally reaching it.

Exhausted but relieved, she leaned upon her stave and set her eyes on a small town situated between a sinuous river and what she guessed was Lake Treyas. Though the afternoon sunlight sparkled on a surface of blue, Elaria knew she had at last reached Greywater.

CHAPTER 3

The town was busy but she found a room at an inn on Saxan street: always the name of the main thoroughfare of any settlement in the three provinces. Eating a fine dinner of fish and potatoes in her room, she also asked for a cauldron of hot water to be brought up. The fish was pink and soft, unlike any Elaria had previously seen or eaten; she wondered where it came from. After washing herself thoroughly, she collapsed into bed.

Leaving the shutters open so she woke at dawn, she felt like she could sleep for the whole day. But her state of mind wouldn't allow her to rest a minute more. She knew from a notice she'd seen the previous evening that Pathfinder candidates were to report to the market square at the third hour for registration. Elaria could estimate time fairly well if need be but she knew Greywater would have its share of sundials, just like Clearwell. She planned to be at the Tournament early; she would be ready.

Other than the weariness and her sore, blistered feet, she had only a few scratches and bruises from her time in Serenity. But her feet were worrying her; she didn't want any distractions during the day. So, once packed up, she headed downstairs and sought out the innkeeper's wife, Arly, who had brought up her dinner and hot water. She seemed a very kind woman and – though busy with breakfast – located a tub of ointment which she said would ease the blisters and heal the skin. Full of thanks, Elaria applied as much as she could, then hurried through to the parlour, barefoot to let the ointment sink in.

Sitting there with her boots, pack and stave on the floor beside her, she could think of nothing else but the bouts. She knew she would fight with a wooden sword and needed to win two of three to secure a place with the Pathfinders. Not easy. Elaria reckoned she was as good a fighter as Tamia, but she wasn't as tough. Her life had been a privileged one by comparison and she'd never really been hurt. Some nasty cuts and bruises and sprains but never a break or a deep wound. What if she was *really* injured? In pain? Would she be able to fight through it?

She would be facing young men as well as young women. The Pathfinders allowed both to compete equally, though in fact females made up only a fifth of their numbers. As in Elaria's case, this was not something most Saxan mothers wanted for their daughters.

When her breakfast arrived, she resolved to put such questions aside and negotiate the day one step at a time. But as she lifted her mug to drink, she found her hand was trembling.

'Are you sure?' said a loud voice.

Elaria's attention was drawn to the group of four men already in the parlour. Their tea had been poured and their breakfast served but they seemed more interested in talking. From their clothing and manner, she guessed they were local merchants.

'Of course. Yaldeer heard it from one of the captains. And it wasn't some rogue group either. Apparently, there were scores of them.'

'By the gods,' said another man. 'No wonder they brought the Tournament forward.'

'A lot of difference that will make.' said a third. 'A bunch of spotty boys who fancy themselves as warriors.'

'Hardly fair, Lorren,' countered the fourth. 'We should be grateful. If not for the Pathfinders, trade would be suffering even more.

'They are little more than a Militia, as well you know,' said Lorren. 'What Saxan needs is a *proper* army. Our borders must be protected. The thought of what those … things could do to us. It chills the blood.'

'You know what chills my blood?' said the second man with a grave expression.

'Your wife first thing in the morning?' said the third.

The men shared a hearty chuckle.

'No,' retorted the second man with a sneer. 'Yours…even on a good day!'

After another round of laughter, the conversation continued. As she ate, Elaria was dismayed by the lack of respect and faith shown by most of the men for the Pathfinders. Garrett had described them as 'over-rated' but she ignored his views as a matter of course. What she heard did not affect her resolve. By the end of the day, she would be one of them. There was simply no other choice.

Having eaten every piece of bread, cheese, ham and fruit on her breakfast plate, Elaria walked through to the bar area and settled her bill with the innkeeper.

'Here for the Tournament, I expect,' he said as he handed over her change.

She nodded.

'Thought so. You've got that look about you.'

His wife emerged from the kitchen and stood beside him.

'I did wonder,' she added. 'Does your mother know you're here?'

'Yes. Though I doubt she's very happy about it.'

'Be sure it's what you want,' said Arly, a grave expression on her face. 'I've seen people come out of that circle in a terrible state.'

'She's sure,' said the innkeeper with a grin. 'Like I said – got that look about her.'

Elaria felt a little encouraged by his words.

'Well, it's not really my concern, is it?' added Arly. 'But come here, young lady, I've something to help you through the day.'

When she opened up the counter, Elaria put her stave and bag down and followed the woman through a narrow doorway into the kitchen. Arly stopped beside a wooden board packed with cakes.

'Raisin buns. Fresh out of the oven. Here.'

She took two of the largest buns and handed them over.

'Thank you. You're very kind.'

Elaria was about to head back to the bar when she heard a familiar voice.

'Morning to you. I'm looking for a runaway.'

Elaria froze.

'Her name is Elaria Rose Carlen. Seventeen. Tall with long blonde hair.'

Garrett's tone suggested this was not the first time he had recited the phrases that morning.

As a tremor chilled her back, Elaria pressed herself against the wall to ensure he didn't see her. Arly watched her and frowned.

The innkeeper turned towards the kitchen. 'Er …'

Moving back so that she was also out of sight, his wife shook her head emphatically. Her husband was not slow to get the message.

'No. Haven't seen her, I'm afraid, young man.'

'You're sure? I've checked all the other inns.'

Elaria realised she could see a blurry reflection of her brother's face in a copper pan hanging behind the counter.

'I'm sure,' said the innkeeper.

Garrett didn't reply.

Then Elaria remembered her stave and bag. They were in plain sight. If Garrett noticed them, he would know instantly that she was there.

She watched the reflection. His head was moving. She couldn't make out his eyes but he seemed to be looking around.

Garrett sniffed noisily. Saying nothing more, he turned and walked away. Only when she heard the inn door shut, did Elaria allow herself to breathe.

***

The Circle was located between Greywater's main square and the edge of Lake Treyas. Ten yards in diameter, the fighting space was marked by a line of red bricks that stood out from the usual grey. It was surrounded by a high, circular stone arena with five levels of seating. Access was via a single, broad arch. The only people Elaria could see inside were a youthful group of Pathfinders hanging blue and white banners.

Outside were a dozen older warriors and a few interested observers. Four officers sat at an enormous table, taking the details of the candidates, of whom there were at least sixty already. Elaria lined up and pulled the peak of a newly-purchased cloth cap over her face.

As she waited, more Pathfinders arrived and they all seemed very interested in the candidates. When she spied Tamia, Elaria turned away and prayed she wouldn't be seen; the last thing she needed was such a distraction. Fortunately, she soon reached the table where the officer asked his questions and made his notes. Fearing the consequences of lying, Elaria gave her real name, age, place and date of birth.

She was then directed towards a holding area, the courtyard of a nearby inn where she found herself standing amidst her competitors. Some clearly knew each other and exchanged tense observations or attempted jokes to ease the tension. But many of them said nothing. Elaria noted two young men – brothers by the looks of them – who were six and a half feet tall and built like wrestlers. They were sparring and already seemed to be working themselves into a frenzy.

Fortunately, there wasn't much time to worry about her rivals. Five minutes after Greywater's bell tower announced the third hour, registration was closed. One desperate fellow clattered into the square on horseback after the four officers had left their table. Despite his pleas, he was turned away.

Three more senior officers – identifiable by the gold trim on their white cloaks – entered the courtyard. The oldest of them was a grey-haired, noble-looking fellow who introduced himself as General Ralk. He then introduced the others, General Vraya and Captain Kano. Elaria remembered Kano from her conversations with Tamia. She had not realised he had Lyther blood in him, though she knew there were many such people scattered across Whispvale. The influence was clear in his pale skin and grey, almost silvery hair. He wore an impressive set of armour, with numerous studs and other adornments.

Ralk was an older man, sixty at least, with a hawkish face and a stern demeanour. 'It is we three who shall judge you today. Our deputies will take you through the drills – marching, swimming and climbing – this morning. These are all important, and anyone who doesn't reach the passing level will be disqualified. But as you will know, the Pathfinders are a fighting force and the most important criteria of all is your performance in the Circle. Two victories from three are required for you to be accepted. Exceptions are occasionally made but only in very unusual circumstances. In the unlikely event that any of you youngsters possess ability with the Way, you are *not* to use it. This is considered cheating. We have several practitioners present and be assured that any attempt to do so will be noted. Any questions may be directed towards Sergeant Lallik here.'

A broad man with a thick, dark beard nodded respectfully to General Ralk as the senior officers left. His accent was as rough as Elaria had ever heard.

'Right then, you lot, I hope you're feeling strong because that lake is bloody cold today. Your gear can stay here in the courtyard. Follow me.'

***

Two hours later, Elaria slumped down against the courtyard wall. She didn't even have the strength to fetch her pack but thankfully the younger Pathfinders came around with mugs and a pail of water. Along with the other remaining candidates, she sat there in silence, breathing hard, relieved that she had got through.

Informing them that they could remain seated, Sergeant Lallik ambled into the centre of the courtyard holding several sheets of paper. He told them that of the original ninety-one candidates, fifty-two had failed to meet the basic standard in one of the three disciplines. He then read through the finishing positions for the one-mile swim, the three-mile run and the wall-climb.

In the swim, Elaria had finished twenty-third, with only two women ahead of her. In the run, she had finished seventeenth, the first female. And in the climb, she had reached the ninth hold, which put her in the top quarter of all candidates. The holds were tiny wooden knots attached to a thirty-foot climbing board. As with the run, this task was not easy in soaking wet clothes. Each candidate had been supported by a rope and harness but Elaria was not fond of heights; she had not looked down once.

'You did well,' said a youth sitting close by. Elaria had seen him at the finishing line of the run looking barely out of breath.

'Not as well as you. Anyway, it's the fights that count.'

Though the young man nodded, this was clearly not a source of confidence for him.

Sergeant Lallik returned a short time later. 'You have one hour until the fights begin. You'll be called out as pairs. Dry yourselves off, get some water down and eat if you wish. Remember, you'll have helmets and the armoured coat. They're coloured red. Any clean hit on the red counts. The first to three hits wins. The swords are wooden and blunt so it's all about technique. Any questions?'

When no hands were raised, Sergeant Lallik strode out of the courtyard, leaving two men behind to guard the entrance. A curious candidate went to look out at the crowd now gathering outside the Circle. One of the guards slammed the door shut.

***

Dozens were called out to fight before her but to Elaria the time passed quickly. Once she'd dried herself off, she drank some water and ate one of

Arly's raisin buns. She sat alone in a corner, staring at the ground, running over all she had learned about sword-fighting: footwork, counter-attack, parries, blocks, watching the eyes, watching the weapon. She tried her best to ignore those returning from the Circle but it was easy to distinguish winners from losers. Despite the helmets and coats, there were a few injuries too: a couple of broken noses and fingers and several damaged limbs.

She didn't even hear the name of her first opponent. When hers was called she simply hurried through the doorway and marched towards the Circle. She barely noticed the hundreds of people hanging around outside or the weary competitors going the other way. At the arch, she gave her name to the Pathfinder officer in charge and was shown to a table just outside the fighting area where several more junior officers were waiting.

'Name?' asked one.

'Elaria Rose Carlen.' She decided there and then not to look at the sea of faces surrounding her.

The officer made a note while another ushered her forward to a wooden rack full of red helmets and armoured coats.

A female Pathfinder sized her up and handed her an archaic-looking helmet. 'Try this.'

Elaria tried it on and found it too big. While the woman searched for a smaller one, Elaria noted the three senior officers from earlier in the day. They were sitting on the bottom row next to a grand-looking fellow who had been furnished with a cushion. He possessed an impressive moustache and wore a golden chain around his neck.

'Pretend he's not there,' advised the woman as she offered Elaria another helmet.

'Who is he?'

'Jaremy Saxan.'

Elaria had never seen the mayor of Saxan. The noble family was revered throughout their lands but, on this particular day, she could not have cared less who was present.

The second helmet fitted well. The weight was unpleasant but she was grateful for the protection. The woman helped her with the straps and then put the coat on. The sleeveless armour was rudimentary; two iron plates connected by worn leather straps. Elaria felt rather cumbersome with it on but guessed her competitors would feel the same. And only now did she meet hers.

'Grayna Tille.'

The officer noted the name. Grayna Tille was younger than Elaria, shorter too; but that did not stop her glaring at her opponent as her coat was put on. She was a rough-looking character with close-set eyes and spiky black hair. Elaria did not recognise her from the trials but she was relieved to be facing another female in this first bout.

'Where are the swords?' she asked as a method of response to the glare.

'Eager to get started?'

A smiling Pathfinder with a well-trimmed beard approached, two of the wooden weapons in his hands. He handed one to Grayna and one to Elaria. 'I'm your judge. Any clean hit on red is a point. I'll call them out. Three points and you win. Leave the circle – your opponent gains a point. Lose your sword – your opponent gains a point. Clear?'

Elaria nodded.

'Clear'. Grayna was breathing in through her nose and practising swings with her sword. Elaria moved aside and stretched her arms and legs.

The officer that stood up from the table had to shout to make himself heard above the crowd. 'Bout thirty-five. Elaria Rose Carlen against Grayna Tille. First fight for both.'

'Follow me.' The bearded warrior led them across the stone floor and over the red line. He positioned them six feet apart then stood between them.

'Fight.'

The Pathfinder had barely stepped aside when Grayna darted forward, swinging manically. Elaria parried two blows with relative ease but was late to realise she'd retreated close to the red line. Grayna cut off her attempt to side-step to the right and lunged at her. Elaria knew she had to block rather than evade but watched helplessly as the blade slid through her defences and tapped against her armour.

'One to Grayna,' announced the bearded judge, sounding rather bored.

Elaria had half-expected them to be summoned to the centre but then she realised the fight was continuing. Somehow batting away Grayna's next lunge, she swung one handed and won herself some more space.

Spinning away from the edge of the circle, she reminded herself to use her reach against her shorter opponent. Before Grayna could get too close, she swept at her head. Grayna ducked neatly beneath the blow, scurried forward and lunged once more, sword straight. Again, the clank of wood on iron.

'Two to Grayna.'

Enraged by her own failure, Elaria swung again – lower this time. Grayna retreated nimbly and easily evaded the three swings that followed. Elaria knew with a horribly certainty that she was outclassed. But she still had the reach: she could keep Grayna at bay, waiting for an opportunity.

Her next swing was met by a solid block, and her opponent countered aggressively, battering Elaria's blade until it shivered. The fifth blow landed low, knocking the sword clean out of her hands. Stunned, Elaria stood there motionless. Then she turned and saw her weapon lying some distance away, at the feet of two grinning youths in the first row.

'Three and the bout to Grayna.'

Elaria turned back in time to receive a cordial nod from the young woman, who then calmly walked back to the table, already removing her helmet.

'Come on,' said the bearded Pathfinder, beckoning to Elaria. 'That's it. Out.'

***

During the next hour, Elaria gave serious thought to giving up. She returned to her corner of the courtyard and sat there, once again gazing at the ground. She wouldn't go home but perhaps she might find work in Greywater; maybe the kindly Arly might give her a job?

She just could not come to terms with the speed and manner of her defeat. She had done nothing; failed completely to impose herself on the bout. It was embarrassing and the very thought of it brought a flush to her face. What had she been thinking coming here? She wasn't ready. She wasn't up to it.

But when her name was called for a second time, she stood without hesitation and crossed the courtyard once more. There were only about thirty candidates left now and she found herself walking behind her opponent, a young man named Bray. She remembered him from the climb; he had almost reached the top of the wall. No shortage of bravery then.

She heard a few comments thrown her way as she neared the arena, most of them encouraging. Then a hand grabbed her arm. She wrenched it away but found herself staring at Garrett.

'Rosie, don't go in there again,' he said, his voice gentle. 'I don't want to see you hurt.'

Her older brother seemed to have lost a little of his usual composure. His hair had not been combed and he was sweating.

Even though she detested him, Elaria felt a brief, strange pang of relief at seeing a familiar face. It did not last long.

'Come on, now,' he said. 'Don't embarrass yourself.'

'Go ...' Her voice sounded thin and weak. She cleared her throat. 'Go home, Garrett.'

With that, she strode on to the arena: under the arch, straight up to the table. When Bray turned around, Elaria copied Grayna and offered only a glare. Lean and athletic, the young man simply grinned. From that moment on, he and Garrett became the same thing: an enemy to be overcome.

Elaria felt a strange calm as she again put on the helmet and armour and took up her sword. It was a different judge this time, but the procedure was the same. In moments, she was back within the Circle.

'Fight.'

Bray was careful; always on the move, always watching. Elaria told herself to take her time, work out a strategy. As they circled each other, some in the crowd began to boo, urge them to strike. She resisted the temptation, as did her opponent.

Elaria had been focusing on his sword and his feet but when she looked into his eyes, she now saw an unmistakable fear. The grin had been bravado. He was an excellent climber but was he really much of a fighter?

Now Elaria took the initiative. She chopped at his shoulder, lunged at his stomach. Bray parried both attacks but she saw his jaw trembling. He was unsure of himself, unsure how to get into the fight. Elaria feinted a low sweep, then cut up towards his face. The tip of her blade clanged against the cheek-guard.

A cheer from the crowd.

'One to Elaria.'

Bray looked shocked; paralysed. She repeated the move. He saw it, twisted his blade to protect his face. But this was no feint. She hit his flank hard.

'Two to Elaria.'

'Fight, boy!' someone bellowed.

Bray launched himself forward, face contorted, and unleashed a flurry of blows. Elaria countered but he was quick on his feet and she soon found herself close to the red line. As she tried to twist her way out of the trap, he caught her across the shoulder.

'One to Bray.'

The crowd were getting into the bout now. Individual comments were drowned out by the growing noise.

Bray came at her again. She knocked his sword to the left, then the right. He went for her head. She held her ground and the blades met. Elaria saw her chance. She grabbed his wrist; held his blade-hand. He was already pulling free but she jabbed at him one-handed. Clumsy and slow, the strike nevertheless connected with his chest.

'Three and the bout to Elaria.'

Bray turned to the judge. 'It didn't touch me! I swear!'

But his complaints were drowned out by the crowd.

Elaria felt her spirits surge as she walked back to the table. As she went to remove her helmet, the bearded Pathfinder intervened.

'Might as well leave it on. You're fighting again soon.'

***

His name was Kryk; and Elaria couldn't believe he wasn't already a Pathfinder. Tall, muscular and exuding confidence, he looked to be in his mid-twenties. She heard from someone behind her that he had won his first two fights.

'Unlucky,' said the bearded officer as he handed over her sword. 'The matches are selected by lot. Just do your best.'

'Any advice?' she asked as Kryk tapped his sword tip against the red line.

'Win.'

There was something about the sarcastic comment that made Elaria feel a little better. The judge was the same as the previous round and she followed him out to the centre of the Circle beside Kryk.

'May as well relax,' Elaria said to her opponent, if only to draw a response and remind herself that he was just another person. 'As you're already through, I mean.'

'Don't expect me to go easy just because you're a girl.'

To his credit, Kryk was true to his word. Within half a minute of the fight commencing, Elaria was a point down. Her foe was not only large but quick and she could do nothing about the angled jab to her chest.

She was still trying to settle when he feinted twice, then swung hard at her head. The sword struck the helmet just above the ear and sent her staggering across the circle. In trying not to cross the line, she stumbled and fell. When she looked up, half her arm was outside the Circle.

It was over. She had lost.

'Only one point at a time,' explained the judge, standing between them while she was on the ground. 'Two to Kryk.'

A glimmer of hope returned. She could fight on.

The crowd had gone quiet to hear his comment. Another voice spoke up, a familiar voice.

'Go on, Elaria – you can do it!'

Tamia.

Emboldened by her friend's encouragement, Elaria shook the dizziness away and got to her feet. The judge withdrew and gestured for them to continue.

Kryk came on again, flicking the blade around with practiced ease. He even threw in a couple of elaborate foot shuffles which drew a mixture of cheers and boos. He seemed to be enjoying himself.

Elaria forced herself to advance. She blocked twice, only just able to absorb the weight of the impacts. Kryk spun through a hundred and eighty degrees and launched a double-handed swing at her head. The blade missed her helmet by an inch. And now he was off-balance.

She swept at his back and –

though he nearly threw himself clear – wood struck iron.

The roar from the crowd was as loud as she'd heard that day.

'One to Elaria.'

Kryk drew in a deep breath, as if to calm himself and avoid another mistake. He attacked with controlled aggression, quick and strong enough to keep her completely on the defensive. He cut off every attempt at escape and forced her back towards the line again. She actually had to look down to see where it was: inches behind her heels.

Kryk raised the sword high and swung down at her head. Elaria got her weapon up and blocked but the handle of his struck her fingers. She heard herself cry out but she somehow kept hold of the sword. Kryk did not hesitate. He batted away her feeble attempt at a counter and swung back the other way.

Elaria threw her head back too late. The sword hit her nose. Pain blazed into her as she fell backwards. Somebody grabbed her and held her up. Feeling blood flow from her throbbing nose, she put her hand to it.

Her vision cleared slightly and she realised just how far over the line she was. She hadn't heard the announcement but saw Kryk raise his sword in triumph as he marched back to the table. Gripped by anger, Elaria dragged herself away from the man holding her.

But she saw he was just a kindly member of the crowd: a bald, middle-aged man who then took a handkerchief from his pocket and handed it to her. As blood continued to spill through her fingers, she grabbed the handkerchief and lurched towards the table.

The bearded Pathfinder took her by the arm. 'Tip your head back. Give me that.'

He held the handkerchief against her nose.

As the pain diminished, Elaria felt nothing but an empty sadness. It really was over now.

The warrior cleaned away some of the blood. 'Don't think it's broken but you've lost a big chunk of skin. Come and sit down.'

'No. I'm fine.'

'As you wish.' He returned the handkerchief.

One of the female Pathfinders helped her remove the helmet and the coat. 'You really should sit down for a bit.'

'No. No, thank you.'

She staggered towards the arch, clutching the handkerchief to her nose. All she wanted was to get back to the courtyard; get away from these people.

A hand gripped her arm. Fearing it was Garrett, she spun around, ready to strike him. But it was Tamia.

'Lari. You fought so well. Just unlucky.'

Elaria couldn't find any words. She felt warm tears upon her cheeks. All she could do was point at the courtyard.

Tamia nodded and put her arm around her. 'Let's get you cleaned up.'

***

The courtyard was deserted. Elaria wasn't sure how much time had passed but Sergeant Lallik had been in earlier to list the names of those who had passed. This group had been taken into the arena and Elaria had heard a great cheer go up. The others had gradually sloped away, though many of the Pathfinders met them at the door to offer consoling words and encouragement.

'Come on then,' said Tamia – for the third time.

Elaria stood. Her nose was still throbbing but at least the bleeding had stopped. She put her bag and stave over her shoulder and walked alongside Tamia towards the door where two guards still stood.

'What are you going to do then?'

Before she could answer, Elaria spotted Garrett lurking outside the courtyard. She felt tears coming again but her attention was then drawn to the bearded Pathfinder from the arena. He strode past Garrett and into the courtyard alongside General Ralk.

'Ah, there you are,' said the officer in his martial tone, 'we were told you were still here.'

Elaria was not entirely sure he was addressing her but there could be no doubt when the general came to a halt two paces away. As a breeze wept across the courtyard, he patted down his grey hair.

'Candidate Carlen, isn't it?'

Tamia gave her a nudge.

'Yes, sir.'

'Well, I've some good news. Despite your losses in the Circle, your performance elsewhere has served you well. General Vraya is a stickler for the rules but he was outvoted by myself and Captain Kano. I don't believe we've ever seen a girl do so well across the non-fighting disciplines. It would be remiss of us to overlook such natural ability and you were damned unfortunate to come across that big brute. Congratulations.'

General Ralk offered his hand. Elaria shook it, still trying to absorb what he'd told her.

'You can attend the formal induction ceremony with the others tomorrow. Sergeant Malcanoth here will tell you what to do. He helped you out too, by the way – very impressed with your attitude.'

The bearded warrior looked away as Ralk turned on his heels and marched back across the courtyard. Elaria noticed a little of what she presumed to be her blood on Malcanoth's white tunic sleeve.

'Thank you.'

'You might change your mind when you do your first drill with Sergeant Lallik,' he said. 'Come on, you'll stay at Greywater Barracks tonight.'

Elaria and Tamia exchanged a smile then followed him across the courtyard.

'Your brother's still here,' said Tamia as they reached the doorway. 'I assume he wants to take you back?'

Elaria nodded.

Once outside, she did not even look at him.

'Elaria, can I speak with you?' Garrett tried hard to sound polite and reasonable.

She kept walking.

'Elaria.'

Sergeant Malcanoth stopped and turned.

'I'm her brother,' Garrett told him. 'She's a runaway.'

'She's seventeen,' said Tamia.

'Then what she does is up to her,' said Malcanoth.

Garrett tried to match the sergeant's implacable glare but he couldn't do it. Malcanoth raised an eyebrow and went on his way.

Now Elaria did look at her brother. His hands were bunched into fists and his entire face was rigid with anger.

'I'll find you, Rosie,' said Garrett. 'Wherever you go, I'll find you.'

CHAPTER 4

Xalius awoke to find himself bathed in the sunlight emanating from a high window. He was sitting at the azure oval table in the palace's great hall, a pile of the ancient texts before him. At the far end of the table, Ogon was making notes. The young warlock had made enormous progress in the previous week, creating an index of the pertinent passages within the books.

'Ah, do you feel better now, sir?'

'I was merely resting my aged eyes.'

'Of course.'

Aged *eye* in fact; the right one was virtually useless.

Though he knew he should be devoting more of his time to the administration of Shya, Xalius and his young apprentice had studied the texts into the early hours. Unless they were excessively fond of fabrication, it seemed that the ancient Shyans had indeed achieved some remarkable results; transforming utterly ordinary beings into weapons of war. Though much more research was required, Xalius was already beginning to consider the possibilities of some exploratory experimentation.

One of the doors creaked open and Darian poked his head in.

'General Siad is here, sir. Shall I show him in?'

'Of course.'

Ogon pushed his chair back and stood.

'Keep at your work,' insisted Xalius, wincing as he rose. 'I shall confer with the marshal outside.'

Fortifying himself with some black brandy and a handful of dried fruit from his breakfast tray, Xalius made his way towards the balcony. By the time he reached it, Siad had already entered the great hall and marched across it. Despite the heat, he wore a bulky silver cuirass with the Sign engraved in red. For once he was without his axe, armed only with a small cleaver hanging from his belt.

'Good morning,' said Xalius as they both stepped outside.

Siad answered with a cordial nod. There was no formal hierarchy within the Haar Dari command structure. Xalius was certainly Atavius's most trusted deputy but Siad was without doubt his greatest military leader. Xalius did possess the title of chancellor but preferred not to be addressed by it; a simple sir was sufficient for him. When the Imperator was present, the lack of clarity was not a problem; when he was absent, it could cause difficulties. But the takeover of Shya had been achieved easily and – for the moment at least – relations were good. Xalius respected Siad; his personal valour and ruthlessness were beyond question. His intellect and wider understanding of the world, however, were somewhat limited.

Siad scratched his great, hairless head and placed his enormous, battered hands on the balcony. He grunted; presumably a note of appreciation for the view.

'If you'd like some quarters here, there are plenty of rooms on the level below.'

'I'll stay at the gatehouse. Close to trouble – in case I'm needed.'

'Very well, though that seems unlikely. The priests have been tamed and the third Ceremony of Acceptance is next week. Not much to concern us is there?'

Siad turned to him. 'Regarding the Shyans, no.'

'Ah, you mean your men.'

Siad was keeping them occupied with a punishing schedule of patrols but they had encountered no enemy force or scouts. It appeared that those to the north didn't care enough about Shya to intervene.

The marshal nodded. 'I have barely enough room to house them. They have been training for months and are thirsty for conquest. A few hours fighting this rabble and now here we are kicking our heels again.'

'Until another silver eagle arrives, we have little choice.'

The giant tapped a thick knuckle against the balcony. 'Ours is an army of many races. We all fight under the Sign but I have Sand Lions, Irregulars from all over and more bands, groups and cults under my command than I can remember. There are old enmities and suspicions based on past conflicts. Inaction is not helpful.'

'I understand. And that we would be wise to exploit this success and move before our enemies can organise themselves. But we cannot predict with any certainty how any such advance might develop. We cannot be sure who will fight us.'

'So far I've allowed my patrols only as far as the Skornish border. We could perhaps scout further afield, identify the best route north?'

'Word of our victory here will have travelled as far as Whispvale by now. Perhaps we should allow our enemies to believe that this is the limit of our ambitions.'

'There are several small towns just over the border.'

'We were told to consolidate here. Nothing more. Siad, I cannot stop you; you command our army. But if asked, I will be forced to disclose that it was *your* decision. Yours alone.'

Siad grunted; not a pleasant grunt.

'Who knows,' said Xalius, attempting to lighten the mood, 'Perhaps a silver eagle will arrive tonight.'

Siad cleared his throat. 'No one understands Rael's will better than the Imperator but sometimes I wish our path was clearer.'

Xalius almost raised an eyebrow. He had long suspected that Siad was far from a true believer; more a warmonger interested in prestige and personal power. If honest with himself, Xalius could not claim to be immune to such notions himself. However, he did believe the Imperator to be an individual of rare quality and strength; and who was he to doubt that Rael's hand guided him?

Xalius pointed down at the wall. 'There is more than one way to keep our army occupied. The defences were badly damaged during the assault. The mayor has crews at it but there is plenty of work to go around.'

Siad furrowed his brow before relenting. 'You're right. If they're not on patrol or drilling they can shift stones. We'll keep them disciplined. Hard.'

'Without forgetting the odd reward, of course. It's time we took advantage of some of the local womenfolk. I'm sure your senior officers would appreciate a bit of female company. Some dusky beauties here, eh?'

'Quite so.'

'When things have settled down, we shall start amending local laws; marry our men off; begin breeding the next generation of Haar Dari.'

While gathering strength in the Madlands, Atavius' forces had not been so restrained with the female population. Recent discussions had focused on the need to appease where possible. Why add to their list of enemies?

'The Imperator would approve.'

'Indeed, he would.'

Darian appeared at the doorway. 'Sir, there is a young woman demanding to see you.' The old man was quite out of breath.

'Must be your lucky day, Xalius,' said Siad. 'A dusky beauty, perhaps?' With a grunt of laughter, he strode past Darian. 'I shall brief my commanders.'

Xalius peered at Darian, who was shielding his face from the sun. 'What does she want?'

'She claims she has uncovered a traitor in the city. Her name is Lishara.'

The name meant nothing to Xalius, but he had an inkling who she might be. 'Red hair?'

'Why yes, sir. How did you know?'

'A hunch. Send her up.'

***

Xalius was surprised when four individuals entered the hall. The first to enter was Verris and his boots tapped on the bright redwood floor as he marched up to Xalius's chair. They had actually found several thrones in the palace, but Xalius didn't for a moment entertain the idea of sitting in one, even though the city was his.

'I wouldn't trust either of these two, sir,' said the captain, aiming a thumb over his shoulder. 'But they've both been thoroughly searched.'

Xalius detected a lascivious edge to the comment as Verris waved the two newcomers forward. Another senior guard stood behind them, watching intently.

The girl could not have been more than twenty: she was tall, rather elegant, with an unusual combination of dark skin and red gold hair. She wore a long, stylish dress; light brown with dark vertical stripes. The overall effect was quite striking; so much so that Xalius gave the second individual only a cursory examination. He was dressed well in the robes of a local but was so short and pale that he seemed thoroughly out of place.

His expression seemed to be a combination of fear and curiosity, his gaze shifting around the room.

Fear did not seem to be a problem for Lisahra. She bowed low.

'Chancellor, it is a great honour to meet you.'

'I care not for that title, young lady.' Xalius could sense this was an individual with some power with the Way: raw perhaps, but tangible. 'Why are you here?'

'Firstly, to pay my respects,' she said. 'And secondly to bring you this spy.'

The man shook his head.

Verris added, 'she was holding a knife on him until we took it off her.'

'So who are *you*?'

He also bowed. 'Vikter Agorr, sir.'

'And are you a spy?'

'No.'

Xalius had been quite an accomplished truth-teller in his younger years. The ability was long-neglected but he sensed no deceit from the man.

'He lies,' said Lisahra. 'He arrived not long after you, sir, and he has been snooping around the city ever since-'

'-Gathering information, actually,' said Vikter. 'If I might explain myself?'

Despite the evident frustration of young Lisahra, Xalius gestured for him to continue.

'Much obliged. I am a trader, a translator, a negotiator, a facilitator. I know every man and woman of import between here and Port Llanos. I am well informed, well regarded and well intentioned. I-'

Lisahra snorted derisively.

'Shall I have them removed?' asked a clearly annoyed Verris.

'Not yet.'

At a nod from Xalius, Vikter continued.

'I look for opportunities – for myself and for others. Upon hearing of the progress of the Haar Dari, I struck upon an idea; an idea that could be of great benefit to two notable groups with some ...similar aims.'

Lisahra was now struggling to maintain her composure.

'Get to the point, man,' said Xalius. 'What do you know of our aims?'

'If your recent history in the Madlands is to be believed – conquest. I believe I can help you with the next phase of your advance.'

'How exactly?'

Vikter clasped his hands together. 'Unfortunately, I would have to be confident regarding my own interests to go into any more detail. Perhaps we could talk alone?'

Xalius sighed.

'I can assure you it would be to your great advantage,' added Vikter.

'Why do I feel like a customer at a market stall?'

Vikter attempted a genial smile.

Xalius leaned back into the chair and turned to Lisahra. 'He seems rather talkative for a spy.'

Vikter answered before she could. 'Sir, she knows I'm not a spy. It seems to me that she simply needed a reason to come here. I have no idea what her-'

Vikter stopped, his face suddenly ashen. Two seconds later he dropped to his knees, fingers digging into his scalp. His mouth clamped shut and his teeth began to grind. Tears fell from his eyes and blood trickled out of both nostrils.

'Please, stop. Please!'

Verris and his guard exchanged confused glances. Lisahra was gazing at the far corner of the room, face impassive.

'Stop,' said Xalius, suppressing a smirk.

She obeyed his command immediately.

Vikter fell onto his side, sucking in breaths and whimpering.

'Quite impressive,' said Xalius, 'though the trembling in your finger was rather obvious.' Upon that finger was a small ring with a purple gem, clearly the artefact through which Lishara channelled the Way.

She gave another little bow and several strands of red gold hair fell across her shoulder.

Xalius admitted to himself that he rather liked her already. 'So why *are* you here, young lady?'

She gazed back at him with wide, unblinking eyes. 'To learn.'

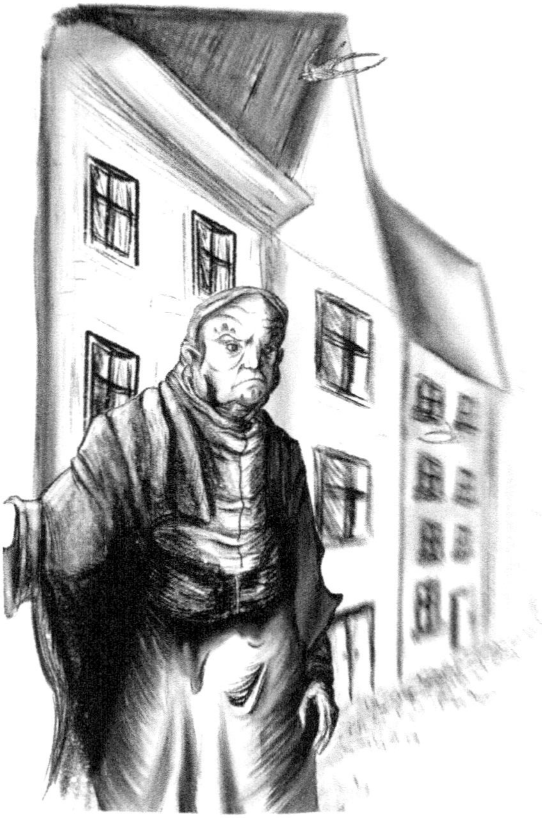

CHAPTER 5

Though the camp was temporary, tidying it was not easy. There were tents to dismantle, fires to put out, pots and pans to collect, blankets and sleeping mats to roll, saddlebags to pack. And all of this had to be accomplished within an hour of dawn. Everybody knew how long they had because a large hourglass placed in the centre of the camp was turned over at sunrise.

Elaria had just packed the last of the eight saddlebags assigned to her when a soldier on horseback threw a blanket in her direction.

'Hey!'

The soldier ignored her and rode out of the clearing to join the others congregating near the path. Cursing under her breath, Elaria unbuckled the saddlebag, rolled up the blanket and somehow squeezed it in. She carried the bag over to an old tree stump where the pack-donkeys were tethered. Three of her fellow recruits were already loading them up.

'Another wonderful day,' moaned Kryk. Elaria had been dismayed to find herself in the same regiment as her former foe. But as the two had got to know each other, she noted that – though prone to arrogance – he seemed a decent enough man. Those who had succeeded at the Tournament had been divided between the three regiments of Pathfinders that protected Whispvale. Elaria had been glad to find herself with Tamia under the command of Captain Kano but she only saw her friend in the evenings.

For their first fifty days, the new recruits would be limited solely to menial tasks. As well as setting up and clearing the camp, these included cooking, washing and digging latrines. The work was tiring, repetitive – and often smelly – and Elaria complained as much as the others.

And yet she had never had such a wonderful time. From the very first night at the Greywater barracks, she had found herself among men and women with whom she shared so much: a love for their homeland, a commitment to protect it, and a determination to do good. Clearwell and everything connected to it already seemed so very far away.

Almost two weeks had passed since the Tournament. After some days of training that included all the Pathfinders – from newest recruit to oldest veteran – they had been briefed by Sergeant Haskey.

They were tasked with patrolling the coast south of Heartsong, to protect and reassure several fishing villages that had been raided by the Beastkin. These attacks had been opportunistic, with only a handful of raiders involved, but the creatures had caused considerable damage and escaped with livestock, food and treasure.

Elaria knew it would be weeks before she would even be given a sword, let alone taught anything useful like map-reading, tracking or combat tactics. They had at least all been given daggers. The recruits were also not yet deemed worthy of the expensive and well-drilled patrol horses that their superiors rode. Elaria and her nine fellow recruits had each been given a pony. They were also all responsible for a pack-donkey.

'Thanks,' she said, as a male recruit named Dawin handed her the reins of her pony. He was a short lad with an unruly thatch of curly, auburn hair. Elaria's mount was named Stripe on account of the line of black fur across his right flank. Stripe was strong and good-tempered but would eat absolutely anything. Elaria spent much of her day tugging on his reins as the animal tried to sample every plant in reach of whatever path they were on. As she tied a line from his saddle to the donkey's bridle, Dawin was unravelling his own rope.

'Apparently we'll see the sea today.'

'Really?'

Elaria had been interested to discover the lands north of Greywater but it had mostly been forest and moorland.

Dawin continued: 'From today we follow the coastal path all the way to Heartsong.' He always seemed to know everything that was going on, so Elaria had made sure they were on good terms. In general, the recruits were keen to help each other out, knowing that they needed to do their best to impress their instructors. Sergeant Malcanoth in particular was fond of reminding them that a third of recruits never became Pathfinders. He had spent quite some time with the youngsters at the barracks but in recent days always seemed to be off scouting and tracking.

From what Elaria had observed, Malcanoth was respected but far from the most popular member of his regiment. He had a reputation for moodiness and the male recruits seemed convinced that he consistently favoured his female compatriots, both recruits and Pathfinders.

Elaria was more interested in his ability with the Way. Most Pathfinders relied on their swords but Malcanoth was known to be quite gifted. Elaria put him in his late twenties, which was indeed young for a Waymaker of any skill. She had seen the occasional mage's show back in Clearwell but could never really imagine some of the more impressive abilities she had heard of. It was still unlikely that she would: according to Tamia, Waymakers had to use their skill sparingly, for invoking such power came at a cost to their health.

Stripe's determination to struggle through nettles to consume a nearby halfpenny fruit dragged Elaria back to more mundane concerns. She belatedly realised that Dawin, Kryk and the others were already leading their ponies towards the path. Further along it, the first of the Pathfinders were on the move.

***

As they neared the coast, the column was gradually enveloped by fog and Elaria recalled getting lost in Serenity before the stag had appeared. By the time the Pathfinders passed over several small dunes and reached a narrow sandy beach, hardly any of the Green Sea was visible; and what Elaria could see of it was grey. When the call to halt came back around the fourth hour of the day, she swiftly dismounted and examined a handful of sand. It was fine and white, unlike anything she had seen before, and she felt a smile forming on her face.

'Typical,' said Kryk as he also dismounted. 'Can't see a bloody thing.'

Dawin pointed north. 'Sarli Rock is about ten miles hence. Saltsand not far after it.'

'What's that?' asked Elaria.

'Headland. Pokes a couple of miles out to sea. The actual rock isn't there anymore – been worn away by the water.'

'Shredders in there,' said Kryk, gazing at the sea. There was only a light onshore wind and the breaking waves were no more than a yard high. 'Some of 'em can eat a man whole.'

'No, the shredders round here are small.' The quiet voice came from Remy, the female recruit directly behind Elaria. She was only a little older at nineteen; good with a blade but rather lacking in confidence.

Elaria had heard of shredders, and even seen the carcass of one that washed up in Lesser Saxan when she was a little girl. They were similar to sharks but far more colourful, and with larger teeth. They also apparently hunted in groups.

'Even the air tastes salty,' said Elaria. Her hand drifted to the thick scab that had formed on her damaged nose but she resisted the temptation to touch it – her constant picking had denied it the chance to heal.

"That's because this is the Salt Coast,' said Dawin. 'Most of the country's supply is harvested right here from these waters and shores.'

Elaria had been told a little about the Salt Coast by her father. The first settlers in Saxan had developed a trade alliance with Saltsand. The exchange of salt and meat had made both contributors richer.

Suddenly two horses trotted out of the fog behind them. Turning, Elaria was relieved to see it was only Sergeant Malcanoth and Sergeant Haskey. They had been riding up and down the column most of the morning and now continued north along the beach. Not far behind them were the two Pathfinders tasked with guarding, or more likely observing, the rear of the column – the new recruits and their four-legged charges. This pair halted near the trainees.

Dawin approached the nearest soldier. 'Sir, can we water the mounts?'

'Not now,' said the Pathfinder sharply.

Like Dawin, Elaria examined the faces of the pair; they looked preoccupied.

'Is something happening, sir?'

The soldier ignored him and wheeled his horse around. He looked back to the south. Nothing more than forty or fifty feet away could be made out through the white wreathes of fog.

As the wait for orders continued, the tension rose. Dawin, Kryk and the others fell silent and even the ponies and donkeys seemed uneasy, shuffling their hooves in the sand, huffing and shaking their heads.

Standing with a hand on Stripe's back, Elaria decided to watch the waves, which did ease her nerves a little.

She now knew a little more about the Beastkin. Back in Clearwater they were referred to as 'man-rats' and sightings were so rare that only a few claimed to have seen one; and their descriptions often didn't match. Indeed, many of the Pathfinders like Tamia hadn't actually seen one either. But several – Malcanoth included – had encountered and fought them several times. Dawin seemed to have absorbed every detail and had recounted them the night before as he and Elaria washed dishes.

The creatures stood about five feet tall when on their back legs but sometimes used all four like their smaller cousins. They were covered in fur and possessed snouts, whiskers and claws. Yet they also had a basic language, wore clothes and armour, and fashioned their own weapons. To Elaria, they sounded almost comical, yet she knew they could inflict terrible damage with their sharp teeth and long claws. Though smaller and lighter than a full-grown man, they were also quick, agile and notoriously hard to kill.

For centuries, the Beastkin had lived as scavengers, mainly in a distant area of woodland north of the city of Bruj. But according to Sergeant Haskey, many of the creatures were now under the control of a man named Sawfang. This character had supposedly organised them into a fighting force, and was using them to attack travellers and raid villages and towns. It was said that Sawfang was amassing quite a fortune, though no one was entirely sure if he was also motivated by some greater aim.

'Something's definitely up,' said Dawin as two more officers rode past and conferred with Malcanoth and Haskey. As he listened to the others, Malcanoth sat calmly on his mount, stroking his beard with his fingers. The officers were too far away to be heard but there was no mistaking the anxiety in their faces. After a minute or so, Haskey turned his mount away and addressed the recruits.

'Listen up – Beastkin tracks spotted in the sand. Looks like a large number. They generally don't attack in daylight or unless they feel sure they can win but this fog doesn't help us. We're moving out soon – stay close to whoever's in front of you. We're also sending back a squad to protect the rear. I very much doubt anything will happen but make sure you have your daggers at the ready.'

Elaria's blade was well-oiled and within easy reach in the sheathe attached to her belt. She had spent several hours in the dark practising her draw. She also had her stave across her back, despite being told by several Pathfinders that it was a needless weight to carry.

She exchanged an anxious glance with Dawin but soon the call came from ahead. As she mounted up and set Stripe away, a six-man squad rode back past them and took up a position directly behind Kryk at the rear, who seemed excited by the prospect of action. Elaria imagined that he would like nothing more than to kill a Beastkin. Stripe ambled slowly across the soft sand and Elaria fixed her eyes on Dawin's back. There was something about the chilly fog and the eerie quiet of the beach that made her feel more frightened than she'd felt since the Tournament. She prayed no blood would be spilled today.

***

Somehow the fog grew thicker; so thick that after an hour or so Elaria could see only Dawin ahead of her. He had earlier pointed out tracks in the sand on the shore side; tracks utterly unlike those made by boots and hooves. Once again, a halt was called.

'I don't like this,' said Remy, who was still behind Elaria. 'There, there,' she added, seemingly for herself as much as her mount.

As for Stripe, he suddenly began to tug at his bridle and veer towards the water. Just as Elaria got him under control, she heard a shout from the front of the column. She turned to her left. Were those shapes in the fog? She thought again of the stag in the forest.

'Look there!' Dawin shouted. More shouts; but too far away for the words to be clear.

'Beastkin!' yelled someone. 'Weapons at the ready!'

Elaria could hear something pounding across the sand.

'Recruits, off your mounts!' came the order from behind them.

Elaria slid off Stripe and took her stave from her back. The pony shied away from the murk again, taking the donkey with him towards the water. Elaria let them be.

'There,' said Dawin, pointing inland.

A dark shape burst from the fog with astonishing speed: first on all fours, then leaping. Dawin ducked behind his mount but the creature dived under its legs and came up at him, swinging with a black, crooked blade.

Dawin tottered backwards before crashing into the surf. The creature leaped after him.

Elaria realised she still hadn't moved.

Go! Help him!

The creature gripped Dawin's tunic with one clawed hand and raised its blade with the other. Whatever the jagged sword was made from, it was unlike anything Elaria had ever seen.

Darting forward, she heaved the stave two-handed at the weapon and knocked it clean out of the creature's grip.

The head snapped towards her: a snarling, yellow-toothed horror. Three claws came at her but before they could connect Dawin stuck his dagger into the Beastkin's gut. Dark blood coloured the blade.

The mortally wounded creature flailed at the recruits. Elaria drove the stave at it, catching its furred head above a fleshy ear and sending it sprawling onto the sand. She was about to step over Dawin and strike again when something struck her left shoulder.

She was thrown several yards. Though the soft sand broke her fall, she was winded by the impact. She had lost the stave and her right arm was lying in water.

'Help me! Someone help!' Elaria knew the voice. Remy.

Though she could hardly breathe, Elaria rolled on to her front and pushed herself up. Once on her knees, she hauled herself to her feet. She looked around; the stave was nowhere to be seen. Drawing her dagger, she spied Dawin, spitting curses as he stabbed the prone creature that had almost killed him.

Elaria turned to her left. Remy was backing away from a hunched Beastskin, short dagger against long blade. Only then did Elaria realise that Remy must have drawn the creature off after it had charged her.

'Elaria!'

'I'm coming, Rem-'

But another of them shot out of the fog, dodging between two of the panicked, shrieking mounts. Apparently unarmed, it splashed through the water and leaped high in the air. Elaria slashed at it; but too early. Clawed hands on her shoulders, the Beastskin knocked her over.

Elaria landed in a foot of water with the creature on top of her. Spitting out a mouthful of brine, she slashed wildly with the dagger that she'd somehow kept hold of. All she could see above was a long snout and two curved, protruding teeth. The thing stunk. Its clawed hands were still on her shoulders, pinning her. Water filled her nostrils, then her mouth.

Suddenly the claws scraped at her hand and the Beastkin snatched her blade.

Killed by my own dagger: all she could think as she struggled and strained for air.

She tried to hold the creature's arm, to stop it driving the blade downward. As water rushed into her throat, she felt her fingers sliding off the monster's oily fur.

She glimpsed movement on the beach.

Sergeant Malcanoth was sprinting towards her, one hand outstretched towards the creature. She could just about hear him shouting something.

Suddenly the Beastkin was still. As it froze, the dagger dropped harmlessly into the water.

Malcanoth's swinging sword almost took its head off. Elaria tried to turn away as blood filled the air but some of it struck her face: warm and bitter. Malcanoth kicked the lifeless creature off her and dropped to his knees, holding her as she coughed and heaved out the salty water.

'Are you all right? Are you hurt?'

She managed a nod.

It had started and ended so quickly. There seemed to be no Beastskin left alive. Several Pathfinders and recruits were close by, blades drawn, watching for another attack.

Sergeant Haskey was also kneeling in the water, holding Remy. Her neck was a ragged mess of pale skin and bloody wounds and the water all around her was turning red. Her eyes were open and still and staring up at the sky.

***

The gatehouse was a broad, stone structure equipped with dozens of rooms. The arched gateway itself was fitted with tall, wooden doors and an iron portcullis. Upon the doors was yet another intricate pattern of the Shyan red triangles. Not for the first time, Xalius reflected that the 'good luck' symbols had brought the locals little fortune of late. As was usual since the Haar Dari's arrival, the doors were open, and beyond lay the endless expanse of the Madlands. The sun was close to the horizon, casting an orange glow over the pale desert sands.

Xalius was still admiring the view when Siad lurched out of the gatehouse, doing up his tunic.

'I trust I haven't inconvenienced you, marshal.'

'Not at all.'

Xalius knew from his informers within Siad's ranks that the commander had followed his suggestion regarding the Shyan womenfolk with some enthusiasm. Apparently, he was "entertaining" a different girl every night.

'I took a walk and decided to apprise you of some developments.'

'Of course.'

Xalius gestured to the gateway. 'Shall we?'

'As you wish.'

Xalius had Ogon and two bodyguards with him. They followed the leaders under the great arch at a respectful distance. Within the gloom, an elderly Shyan man was lighting several lanterns. Upon spying Xalius and Siad, he halted his work, bowing as they passed.

'Carli had one of her premonitions last night,' said Xalius. 'She claims we should expect contact from the Imperator within a day or two.'

Siad nodded enthusiastically. Carli was not infallible but both men knew she was right more often than she was wrong.

'Anything else?'

'She foresaw a great column of our warriors on the move. She believes the eagle will carry urgent instructions.'

'I shall ensure my men are ready. We have gathered a good stock of provisions but I will need more, especially fodder for the mounts. We are running very low; the nearest grassland is forty miles away.'

'Of course. Have your deputies liaise with Darian.'

The two men emerged from the far side of the arch, facing the plain. Gathered on either side of the gate was a squad of Siad's troops. He inspected them briefly, admonishing several for minor infractions. Xalius kept walking then turned and looked up at the great walls. There was now only one damaged section: he could not fault the contribution of the marshal's men in recent days. Siad gave some more orders and soon many of the men had located brushes and were shifting drifts of sand away from the gatehouse. Joining Xalius, he cast an eye at a mounted patrol trotting along about a mile away.

'If we're sent north, will you accompany us?'

'That depends on our orders,' said Xalius. 'I must admit I am rather busy.'

'Your research?'

'Indeed. I believe it is Rael's will that I take full advantage of the library's contents.'

'How exactly?'

'When the time is right, I will let you know. For now, we are doing nothing but reading. You are aware of this man, Vikter Aggor?'

'The spy?'

'Actually, he is more of an opportunist. A conceited fellow but he has added considerably to my knowledge of the Skornlands. Have you heard of an individual named Sawfang Mawraze?'

'No.'

'Aggor refers to him as an ogre – possibly a gragg, though I'm not sure what he'd be doing so far north. Apparently, he has taken charge of a massive group of Beastkin. This Mawraze has also amassed considerable wealth and power.'

Siad grunted, clearly unimpressed. 'Beastkin are no match for us. Vicious creatures but they are more animal than man – they have no understanding of organised warfare.'

'Quite so. But Aggor believes Mawraze may be open to some kind of accommodation. He is hated by the Skornish and the men of Whispvale. I have not heard before of anyone being able to control the Beastkin in such a way. He – and they – could be of use to us. There are precious few north of the border who we might ally with.'

'True enough. How is Aggor involved?'

'As I said – an opportunist. If an alliance is made, he will expect some form of compensation. He claims to be a friend of Mawraze.'

'Could be a northern spy. Could be a trick.'

'Unlikely. I sensed no deceit.'

Siad raised an eyebrow at this and wiped away the sweat upon his hairless head. Even at this late hour, Shya was hot. Xalius didn't mind it; his aged body usually felt cold.

'You should be careful,' said the marshal, 'surrounding yourself with strangers. We left many enemies in our wake and we will make many more. What about this girl – the redhead?'

It was clear to Xalius that Siad also had his sources at the palace. Fair enough; he would expect nothing less.

'Lisahra is no threat to me. An enthusiast for the Way. She has some ability and is a quick learner. Given time, she may also become useful.'

Siad did not reply.

Xalius turned his attention to the distant patrol. 'Anything from your scouts?'

'Our way north is clear. No threats from the Madlands – my patrols to the south rarely encounter more than the odd traveller or refugee. The rear is secure.'

'Probably because you had your men kill every last one of our enemies.' This was not a policy Xalius had entirely approved of, though the logic was clear.

'*Definitely*. Anything else?'

'No.'

'Then I shall bid you goodnight.'

As Siad strode away, Xalius turned to the setting sun. Half of the orange ball had now disappeared below the horizon. The patrol – a squad mounted on camels – passed in front of it, their silhouettes a beautiful and impenetrable black.

CHAPTER 6

Elaria was about to help Kryk feed the donkeys when Malcanoth came to fetch her.

'That can wait,' said the sergeant. 'Captain Kano wants to speak with you.'

Malcanoth led her back across the darkened sandy cove where the Pathfinders had made camp. It was a sheltered and easily-defended position. But even though three days had passed since the Beastkin attack – and there had been no further sightings – Elaria found herself constantly looking up at the cliff face above, fearing the horrible creatures would suddenly appear and fling themselves upon her.

That day on the beach, Malcanoth had used seawater to wash the blood off her face before handing her over to Tamia. Elaria had not been able to find the right opportunity to speak to him since.

'Sergeant.'

He glanced over his shoulder as they neared one side of the cove.

'What?'

'I just wanted to say thank you – for what you did.'

Malcanoth nodded but said nothing. Elaria concluded that perhaps he was in one of his moods. She also wanted to ask him about the Way, but this clearly wasn't the moment.

They reached a small fire made of driftwood, where Captain Kano sat alone on an outcrop of rock. Gathered nearby was a squad of guards bearing torches. Even though she knew there were also several patrols out, Elaria felt uneasy.

'Thank you, sergeant,' said Kano. As Malcanoth departed, the veteran gestured to a mat close to the fire. 'Please, sit, Elaria.'

'I can stand, thank you, captain.' She worried instantly that this sounded rude. She had never spoken to Kano before.

'Please.' The Pathfinder moved from the outcrop and knelt on the mat himself. He then reached into a nearby pack and took out a flask and two mugs.

Elaria sat down, making sure she kept her dirty boots off the mat. She looked sideways at Captain Kano as he poured some of the flask's contents into the mugs. His face seemed rather lined up close, and she had noted before how his long tail of fair hair was in places almost white. He was not a large man but he carried himself with such poise and confidence that others somehow seemed smaller around him. Elaria knew from Tamia that he had been with the Pathfinders for more than three decades and had developed many of the strategies that had successfully defended Whispvale for so long.

Captain Kano passed her the mug. 'Sailor's rum from Port Llanos. Sweet but quite strong. My wife sometimes has a mug when she can't sleep.'

'Thank you, captain, but I don't really drink.'

'Ah. Leave it if you wish.'

Elaria took a sip. The rum was strong and sweet – but she preferred it to what little wine she had sampled.

The captain turned towards her. 'I must apologise. It is my responsibility to protect recruits and I failed. Rest assured that when next I return to Saxan, I will write to the families of all four who fell.'

Elaria didn't know what to say. She could not believe the veteran was talking to her in such a way.

'I ... we must always expect danger, I suppose, sir.'

'Quite right. And in that we failed.'

'I didn't mean-'

'We failed. Of that there is no question. In truth, none of us believed we were at risk that far south. You know that we found two men fighting alongside the Beastkin?'

'Yes, sir.'

When the fog had cleared after the attack, Kano led half the column away to check the surrounding area. They had come across a large group of the creatures and launched a mounted raid with their long blades, slaughtering them on open ground. Including those killed at the beach, forty Beastkin had been slain. The Pathfinders had lost five in addition to the four dead recruits. Three seriously injured soldiers had also returned south with the bodies of those lost.

'I've rarely seen men fighting with them.' Kano sipped his rum and gazed at the fire. 'We must assume that is why they were so brazen.'

What they had found at the fishing villages confirmed how badly the situation had deteriorated. One was abandoned completely and many of the occupants of two others had already left for Heartsong. At the largest settlement, Saltsand, the villagers were spending so much time patrolling and bolstering defences that they had barely any time to fish. The only people Elaria had seen smiling there had been children too young to understand the danger.

'If they come again, we'll be ready,' added the captain.

'Yes, sir.'

'You have your sword?'

'I do, sir.' These had been doled out to the recruits several hours after the attack. Kryk was not the only one angry that they had not been provided sooner.

'Once in Heartsong, we will begin instruction. You will learn quickly. It is already clear that you do not lack courage. Who was the recruit you saved?'

'Dawin, sir.'

'Dawin, yes. Quick thinking. Decisiveness. That's what we look for.'

Elaria didn't doubt the captain's motives but he seemed preoccupied and was still staring at the fire.

'It felt like I was moving slowly, sir. Everything went slowly.'

'That's the gods helping you, Elaria – when you need them most. How are you feeling, now that a few days have passed?'

'Not too bad, sir. It helps to have Dawin and Tamia and the others to talk to.'

She didn't want to tell him that she could not forget the sight of poor Remy: her bloodied neck and lifeless gaze. It was all she saw when she closed her eyes.

'I don't suppose you've ever witnessed anything like that before?'

'No, sir.'

'I apologise again that you had to so soon.'

'That's really not necessary, sir. When I joined, I knew I would see such things. It just makes me want to fight them. Avenge Remy and the others.'

Kano turned to her. 'If you face the Beastkin again, don't let anger cloud your judgement. Keep a clear head.'

'Yes, sir.'

Elaria did not want to waste an opportunity to learn more about the coming days; she wanted to tell Dawin something, for once.

'Sir, what will happen now? After we arrive at Heartsong?'

The captain put down his empty mug and stared at the fire once more. 'That depends. It is one of the few places where we still have more friends than enemies. But like any town it is always full of rumour. And I have never known a time when rumour and speculation was so rife. The Pathfinders will not act until we have separated lie from truth.'

***

By early evening of the following day, Heartsong was in view. Approaching via a windblown clifftop path, those in the column were able to look down upon the whole town. It had been constructed on both sides of the River Rindan, a sprawling settlement with cobbled streets and buildings painted a dull red in the style of the region. The western half was a mass of green – Tamia had told Elaria how the gardens of Heartsong were made up of trees and plantlife from all over Kyseran. She immediately noticed a trio of behemoth Blackwood trees standing tall above all else.

'It's beautiful.'

'It is,' replied Tamia. 'Bit more dirt and rubbish when you get down to street level but you can see why so many people want to live here. There's nowhere else like it in Whispvale and there's nothing even close in the Skornlands. Won't find many houses that the likes of us could afford.'

Elaria could feel a different mood among the Pathfinders on this day. The sky was bright and they'd been protected by open ground on one side and the precipitous cliffs on the other. Surely, they were safe from the Beastkin now.

As the path began to descend, they passed a party of robed figures kneeling around a stone plinth. The group paid no attention to the soldiers and continued their low, insistent chants. Emblazoned on the back of their dark green robes were numerous swirling symbols of red, orange and purple.

Tamia noted her friend's curiosity. 'Druids. Heartsong Grove is their most sacred place – the rest of the town grew up around it.'

Elaria had to coax Stripe away from a lush plant before continuing. 'They follow the Espheral gods?'

'I think so. Actually, I'm not sure. You know you should really get that cut.'

Tamia nodded at Elaria's hair, which was blowing around her face. There was apparently no specific rule regarding this but all the female Pathfinders kept their locks no longer than collar length.

'I haven't decided yet.' She could tell from Tamia's face that she did not approve. 'What?'

'It's your decision, of course, but some of the other girls don't like it. They think it's distracting.'

'What do you mean?'

'For the men.'

Elaria and Tamia stopped their mounts due to a delay up ahead. Elaria turned to check that her pack-donkey had stopped too.

'Anyway,' said Tamia after a time. 'Are you going to tell me what he said?'

She had already questioned Elaria once about her meeting with Captain Kano. Elaria felt that she shouldn't divulge what he'd mentioned about truth and lies; and she also felt a little resentment towards Tamia.

In the immediate aftermath of the attack, the older girl had been very kind but since then Elaria had sensed a certain jealousy: firstly, over her actions in defending Dawin, and secondly over her contact with both Malcanoth and Captain Kano. Tamia had been near the front of the column and had no opportunity to fight the Beastkin. That was not Elaria's fault, and she was in no mood to oblige her.

'It was nothing important.'

'Why not tell me then?'

'I don't think he'd want me to.'

'You're just a recruit. He can't have told you anything that serious.'

'Then you don't need to know.'

Tamia shook her head, then coaxed her horse out of the line and trotted away down the path. Elaria watched her, confounded. They had been so close in their younger years but it just wasn't the same now. Had Tamia changed? Had Elaria? Perhaps they both had.

***

The Pathfinders were welcomed by Heartsong's local militia and given an escort as they followed a broad avenue into the centre of the town. They were to be housed at the Militia's headquarters, Fort Havath: a hollow rectangular structure with a vast interior parade ground. Once inside, Elaria led her pony and donkey to a large stable where dozens of grooms were at work. It was clear that a good portion of the town's wealth was spent on the Militia. Though it was a relatively small force, the fort was impressive and imposing, and all the men's equipment, clothing and weaponry was of the highest standard. Their main weapon was a seven-foot lance, and each soldier wore a tunic of diagonal red and white stripes.

Once they had taken their gear to the barracks, the Pathfinders were invited into the fort's dining hall. Sitting on a long bench between Kryk and Dawin, Elaria listened with hundreds of others to a brief speech from the First Lance, Heartsong's senior soldier. He welcomed the Pathfinders enthusiastically, describing them as the Militia's closest and most long-standing allies. Captain Kano spoke briefly – somehow both shy and authoritative – full of thanks for the First Lance and his men. Once the formalities were over, a hearty meal of fish pie was served, accompanied by something that Dawin eventually identified as spiced seaweed. The senior officers from both the Militia and the Pathfinders were seated at their own table and left as soon as they'd eaten.

'Wish I could earwig on that conversation,' said Dawin.

Kryk had just slurped down his last spoonful of fish pie. 'We'll not be here long. I reckon we'll be heading back south tomorrow.'

'South?' said Elaria. 'But we only just got here.'

'Think about it. Beastkin are moving down into Whispvale. Are we really going to stay here and leave the other regiments to it? We'll be out hunting. Mark my words.'

'Don't be so sure,' said Dawin, who had just concluded a conversation with an older Pathfinder sitting behind him. 'Serek's been talking to some of the Militia sergeants. He reckons we might be headed north. Some band of brigands from the Madlands is running amok in the Skornlands.'

'How does that concern us?' queried Elaria.

'It'll concern us if they come our way,' replied Kryk. 'We're bound by treaty to help the Skornish.'

'Those treaties haven't been honoured in decades.'

'Don't worry, Dawin. If it comes to the rough stuff, Elaria will protect you.'

'Very funny.'

A grim-looking Militiaman on the other side of the table leaned over to grab a jug of water. 'Big lad's right. There's some barbarian army on the move. And nothing that ever came out of that dusty hell-hole was friendly. Rumour has it they've already taken Shya.'

As the others continued their discussion, Elaria sat back in her seat and gazed up at one of the hall's high, circular windows.

Barbarians. Madlands. Shya.

In Clearwater, these beings and places were spoken of mainly in legends and tales. Elaria had never even heard of anyone who'd actually seen the Madlands. The thought of taking on the Beastkin was bad enough. To face the creatures that dwelt in the most forsaken part of the world?

Despite the warmth of her surroundings, she shivered.

***

First came the vanguard: Marshal Siad Borshan himself, flanked by two veterans and four bannermen, each carrying the Sign upon a great standard. Then came the Ironhands: two-hundred hand-picked warriors, each of whom Siad claimed to know by name. Every single one was a Gragg.

Many centuries ago, they had been slaves bred selectively for size and power – to be used in fighting pits for their masters' entertainment. No one recalled much about the masters any more but the Gragg were known as the biggest, fiercest warriors in all Kyseran. There were never many available, for only infants of a certain size were left alive; and this ongoing process of selection continued the enlargement of the warrior race. Most Gragg women were over six feet in height. Siad was almost seven feet tall and a handful of his men were over eight.

When in battle, they wore goldsteel armour and were armed with great shields and axes almost as large as their commander's. They rode tall, sturdy horses specially bred in the east Madlands by the Zerfa tribe. Each of the Ironhands was trailed by a man-at-arms who towed two pack animals carrying their masters' equipment. Xalius noted the sour looks on many of the heavy-browed Gragg faces. He imagined they would have been "enjoying" the Shyan womenfolk and were not particularly keen to leave the city.

A quarter of the Haar Dari remained in Shya. Six Ceremonies of Acceptance had now been carried out and there had still been no major acts of rebellion. Better still, the first caravans had begun to arrive, generating much needed trade to fund their upcoming war effort. It seemed that the Shyans had accepted their fate.

Xalius had appointed one of his deputies to administer the city and Siad had done likewise with the military force. The two leaders commanded the bulk of the Haar Dari army but there were other detachments south of Shya if Atavius wished to use them. Xalius did not know when the Imperator himself might return. The silver eagle had arrived four days earlier, and had contained only two lines of instruction.

Xalius adjusted himself. His bony frame ached, even though he was sat upon a cushioned seat. He was not looking forward to moving again. Camels were ideally suited for travel across the sandy dunes but their awkward gait made it hard to ever feel comfortable. He and his animal were currently located on a low dune to the side of the dusty road north of Shya. Adjusting the parasol that shielded him from the burning sun, he watched the last of the Ironhands walk by.

Next came the Sand Lions. They were the largest and most civilised of the tribes, from the eastern reaches of the Madlands. Lean and muscular, these black-skinned warriors wore only hide to cover them and usually carried a collection of spears that could be thrown or used at close range. Quick but lightly-armed, they were best suited to skirmishing. They were also ideal for scouting duties: the Sand Lions could live on almost nothing, march for a whole day and fight at the end of it.

Once they had passed, Xalius gave a gracious nod to his warlocks. Ogon and Carli were with him, but the rest rode together in four ranks of five. His gaze moved across familiar faces. Many of them had studied under him personally though some had been highly adept with the Way before joining the Haar Dari. Between them, the warlocks possessed a remarkable range of abilities. Each wore a silver cape over their tunic so their leader could easily identify them in battle.

Xalius glanced to his right, where young Lisahra sat atop her own camel, observing the warlocks with jealous eyes. Though her talent for the Way was obvious, Xalius had already detected other traits within her that might prove equally valuable: she seemed highly ambitious and utterly ruthless. Watching the column pass by beside her was Vikter Aggor. He seemed happy that the Haar Dari were moving into territory he knew well.

Behind the warlocks were the Irregulars. Xalius had been surprised to note over the years that its members were some of his most loyal servants. Most were Madlanders but there were northerners too; men who'd had cause to leave their birthplaces far, far behind. Other than their Haar Dari tunics, the Irregulars clothed and armed themselves however they pleased. They were led by two twin brothers from the islands off the Madlands' north-east coast. Xalius never had a problem telling Yakin and Yala apart. Yakin was missing an eye; Yala a hand. They were both shifty characters, rarely seen apart and always with a pocket full of *oruba* – a narcotic that flourished in certain areas of the Madlands.

Next came two dozen desert dogs – each attended to by a team of Irregulars. As well as the chains attached to each leg, every beast was ridden by a man armed with a whip in reach of both ears. This was the most sensitive part of their bodies and a blow usually calmed them. Occasionally, however, the pain would send them into a mad frenzy and they would attack any living thing in range, including their handlers. Still, as Atavius and Siad contended, these rare incidents were counterbalanced by the terror that even a sighting of these beasts could invoke. Xalius almost felt sorry for the "civilised" folk his master had sent him against; if the desert dogs didn't terrify them, the Ironhands would.

Behind the dogs – at a *very* respectful distance – came the baggage train. Darian had informed his master that they were bringing three hundred spare mounts, two hundred carts of food and fodder and five hundred slaves, many of them Shyans. Xalius didn't feel a need to observe these people, nor the rearguard Siad had posted. He turned and caught the eye of Darian, who was seated on his own camel at the bottom of the dune. In close attendance were Carli and Ogon and two large carriages. The first vehicle contained Xalius' bed and tent and the other luxuries he needed while on the move. The second was packed full of books liberated from the palace library. He felt confident that Ogon had brought all the texts they would need to continue their study.

As if sensing his master's intention, the driver turned. Xalius gave a nod and readied himself. With a great snort, the camel lolloped down the dune. When the beast reached level ground, Xalius turned once more to observe the distant walls of Shya. Somewhere beyond the conquered city, the Imperator wandered the Madlands as he had for decades: gathering allies, knowledge and power. Xalius hoped he would return to their ranks before they attacked their next target.

Despite a detachment almost seven thousand strong, this would be no easy victory like Shya. Crossing into the Skornlands and striking at its people would have far-reaching consequences. The Haar Dari were no longer a cult on the fringes of the world. They were a power now; and they were going to war.

CHAPTER 7

Malcanoth had never particularly liked Heartsong. There were far too many rich people for his liking; and an air of smug complacency about the place that annoyed him. Even though the villagers had carried news of the Beastkin threat to the town, the people were going about their business as usual, as if nothing could touch them. Malcanoth respected the First Lance and his Militia but they were not a large force, and would struggle to contain a concerted attack by any foe. And while most of the population knew of this danger, few were aware of the growing threat to the east. In truth, even the likes of Captain Kano had no clear idea of the details. But if some Madland army really had taken Shya, the free peoples of Whispvale and the Skornlands might soon find themselves facing two enemies.

The Pathfinders had been in the town for a week and Malcanoth had spent much of his time with the recruits. The beach attack had hit the officers hard and they all felt guilt at the loss of their young charges. Malcanoth could still not believe he had left the rear of the column so vulnerable. Kano had told him that the fog had made their job almost impossible – and that no one could have seen it coming –but he found himself tormented by the faces of the dead youngsters. He had pledged to himself that he would never let anything like that happen again.

With all that was going on, the sooner they could get the recruits up to a decent standard, the better. Malcanoth had taken it upon himself to ensure that their comfortable surroundings didn't weaken their commitment and resolve. He'd led the youngsters on long runs along the banks of the River Rindan and overseen numerous drills at Fort Havath, often with Militia volunteers acting as the enemy. As Captain Kano had made clear, the Pathfinders had to use every hour of every day. Until decisions were made by those in charge, it was not clear where or how they would be deployed. But when the order came, they had to be ready.

Malcanoth wasn't all that happy about leaving the fort, but the other officers could handle training without him for a while and he had an important visit to make. Relaxing slightly as he left behind the centre of Heartsong and approached the western quarter, he began to see more and more druids. Clad in their traditional dark green robes, every man and woman seemed occupied with some meaningful task. Most of the younger folk were tending to sacred groves, gardens and water features. More senior individuals were identifiable by the numerous adornments on their robes; and they could be seen teaching or leading prayer and worship. Malcanoth liked the peace and simplicity of the place; such a contrast to the opulence and finery on show elsewhere in Heartsong. He had left his sword back at the fort, knowing that a display of weaponry would offend the holy people.

If life had turned out differently, he might have found himself here among them, communing with Rhoioll, the god of life; seeking no more than peace and enlightenment. But Malcanoth didn't like the idea of leaving the protection and law enforcement of his country to anyone else. It was a job he knew he could do; and though he'd never thought himself a leader, he'd been a Pathfinder long enough to rise to the rank of sergeant. He often found it difficult to bite his tongue when dealing with his superiors. He often found the new recruits frustrating and annoying. And he often wanted to be on his own instead of surrounded by others all day and all night. But he didn't have many friends outside the Pathfinders, and not much family at all. It was more than a job to him; it was his life.

One of the few family members Malcanoth did have left was his cousin, Nelaruin. He too had done well in his chosen field: exceptionally well, in fact. Even as a boy, Nelaruin had always been kind, caring and thoughtful; good with people of all ages and types. And when he'd announced his intention to become a druid upon his fourteenth birthday, everyone agreed that he was well suited to the life. At sixteen, Nelaruin had joined the Druids of Abettari, the most prestigious and prominent sect in Heartsong. This group was devoted to a long-dead saint who had been a gifted healer and had formalised many of the key tenets of druidism as practiced in Whispvale.

Fifteen years later, Nelaruin was now deputy leader of the Druids of Abettari and a man of great importance and influence within the town. As a Waymaker, Malcanoth was interested in how his older cousin had developed his own abilities; in both healing and premonition. This second skill was currently of particular interest to Malcanoth. Taken in combination with Nelaruin's political connections, it made him an excellent source of information. Malcanoth was always happy to see his cousin, but this was not purely a social meeting.

He halted outside a large, arched doorway and rang the bell mounted in a niche. While waiting, he paced back to the cobbled street then turned and surveyed the great blackwood trees visible above the walls of the Grove of Abettari. After what seemed like several minutes, one of the wooden doors creaked open and a young druid showed his face.

'Good day to you.'

'Good day. I'm here to see Nelaruin.'

The druid frowned. 'The Deacon Islorath, you mean?'

'I know exactly what I mean.'

'Can I ask the purpose of your visit?'

'No. But the name's Malcanoth. Malcanoth *Islorath*.'

'Ah.'

'Exactly – ah. Now open the bloody door. I don't have all day.'

***

Malcanoth drank the foul-smelling green liquid all in one go. He knew this was usually the best way when given something by Nelaruin.

'Yuk.'

His cousin smiled. 'An acquired taste perhaps, but the restorative qualities are beyond doubt. And you seem in need of some restoration, Mal. You look tired.'

'Rough couple of weeks.'

They were sitting in a three-walled courtyard that faced onto a pond. A trio of young druids on the far side of the water were tending to a flowerbed. Behind them was the imposing line of blackwoods, currently blocking out the sun.

'As for you, I swear you're getting younger.'

Nelaruin smiled. 'I can't say I feel it.'

In their youth, it had often been said that the cousins looked more like brothers. Nelaruin had darker hair and was not quite as tall as Malcanoth, but there had always been a strong resemblance. These days, however, Malcanoth's weathered, scarred features made him look older, though he was in fact a year younger.

'Must be the purity of your existence.'

Nelaruin adjusted one of the silver broaches on his cloak. 'I barely get any sun on my face or wind in my hair these days. Too many meetings.'

Malcanoth knew that his cousin was now in practice the leader of the Abettari. The Arch Deacon, Caiman Hardwicke, had been afflicted by infirmity for several years, and was seldom seen in public.

'How is he?' asked Malcanoth, still grimacing at the after taste of the herbal concoction.

Nelaruin's face grew grave. 'Not good. We had believed his condition to be the result of his seizures; or simply of old age. But his words have taken on another character of late. He talks of something called the 'black god' – an evil presence of some kind. He talks of it when asleep and when awake, and he thrashes about in his bed, as if possessed.'

'Forgive me, but I am surprised he has lasted this long.'

'So am I. Strangely, this change to his mind seems to have reinvigorated his body.'

'Do you ever get any sense out of him?'

Nelaruin shook his head. 'He knows none of us. He remembers nothing of who he is; not even the name of Rhoioll.'

'It might be better that he die.'

Nelaruin's eyes narrowed at this.

Malcanoth shrugged. 'I know that's against your teachings but sometimes it's for the best. All these meetings you've been too– any of them in town?'

'Most. Mayor Sycamor is rather more open to us than his predecessor.'

Malcanoth knew this was a source of some tension in Heartsong. All the residents respected the druids; but not all agreed with their influence over the town's political leadership.

'You'll know about the Beastkin then?'

'Indeed. We've been treating the victims, helping some of the refugees find housing.'

'I've spent quite a bit of time with the Militia officers. I'm not sure they – or Sycamor – really understand how bad this is. If the Beastkin are being controlled and directed, Heartsong itself could be under threat. If properly organised, they could overrun this place in hours. I don't see a town ready for a fight. How many in the Militia? Six hundred? Seven?'

'Five hundred and sixty. Sycamor understands the threat, believe me. If not for…other matters…he would have ordered an attack on the Beastkin already.'

'Other matters?'

Nelaruin looked over his cousin's shoulder at the functional but sprawling complex of timber buildings where the Abetarri resided. It seemed to Malcanoth that he might be thinking of Caiman Hardwicke; or the weight of the role and responsibility now upon him.

'Well?'

'Must we talk of such things? Why do we never talk of old times - good memories?'

'I want to know what's going on.'

Nelaruin let out a long breath.

'We're blood, Nel,' added Malcanoth. 'You owe me that much.'

His cousin leaned onto the table between them, hands clasped together. 'Very well. You'll likely hear of it before long anyway. I met with Sycamor yesterday. He had news from Militia scouts who'd encountered a party of Remmari warriors east of Slate Tower. A great host crossed the border into the Skornlands three days ago.'

'The army that took Shya?'

'Yes.'

'We don't know where they have come from or who leads them. All the warriors knew is that there are thousands of them. *Many* thousands.'

***

Elaria held the cloth firmly against the cut, waiting for the blood to stop. She had sustained the injury while sparring with Kryk three days earlier and now a fresh blow had opened it up again. She knew she should have protected it but she already had a bandage on her other arm after getting a kick from a Militia horse during a drill. Letting out a long sigh, she sat on her bed, one of four in the barracks room. She was tempted to lay back and doze but there was half the afternoon to go yet.

Sergeant Haskey was in charge today. Elaria liked him; he was a friendly, enthusiastic character who took the time to listen to questions and give individual guidance. Even so, she somehow missed the glowering, intense presence of Sergeant Islorath, who she hadn't seen in the fort since the day before. Elaria was yet to summon the courage to ask him about the Way. He had a habit of dismissing any question not strictly related to whatever they were practising.

She removed the cloth but her left wrist was still bleeding. She was about to look out of the window at the training ground when Tamia walked in. She looked down at the bloodied cloth.

'Bad?'

'No.'

'Lari, listen. I came to talk to you about this before anyone else does – your hair.'

'This *again*?'

Since their last conversation, Tamia had largely ignored her. Even when Elaria had gone to sit next to her at dinner, the exchange had been stilted and strained.

'Listen, Tami, I don't know if I've done something wrong and ...I know I'm only a recruit but...we are still friends, aren't we?'

'We're friends.' Despite Tamia's words, Elaria didn't detect much warmth. Perhaps it would be like this until her year was complete; until they really were equals.

'Lari, listen – just cut it, okay?'

'I will. It's just...it's part of me.'

'Without it, you'll feel more a part of *this* – the Pathfinders.'

'I already do. And I know it's tradition but there's no actual rule.'

'You need to get on with *everyone* here. Not just the men.'

Elaria stood up. 'Why do you say that? I don't care about the men.'

Tamia gave a slight grin, then leaned back against the wall. 'You don't mean to. But men can't help themselves. Even in the Pathfinders. Cutting your hair shows you mean business; and what's important to you.'

'Did you see me fight at the Tournament? I think that showed enough.'

'I saw it. You lost two of three fights. And yet here you are.'

Suddenly, several things seemed a lot clearer. 'What are you saying?'

'Who made that decision, Lari?'

'The officers.'

Tamia said nothing; she merely kept nodding.

'You seriously think that's why they did it?'

'No, I don't.' Tamia came forward and put her hand on Elaria's shoulder. 'And I think you are worthy of your place here; and not only because I'm your friend. But not everyone shares that view. And sometimes what people think is more important than the truth.'

Elaria could see the sense in that but she still felt angry. She didn't mind being told what to do by the officers because she knew it might save her life. And she knew Tamia wouldn't do this without good reason but it seemed a little like people were trying to control her. She'd had more than enough of that.

'Anyway,' said Tamia, 'it's up to you. We better get back outside before we're missed.'

***

That night, Elaria struggled to sleep. Sharing the room with her were another recruit, Sharlee, and two experienced Pathfinders, all female. They were friendly enough but had not offered an opinion regarding her hair; and Elaria hadn't felt like seeking one. She enjoyed sharing the room with women. Even though there had been nothing to concern her from the male recruits and soldiers, they had slept close together out in the field. Every night, Elaria had felt compelled to keep her knife within reach. She had no way of knowing how many men like Garrett there were; men who just took what they wanted.

These reflections drew her to other thoughts of home. Upon returning from dinner, she had seen one of her room mates writing a letter. Apparently, the postal carriages were still running despite the Beastkin threat. Elaria felt she should write to her mother but she didn't want Garrett to know where she was. Mother might discuss it with him and he was not above reading other people's letters, especially if he recognised her writing. But Elaria knew that rumours would be reaching Clearwater too now and she could save her mother a lot of worry with a letter. She resolved to write within a few days, sooner if they were to be sent somewhere.

Elaria was surprised they had been in Heartsong for so long. It was generally unusual for the Pathfinders to stay anywhere longer than a few days. Still, it had been an enjoyable and productive time. Her sword work was getting better and every day brought new discoveries about technique and tactics. On the following day, they were scheduled to march through the river country and the recruits were expected to demonstrate their navigation skills. Apparently, the march would take them through some of the most beautiful water-meadows in all of Whispvale. The meadows were clearly well known; there were paintings of them all over Fort Havath.

She thought about what Tamia had said. Perhaps her old friend was right: that this was one of those things you just had to do; like helping around the house or obeying a teacher. Elaria resolved to cut her hair and avoid any more problems with her female comrades. Though reaching the decision had been difficult, once it was made, she instantly felt better and swiftly drifted away into sleep.

***

The guard tower had been abandoned by the enemy as soon as the Haar Dari were sighted. That had been around midday and by nightfall the tall, slender structure was surrounded by tents and groups of warriors gathered around fires. The sands of Shya had given way to an earth orange in hue and covered by mile after mile of thorny vegetation. Thankfully, the road was in decent condition; until recently the traders of Shya had paid for its upkeep. The Haar Dari's target was now only ten miles away, and they would strike the following day.

The lights of the city were clearly visible from the top of the tower but from his current position on the third floor, Xalius could see only the fires, torches and lanterns below. He felt a familiar satisfaction at being amid thousands of loyal warriors; leader of a force dedicated to a single goal. Siad was out with his scouts; and would doubtless return with amendments to their plan of attack based on the latest intelligence. Xalius had every confidence that they would be successful. He had done all he could to prepare: checked in with each commander; examined the logistical details with Darian; given his warlocks specific tasks for the assault. Now he had a little spare time, and he felt he was spending it wisely.

He turned from the window and glanced at the hourglass, which had been adjusted to measure ten minutes. In the middle of the room, dimly lit by two lanterns, was Lisahra. She was kneeling, her green eyes focused on the coin suspended in the air a yard in front of her. Xalius guessed she had about another minute to go. She was doing well. He had detected little uncertainty and a strong level of concentration. He clasped his hands behind him and walked around the small, circular chamber. He passed behind her, wishing his cloudy vision would give him a clearer view of that lovely red gold hair. He began to hum, then to whistle, with increasing volume. The coin trembled. Lisahra raised her arms, aimed her fingers at the object to aid her focus.

Xalius walked in front of her, blocking her view of the coin. As he turned to face her, it struck the floor and rolled away. She glanced at the hourglass and smacked her hand against the stone floor, spitting curses.

'Calm yourself, my dear.'

'I didn't know you were going to do that.'

'That's rather the point.'

'I can paralyse people,' she said proudly. 'Let me show you *that*.'

'You told me that this is the area in which your skills are most lacking and that is evidently the case. What you require is practice – and guidance.'

Lisahra got to her feet. 'Yes, sir.'

'Have you heard of Terr Ventrik?'

'No.'

'By Rael, do you know any of the great practitioners?'

'Not really.'

'Then how did you develop yourself?'

'My father had a little skill, sir. He took me to a man in Shya when I was ten. The man said I had natural ability. He gave me some exercises and I have been developing myself ever since.'

'You have done well, considering.'

Lishara bowed.

Xalius continued: 'It is said that Terr Vintrik was the first to move anything larger than a man by use of the Way. He understood that it is only by devoting all our power to a single task that we can separate ourselves from the unskilled generality. He also postulated that the Way draws on everything: our minds, bodies and spirits. Waylakes are rare and hard to find so we must depend on ourselves. For someone in your position, you are yet to grasp that balance – unlock all three elements. My warlocks are useless to me if they can't focus solely on the task I give them.'

'Sir, I know I do not need to see the coin to keep it in the air.'

'Of course. And yet you could not. You were distracted.'

'But a warlock must also know what is going on around her. In a battle for example, I could not ignore my surroundings.'

'Quite so. And that is one of the reasons why Terr Ventrik compiled the Tables of Tasks. There is no better way to learn how to remain both focused and aware. You should be glad you are female; it comes more easily to women.'

'But the most powerful practitioners are male.'

'The most *destructive*, certainly.'

She took a step closer. 'Will you tell me about the Imperator? Is it true that he once set an entire army aflame? I know that you yourself-'

'I will tell you this – go and see Darian and ask for the Tables of Tasks. Copy them out clearly with good ink and paper. Then practice. Once we have the city and things settle down, we will find you somewhere you can concentrate.'

She bowed again. 'Thank you, sir. Is there anything I can do for you?'

Xalius wondered how his answer might have differed had it been a few years – decades? – younger.

'Simply this: when you see Darian, ask also for the text for the Ceremony of Acceptance. You must become one of the Haar Dari – that is the price of your education.'

'Of course.'

From outside came the faint sound of singing: without doubt the Sand Lions.

'What's the song about?' asked Lisahra.

'Their language is difficult to translate but I believe I recall the tune. It is a prayer for victory in tomorrow's battle. Originally, the song was for their former king. Now it is for Rael. Lisahra, what have you left behind – in Shya?'

'Nothing, sir. That's why I'm here.'

'You do appreciate that many in this world – most, perhaps – will consider us conquerors; invaders? The enemy.'

'Sir, my father was a gambler and my mother left us when I was no more than a baby. My family have failed at everything there is to fail at. I want to be on the winning side. With the victors.'

'For one so young, you have excellent judgement.'

***

By the third hour of night, Xalius had finally concluded discussing points of strategy with Siad in the marshal's tent. The most recent intelligence had revealed several minor but significant concerns and both men were anxious not to make a mistake. They had overwhelming force on their side – and there was no sign of enemy reinforcements – but any error on their part would doubtless be discovered by the Imperator, should he see fit to grace them with his presence. With these changes settled on, Siad departed to brief his commanders.

Xalius – accompanied by his four bodyguards – returned to the tower. He was almost there when Vikter Aggor emerged out of the darkness. Xalius had been too busy to meet with him in the last few days.

'You again.'

'Yes, sir. Might I have a moment?'

'One minute. No more.'

When Vikter tried to get closer, one of the guards raised a hand, stopping him instantly.

'Speak. Quickly.'

Due to his lack of height, Aggor had to shift sideways to make himself visible between two of the hulking Ironhands. 'Sir, the attack tomorrow: if all goes well, will you permit me to despatch a message to Sawfang Mawraze?'

'I shall. How will you do so?'

'I have certain…assets within the city that I can use.'

'I do hope they will still be alive after we claim the streets.'

Vikter was wringing his hands as he spoke. 'I too. May I invite Mawraze to a meeting? I am certain he would be honoured.'

'You may. Once the city is secure, I will provide an escort so that you can find your messenger and send him on his way.'

Aggor gave a neat bow. 'My sincere thanks.'

Without another word, Xalius continued on through the darkness towards the tower. Despite the late hour, the Sand Lions were still singing.

CHAPTER 8

Fort Havath was full of rumours: the druids had foreseen that an attack that would come within hours. Or days. Or weeks. The Militia was about to head east. Or north. Or divide. Or form a combined force with the Pathfinders. The Madland enemy was an army of mages. Or barbarians. Or the undead. Or a combination of all three.

'The only thing we know for sure is that this meeting is going ahead. Probably right now.' As usual, Dawin spoke with complete certainty. He, Elaria, Kryk and Sharlee – one of Elaria's roommates – were sitting on benches in a corner of the parade ground, cleaning and polishing armour. Most of the pieces belonged to the Pathfinder officers: chest-plates, arm-guards, greaves and helmets.

'How do you know?'

'Look around, Sharlee.'

As one hand was holding a helmet and the other an oil-soaked cloth, Dawin used his chin to gesticulate. 'See any of the senior officers? Our lot or the Militia? They're *all* there.'

'All in the tree,' added Kryk.

'What tree?' asked Sharlee.

'The Great Hollow,' replied Elaria. 'The inside of an ancient tree stump – that's where all important meetings are held here.' This much she knew from discussions over dinner with the Militia soldiers. They had mentioned the meeting too, though they didn't know exactly when it would occur. Like the Pathfinders, their chief preoccupation was the next mission.

'Everyone important will be there,' added Dawin. 'The captains, the druids, the mayor.'

Kryk said, 'Even if it comes to a battle, we'll stay here or be sent south. I just know it.'

'How can you be sure?' asked Elaria. As two Pathfinders marched past, all four recruits suddenly paid more attention to their work.

'The Beastkin are *our* problem. Whatever's going on to the east is someone else's. No Pathfinder has fought beyond Slate in fifty years.'

Dawin spoke up again: 'Even if the Pathfinders are called east, we recruits won't be going. We'll probably be mucking out horses while the others have all the fun.'

'Fine by me,' said Sharlee, who came from a long line of female Pathfinders and never seemed particularly happy about it.

'Not me,' said Kryk. 'I'd rather die in a battle than miss it.'

'Brave talk,' said Sharlee.

Elaria wouldn't have put it like Kryk – and she wasn't sure he really meant it – but she understood his devotion to the cause. Unlike Sharlee, he had no family history with the Pathfinders. But, like Elaria, ever since he had learned of them, he'd wanted to enlist.

'Wish I could use the Way,' said Dawin. 'I'd transform myself into a bird and fly across town to the Great Hollow and hear every word.'

Elaria finished polishing an arm-guard and put it down. Stretching out her legs, she winced at several aches from the previous days' march. Before taking up the next piece, she once again touched her newly-shorn hair. One of the women in her room had done it for her and all agreed it was a good job. Even so, Elaria reckoned she looked like a boy; the first sight of herself in a mirror had sent her into a slump from which she'd only just started to recover.

'It looks nice, really,' said Sharlee, with an encouraging smile.

Kryk scoffed at that, to which Elaria replied by throwing a vambrace at him.

Dawin had his own concerns. 'Whatever happens over there today, we'll know our fate soon enough.'

***

Malcanoth was surprised to be at the meeting but he couldn't deny a certain satisfaction at mixing with such esteemed company. He suspected that Captain Kano wanted some impressive characters alongside him and the presence of the very tall Sergeant Crellin and the very experienced

Sergeant Ithys confirmed this. Malcanoth and Kano had always gotten on well; the captain often commenting that he approved of the sergeant because he "only spoke when it was necessary to do so".

Once the four Pathfinders had sat down, Malcanoth looked around. He and his companions were seated at a large, horseshoe-shaped table. Between the two ends of the horseshoe was a small, circular wooden structure that housed a raised lectern and several shelves containing books and ceremonial items. Of the ancient tree itself, not much was left: just an incomplete circle of dark, desiccated wood that at no point reached higher than five feet. The girth of the tree, however, remained impressive: forty feet at least. The residents of Heartsong still boasted that, in its prime, the High Blackwood had stood over four hundred feet above the ground. Not that any of them had ever seen it; over a century had passed since the great tree fell.

A high, conical roof had been constructed containing several glass panels to admit light over the hollowed-out stump. There was a golden hue to this glass that cast an eerie warmth onto everything below. The single entrance was guarded by four Militia soldiers and a dozen more were stationed around the hollow's edge. All were armed with heavy lances and wore green and black cloaks bearing the sigil of Heartsong: a heart upon a cello. These men saluted as one when the First Lance arrived. He was accompanied by four senior officers; and all five wore pointed black caps that almost covered their eyes.

Then came the Druids of Abettari, hands clasped in front of them, cloaks touching the ground. Malcanoth nodded to Nelaruin and the two senior men, both of whom he'd previously met. The trio took their seats as the guests awaited the man who would lead the proceedings: Mayor Sycamor. Glancing at his cousin, Malcanoth began to wonder if their familial connection might be another reason for his presence, even though Captain Kano was acquainted with Nelaruin.

Hearing what sounded like an argument, Malcanoth and the other guests all turned towards the entrance. Facing the guards were an extremely unusual-looking pair. One was a very tall, lean fellow with straggly grey hair hanging down his back. He was difficult to age, but had the look of a man who had endured a long, trying life. He was clad in pale robes and was currently resting both hands on a wizened staff as he gazed down at the armed men blocking his path. His companion was more vocal:

a fat, bald man wearing the traditional leather jerkin and trousers of the Skornish. His voice could now be heard; as could that of the senior guard, who didn't seem keen on admitting him.

Nelaruin swiftly got to his feet, hurried to the entrance and intervened. He spoke briefly to the guard then shook hands with the tall man, whom he clearly knew. Like all those attending the meeting, the new arrivals had to leave their weapons with the guards: this consisted of the tall man's staff and the bald man's dagger.

Just as they reached the table, Mayor Sycamor strode in, eight town officials trailing in his wake. The six men and two women were the last to take their places around the horseshoe. Sycamor composed himself and inspected his guests before stepping up to the lectern. He was a small man with snowy white hair and an amenable face. Around his neck was a silver chain and a large pendant bearing the Heartsong sigil. Despite his diminutive size, the mayor's voice had a certain depth and gravity. He spoke a few lines of prayer, a custom in these parts, before initiating the meeting.

'Welcome all, to this meeting of the Council of Heartsong and honoured guests. I am Mayor Harren Sycamor and I will begin by introducing my officials to those who do not know them.'

As the mayor did so, Malcanoth turned his gaze to the unusual pair. The taller, older man was whispering to his bald companion, who was casting suspicious looks in every direction. They could hardly have looked more out of place and only now did Malcanoth note the amount of dust on their clothes and faces. The tall man in particular could have easily passed as a vagabond.

Mayor Sycamor gestured to Nelaruin and introduced the three druids. Then came the turn of the First Lance and his subordinates. The Militia leader's name was Oakvane; he and his men stood and first saluted the mayor, then the other parties. At a whispered order from Captain Kano, the four Pathfinders did the same. When so many eyes turned upon him, Malcanoth began to really feel out of place. He was very interested to hear what was said but hoped no one asked him anything.

Finally, Sycamor gestured to the vagabond and his companion.

'May I introduce Grogal Norphiem, envoy of Remmar.'

The bald man nodded in acknowledgement.

Now he knew of the man's origins, Malcanoth could understand why he appeared so anxious. Remmar was a city within the Skornlands. Relations between that domain and Whispvale had been poor for some time. The ruler of the Skornlands, King Aryn Flint, had long been convinced that the Pathfinders favoured Whispvale over his realm, even though the force had been formed to protect both domains, as well as the Wildlands. Some years ago, Flint had employed large numbers of mercenaries to curtail crime and guard against the Beastkin; and withdrawn all funding to the Pathfinders. But over time the most ruthless of these mercenaries had become organised criminals who Flint could no longer control. They imposed their services on traders and used them to traffic contraband. The result was a chaotic state which the king could barely govern, let alone protect.

King Darian Blythe of Whispvale believed his fellow monarch's problems were of his own making and – as he had always provided far more funding to the Pathfinders – possessed little sympathy for his current plight. Malcanoth knew that Captain Kano and the rest of the Pathfinder leadership regarded the problems in the Skornlands as a self-inflicted wound.

'And Craggy Kingthyme … er …'

The tall man gave a thin smile. His voice was a low rumble. 'Wanderer.'

'As you wish,' replied Sycamor. Kingthyme seemed unaware of the curious and cynical looks that his comment had caused.

The mayor continued: 'This meeting was originally called to discuss the Beastkin threat but our guests bring us news from the north and what they tell us has been reinforced by information communicated to me this morning. One of our fishing vessels encountered a Remmari vessel south of the Isle of Caves. The captain reported that they had seen the city on fire. That would be three days ago now.' After a grave pause, Sycamor continued. 'This is perhaps now the time for our guests to speak.'

Kingthyme gestured for the envoy, Grogal, to go first. The man stood, his large belly hanging over the table, face already flushed.

'Thank you, Mayor Sycamor, for receiving us…and greetings to the rest of you.'

This drew a few raised eyebrows; it seemed remiss of the man to not acknowledge the other esteemed guests by name.

'The first thing I must say is that I am not an official envoy of Remmar. It seems that King Flint did not wish to send a request for help. I suspect he is regretting that decision.'

First Lance Oakvane spoke up. 'Excuse my interruption but where is the king now?'

Grogal turned to the soldier. 'He and his family withdrew around the same time I left. I expect they have journeyed north to Bruj.'

'We have received no word from Remmar,' said Sycamor. 'How is it that his forces were defeated so easily?'

Grogal shook his head. 'Forces? The king can muster barely two thousand men. Many have defected to the sell-swords. Half of the noble families have deserted him. Nobody knows who will fight for him – for the Skornlands.'

'Why didn't he ask his Highness for help?' asked Sycamor.

'The king is proud. And he knows Blythe wouldn't give it.'

Upon hearing this, Oakvane and Kano both stood but the local man was first to speak.

'You will address his Highness correctly while at this table!'

Turning towards Oakvane, Grogal did not look apologetic. 'He is not my king.'

Sycamor held up his hands. 'Gentlemen, please. Let us first hear what Master Norpheim can tell us about the force that attacked Remmar.'

Kano and Oakvane reluctantly sat down.

Grogal gulped then continued: 'I wish I knew more but I will tell you what I heard before I left. There have been rumours of an army on the move for months but the first real intelligence we received came from Shyan traders who escaped the city when the enemy struck. They described a large, diverse army fighting under the banner of some…cult – the Haar Dari. Little is known of their leadership but they have several powerful mages and made short work of the Shyan defences.'

Grogal paused respectfully when Nelaruin raised his hand. 'Shya has its own council of mages. Lady El-Elzir is *very* powerful.'

'She *was*. The council of mages was wiped out. The Madlanders took control of the city in a single day.'

This comment elicited considerable consternation and discussion.

As Sycamor attempted to quieten the others, Oakvane questioned Grogal.

'Might I ask why it is *you* that comes before us?'

Grogal ran a hand across the little hair he had at the back of his head. 'I was part of a guild based in Remmar, formed to bring the mercenaries to heel, and fight the Beastkin. I was their healer.'

Malcanoth observed his cousin lean forward onto the table, eyes locked on the speaker.

'When we learned the enemy was headed for the capital and that the king and his court had departed, my fellow healers and I also fled. Before long, the biggest pack of Beastkin I've ever seen attacked us. It's only because of Craggy here that I survived.'

Grogal continued to scratch his head. 'Remmar is a city of over fifty thousand. How the remaining people have fared, I…could not say.'

His companion placed a hand on the envoy's shoulder as he sat down.

Mayor Sycamor seemed lost in thought so Nelaruin spoke up.

'Master Kingthyme, can you tell us any more?'

'Perhaps start by telling us who you are,' added Captain Kano.

As Craggy stood up, Malcanoth looked at him and wondered if his first name was a nickname. It certainly suited him well: his long, grim face resembled a pocked, angular wall of rock.

'As well as a wanderer, I am a Waymaker. I don't imagine that will impress you any more than my appearance but I hope you will heed my words. Fate threw me together with Master Norpheim here and I believe we are in Heartsong for a very important reason.' His pale eyes moved from face to face before he continued. 'To warn you of the threat to all Kyseran posed by the Haar Dari. And to implore you to aid Remmar and the Skornlands – before it is too late.'

Captain Kano spoke again. 'And why have you waited until now to do so?'

'The fault is entirely mine. I have been trying to find allies and methods of halting their progress but I have failed. It appears that I underestimated their power and the speed with which they would advance into the Skornlands.'

'How is it that you know so much about them?' asked Kano.

'I know a great many things, though some would say not enough. That is not important. What *is* important is that we fight together, lest we succumb to the devotees of Rael.'

At the very mention of this word, Nelaruin and the other druids spoke the name of Rhoioll.

Malcanoth had not heard the term before and it seemed Captain Kano hadn't either.

'Who or what is Rael?'

'A demi-god,' explained Craggy calmly. 'A man who defied the Espheral gods and made himself one of them through the Way.'

'What nonsense,' scoffed Kano.

'I wouldn't expect *you* to believe him,' retorted Grogal, pointing across the hollow. 'Or give a damn about the Skornlands. Anyone can see you have Lyther blood in you. And what Lyther ever cared what happened to men?'

Kano's only response was to glare across the hollow at the Skornish man. Defeated by the power of his gaze, Grogal looked to the ground, muttering.

Malcanoth wasn't sure what the Skornish meant by the Lyther comment but could not believe the stupidity of the envoy. Did he really imagine his people in Remmar would receive any help now?

Craggy held a hand out to calm his companion. 'Forgive him, please. Old enmities die hard.'

Mayor Sycamor spoke some appeasing words to his officials – some of whom looked as angry as Kano – then gestured for Craggy to continue.

'In the Madlands, they sing songs and tell stories of Rael. Of how he battled Seltan for endless days above the Red Plains. The man that made himself a god was worshipped in the centuries that followed by the Haar Dari. At times there was only a handful of them but they always endured and in the last decades they have grown stronger and stronger. Their leader is named Atavius. You must believe me when I tell you that he aims to emulate Rael, and he has a power with the Way beyond any I have seen.'

'Enough.' Kano was on his feet again. 'Enough. Perhaps the cretins and barbarians that populate the Madlands believe these tales but we do not. You come before this council dressed like some…vagrant and expect us to believe this child's story. I know the Way; and I know its limitations. What right have you-'

Captain Kano desisted because Craggy was now hovering about a yard above the ground, and so too was every single item that had been laid out on the horseshoe table. The man showed no sign of the effort required and simply gazed down at the dumbstruck congregation. Malcanoth had never seen such a demonstration and knew even Kano was incapable of such a feat. To suspend small items was easy, but a person?

'As you can see, I do know a little of the Way,' said the mage calmly. 'But this is trivial compared to the power Atavius wields. Now that he has started on this path, he will settle for nothing less than the conquering of all Kyseran.'

With that, Craggy Kingthyme descended, gently returning the objects to the table with accomplished ease.

The Heartsong officials – Sycamor included – gazed at him in disbelief.

'Not bad,' said Kano. 'Not bad at all. And you make a powerful case. But I do not know you. *We* do not know you.'

'If I may, captain.' Nelaruin stood. 'Actually, I do. Craggy has visited us at the Grove of Abettari many times. He helped us with several very ill patients and was always interested in our healing capabilities and the goings on in Whispvale.'

Craggy bowed his head to Nelaruin and returned to his seat.

Nelaruin continued. 'Some of us here believe the war we face to be simply a matter of men and weapons; others will believe it to be something more. But surely there can be no doubt that the war is here. The only question now is what we do about it.'

Oakvane stood. 'Master Nelaruin, with respect, we are under no obligation to assist the Skornlands. It is clearly the wish of both monarchs that any remaining ties have been severed. We must concentrate on the Beastkin and this Sawfang character. Then we can reinforce our borders without having to look over our shoulders.'

Grogal stood again. 'Remmar is burning. You would use the suffering of your fellow men to buy yourselves time?'

'And if it was us that had been struck first?' added Oakvane. 'Would Remmar now be rushing to *our* aid?'

Grogal shook his head in despair.

Mayor Sycamor raised his hands. 'The decision is not ours. I shall send a message to the king, apprising him of what we face. If others here wish also to advise him, feel free to do so. Whatever he decides, we will obey. I trust we can at least agree on that?'

The mayor looked first at Oakvane, then at Kano. Only when he had received nods from them both, did he look satisfied. Nelaruin also gave his assent.

'Mayor Sycamor, that will take days,' said Grogal.

Craggy added, 'The Haar Dari already have a foothold in Shya. Possession of Remmar opens up the rest of Kyseran. I believe we must strike before they can consolidate.'

'We must attack immediately!' added Grogal.

'"We"?', said Kano.

Sycamor turned to Grogal. 'You are in Whispvale now, Master Norphiem. 'We take orders from our king, and *only* our king. And we obey them.'

***

Malcanoth had seen a few keas in his time. The brightly coloured, elegant birds were uniquely intelligent; quick and reliable in terms of finding their way. He knew that the creatures were now flying across Whispvale and the Skornlands – exchanging crucial messages between King Flint and King Blythe. The fact that the monarchs were communicating had itself been a surprise but there was another shock to come.

It was on the second morning after the meeting that Captain Kano called Malcanoth and his other senior men to one of the four towers at the corners of Fort Havath. Angular rays of sunlight illuminated the circular chamber as the nine Pathfinders entered. Already present was First Lance Oakvane and a similar number of his officers.

The men stood and listened as Oakvane removed his cap then held up a piece of paper. 'A copy of His Majesty's orders – they arrived during the night and I've spoken at length to Mayor Sycamor before coming here. The King has decided that we *will* aid our old allies in the Skornlands. King Flint is assembling his own force and will attack Remmar from the north – at dawn, four days from now. We are to land east of the city in the Bay of Brakken and attack the enemy from the rear.'

Malcanoth was still absorbing this announcement while the First Lance continued. Had he heard this correctly? Blythe was helping Flint? The Pathfinders would be sailing to Remmar?

'The mayor will arrange for the requisitioning of all available sailing vessels – we should have enough capacity. Now, the nature of this force:

His Majesty has pledged half the Militia and all the Pathfinders currently in Heartsong. Additionally, Mayor Gralton of Slate has promised another three hundred troops. Given the gravity of this threat from the east, the king is also recalling the Fleet from the Western Sea but the weather is poor and they will not be here any sooner than two weeks. His Majesty is also re-deploying his other forces. In the event that we are…unsuccessful, he will begin conscription and reinforce the northern border.'

Malcanoth had moved on to a few calculations: Kano had barely two hundred soldiers at his command. Even with the Militia and the Slate men, they would have little over a thousand in total.

Oakvane lowered the hand containing the paper and settled his gaze on Kano.

'Any questions, captain?'

'Not for the moment, First Lance.'

One of the Militia officers who had not been present at the Great Hollow raised his hand. 'Any estimates of King Flint's forces, sir?'

Oakvane shook his head. 'We cannot possibly make an accurate estimate, nor do we know much about our opponents. Now, there will of course be talk about such things: a lot of talk. That cannot be avoided. But none of it will change anything. We have been ordered by our king to attack an enemy and that is what we shall we do. If the Skornlands fall, Whispvale will be next. That is the truth and that is what you will tell your men. We will catch them by surprise and we will send these heathen primitives back into the desert!'

At this, some of the more enthusiastic Militiamen gave a cheer. Oakvane raised a fist and began the inevitable chant.

'For the Vale, For the King! For the Vale, For the King!'

The Pathfinders were not as fond of such martial behaviour but Malcanoth and his comrades joined in. The chant grew in power and vigour but he soon found himself merely mouthing the words, lost in his own thoughts. He was wondering how many of the Pathfinders had ever even been on a ship.

CHAPTER 9

Everyone seemed busy apart from the recruits. The population of Fort Havath had swiftly swollen and all the Pathfinders and Militiamen were charging around the place, most seemingly obsessed with their own equipment. The Pathfinder officers were rarely seen and – if not for Dawin – Elaria and the others would have had no clue what was going on. But the inquisitive recruit had made a valuable contact in Fort Havath's kitchen and it seemed the serving staff were remarkably well-informed. Having received only anxious looks and silence from their officers, the young Pathfinders at last discovered the truth.

With no training scheduled for the day, they gathered under a tree just outside the gates of the fort.

Dawin quickly related all he knew to a rapt audience. 'So that's it. The ships will leave tomorrow morning for Remmar. They reckon it's about seventy miles as the kea flies.'

'They're *all* going?' asked one young man.

'All. And half the Militia, like I said.'

'Do you know any more about these barbarians?'

Dawin shook his head. 'No one seems to know much about them.'

'King's orders?' asked the same youth. 'You're sure?'

'Definitely,' said another recruit. 'I heard that too. The Heartsong folk can't believe they have to fight for the Skornlands.'

'I still can't believe the barbarians have taken Remmar,' added a tall youth with an unruly mop of hair. 'My uncle went there a few years back. It's a *big* city – big as Menelcross.'

'But Flint's army is a mess,' said the lad standing next to him. 'The whole of his kingdom is a mess. Why should we have to save his worthless skin?'

'*We* don't,' said Dawin. 'We're staying here.'

'Good,' said Sharlee, who was standing next to Elaria, close to the tree.

'We should be going too,' said the tall youth. 'It's clear they need every sword they can get. Even the Slate Militia is coming down. I heard they might not make it in time.'

'No one's getting me on a ship,' said a miserable-looking young man behind him.

'So what will happen to us?' asked Sharlee.

Dawin spoke up. 'They'll probably just leave us here until someone decides where we're to go.'

From his tone, Elaria guessed Dawin was disappointed not to be accompanying the attack force. She could not quite decide if she was disappointed or relieved. As the conversation continued, she looked around at her young comrades, all of whom she knew by name. Only one was missing: Kryk.

***

Heartsong's harbour was full. The wealthy town maintained two transport ships and three coastal patrol boats for the Militia. All five vessels carried oars as well as sails. Also pressed into service was the mayor's ship, a ceremonial vessel needed for military duty.

Two large fishing vessels had also been requisitioned and stripped to accommodate the Slatemen. The Pathfinders would be spread across the other vessels alongside the Militia. Anchored just outside the harbour with them were a further two ships belonging to local merchants. Now, as darkness descended, lanterns were lit on the anchored ships bobbing gently under a slight swell. There were dozens of lights within the harbour too: the hours of daylight hadn't been sufficient for every job to be completed.

Standing between two large mooring posts, Malcanoth enjoyed the breeze that chilled his face and ruffled his hair. The refreshing wind somehow made him feel better about the prospect of the sea voyage. He had good cause to be very wary of the sea; and found the thought of sailing beyond the sight of land almost as frightening as taking on this unknown foe. He supposed some of the younger Pathfinders and the recruits might be surprised, perhaps even amused, that he was frightened. That did not concern him; fear was natural and he knew that when the time came it would keep him sharp.

Fear was everywhere in Heartsong. The Militia were a loud, proud bunch but he could see it in their eyes as much as the Pathfinders. Malcanoth was glad he would no longer have to worry about the new recruits; he had enough to concern him with the platoon he would now command under Kano. The captain was one of the few men he'd encountered who never seemed to show fear. Malcanoth tried to hide such feelings – any feelings, in fact – but knew he hadn't always succeeded. Kano was either highly adept at hiding fear or genuinely didn't feel it. Malcanoth reckoned it didn't really matter; the effect on his subordinates was the same.

He had never seen his superior so focused as Kano now prepared to lead an army to battle; in a place few of them had even seen. First Lance Oakvane was to stay in Heartsong. He had wanted to join the Remmar force but the mayor had insisted, even invoking a long-standing rule to ensure his cooperation. So it was Kano that would lead the attack. And he had communicated nothing other than dedication and enthusiasm to all; for an operation he had himself argued against. Typical of the man.

Malcanoth was as prepared as he could be. He wished there'd been time to go and see Nelaruin but at least they'd managed a brief conversation after the meeting at the Great Hollow. He had also written a brief letter and sent it to his home in Riverton. Malcanoth wanted his uncle to know where he was going and that he might not hear from him for a while. He had filled his pack only with essentials and elected to leave his bow behind; they would have to move quickly after the landing and he didn't want a second large weapon slowing him down. His pack also contained two books of instruction. These had cost him a considerable amount and he planned to spend his spare time during the voyage with practice. He would focus solely on the few aspects of Waymaking that could serve him in battle.

Dedication. Concentration. Repetition. Execution. This had been the mantra of Malcanoth's uncle, who had seen his nephew's ability and introduced him to the Way. His parents – like the rest of his family – had been very religious, devoted to the Espheral gods. They had not approved of such things and had asked his uncle not to teach him.

For three more years, this request was obeyed. But by then Malcanoth was fourteen and starting to think about the Pathfinders. He and his uncle agreed that if he was going to be a soldier, he might as well use every asset available to him. Starting so late was not ideal, but his uncle had a good library and they re-discovered their skills together. Malcanoth looked down at his left hand. Unlike his sword hand, it ached. It always ached for a while after he used the Way, then eventually the pain would recede.

He looked down at the harbour and saw a group of Militiamen on a ship's foredeck, practising their sword drills by lamplight. He clenched his fist and almost enjoyed the dull ache; he knew it would get a great deal worse before it got better.

***

Lying in bed in the darkness, Elaria found herself lost in thought, unable to sleep. It wasn't as if she really wanted to go to Remmar and fight this mysterious enemy; it was just that the future suddenly seemed so uncertain. As a recruit attached to Kano's force, the path ahead had been clear. Now, everything had been thrown into doubt.

Nobody knew how many of the Pathfinders would return, and even if they did, what next for the recruits? Only Sergeant Haskey had found time to come and see them, revealing that they were now temporarily under the command of First Lance Oakvane. The young soldiers were to follow his orders, help the Militia and await the return of their older comrades. Dawin seemed convinced that this would mean days of cleaning and cooking, fetching and carrying. All the Militia soldiers had been called to arms and a number of civilians had been brought in to Fort Havath to keep the place running.

At least Tamia had come to say goodbye. With her platoon about to depart, she had rushed into the barracks to find Elaria. She had apologised to the younger girl for the earlier awkwardness and kissed her affectionately. She also confided that she'd sent a letter to her family in Clearwater. Elaria sensed excitement but also great fear; and when they embraced, she could feel Tamia shaking. After she'd gone, Elaria went to the window and watched her climb up into a cart. As the vehicle moved off, not one of the Pathfinders spoke.

Elaria turned over, pulling her blanket up to her chin. Below, Sharlee was quietly snoring. With all the older women gone, there were just the two female recruits now. Elaria had planned to go down to the harbour at dawn to see the ships off but they'd been ordered to gather outside the barracks at first light. Nobody knew exactly what they would be doing but there was a rumour that Mayor Sycamor was diverting all available manpower into renewing Heartsong's outer defensive wall.

Beneath all the uncertainty lay a fear that her past would catch up with her. Without the protection of the Pathfinders, she felt vulnerable and feared that Garrett would still be looking for her. Elaria decided that she would not write to her mother; she could offer her brother no clue of her whereabouts.

She turned over again and had almost drifted off to sleep when she heard someone calling her name. Then whoever it was called Sharlee's name and the girl woke up.

'What?'

'It's me, Dawin.'

Elaria, who was in a top bunk, pushed her blanket off and lowered herself to the floor.

'Dawin?' She hurried over to the window and found him there with his hands on the sill. There was enough light from a nearby lantern to see the anguished look upon his face.

'It's Kryk. He's gone and done it.'

'Done what?' asked Elaria as Sharlee joined her.

'We …we were discussing it – trying to get on one of the ships. We went down to the harbour earlier to see how we could do it.'

'What?' asked Sharlee, sounding as sleepy as Elaria felt.

'Joining the others. He reckoned that if we could sneak aboard and hide for long enough, they'd have to take them with us. Kryk was all for it but I told him we'd likely be kicked out for good – just for trying it. He seemed to agree but I just woke up and found him gone. His gear's gone too. We've got to stop him.'

***

A week earlier, getting out of Fort Havath would have been difficult. Now, with only a dozy, one-legged Militiaman on duty at the gate, it was simply a case of claiming they had to make a last-minute delivery to the Pathfinders. Elaria and Sharlee had swiftly thrown on some clothes and

Elaria was already wishing she'd brought her cloak as they jogged through the dark, chilly streets towards the harbour.

'How long do you think he's been gone?'

'No more than an hour,' said Dawin as they passed a rowdy inn, one of the few places still open.

'What was your plan?' added Elaria.

'With all the bits and bobs being ferried out to the ships at anchor there's a little fleet of rowboats at the eastern end of the harbour. Some of the Pathfinders are on those big fishing craft – they've got low sides, easier to climb aboard.'

'Can't believe you even thought about it.'

'Neither can I now. But you know Kryk – that hothead can't bear the thought of missing a fight.'

As they ran, Elaria realised how much fitter she was after weeks of constant training. They must have covered at least a mile before spying the harbour and not one of them was breathing hard. Passing under a high crane, she noted the chain and hook swinging. The wind had risen since sunset; a strong westerly that was shifting even the boats sheltered by the harbour.

They continued down a steep road, narrowly avoiding the attentions of two watchmen bearing lanterns. Halting by a low wall, they looked out at the harbour, which was formed by two curved breakwaters. The entrance itself was no more than fifty feet wide: beyond was the dark, foreboding sea.

Dawin was already on his way to the eastern side of the harbour.

'What are we doing here?' moaned Sharlee as she and Elaria followed.

Below them were vessels large and small tied to the harbour wall. In some places two or three had rafted up together. The recruits passed a talkative group of sailors walking the other way and then had to run around a malodorous pile of fishing nets and barrels. Dawin stopped beside the wall and pointed towards the entrance.

'Hell, he's already out there. See him?'

Elaria and Sharlee halted and looked down at the dark water. There was some moonlight but it took Elaria some time to identify the little shape and the movement of the oars. Then she found she could make out Kryk's large, upright frame. He was almost to the breakwaters, pulling hard.

'Kryk!'

Elaria had no idea why Dawin even tried. His friend was at least three hundred feet away and the wind was loud. The blow was also helping Kryk on his way, pushing him out of the entrance.

'Bloody idiot. Come on, we'll find a rower to borrow.'

Dawin ran to the closest of the many iron ladders affixed to the harbour wall, only pausing when he realised the girls hadn't followed.

'Please. He'll listen to you, Elaria.'

'It's dangerous, Dawin. You don't know any more about rowing a boat than I do. It's a long way out to those ships – anything could happen.'

'But they'll kick him out for this. You know they will. He'll listen to you. Come on. Sharlee?'

'Not me, Dawin. Kryk wants to drown himself, that's up to him. Don't go Elaria, it's not our problem.'

'Come on, there's no time!'

Elaria knew this situation was only going to get worse if they – if she – didn't act. 'All right, I'll help. Sharlee, run around to the entrance – he might hear you from there.'

'Elaria, don't. You shouldn't.'

But she was already on the ladder, swiftly following Dawin down towards the water. Below were at least a dozen small boats, tied to each other or one of the iron rings affixed to the harbour wall. Dawin dropped into the closest and helped Elaria down beside him. As the boat shifted, they both had to crouch low and throw out their arms to keep their balance.

'There are oars in that one.' Dawin clambered towards a rowing boat on the edge of the miniature fleet.

Elaria was glad to find her eyes adjusting to the darkness; traversing the boats without falling in was quite a challenge. By the time she reached Dawin, he had the oars ready.

'Cast off,' he instructed.

'What does that mean?'

'Untie us!'

Elaria sat in the bow and located the rope connecting them to another boat. Her fingers were cold and the knot would not come undone easily.

'Quickly,' insisted Dawin.

'It's not that easy…ah.' At last, she had it free. She pushed them clear and soon Dawin was able to dip the oars. Elaria was relieved to see that he seemed to know what he was doing.

Considering the number of vessels and people gathered in the harbour, it seemed strange to cross it without drawing attention. But at this late hour, there were only a few lanterns still alight and no one else on the move. The wind had increased again and Elaria narrowed her eyes as she shouted directions to Dawin. She wasn't entirely sure why an oarsman had to face backwards; it seemed very unhelpful.

'Can you see him?' asked Dawin.

'No. Not far to the entrance though.'

As they neared it, the height of the waves grew and water began to strike Elaria's face. Hunched low in the bow, she guided Dawin between the breakwaters. Hearing a shout, she looked up and saw Sharlee waving from the eastern side. Elaria yelled back but heard nothing more over the howling wind. The gusts were however blowing them outward and within a couple of minutes they were clear of the harbour.

Dawin shipped his oars and turned around, breathing hard. He and Elaria could see the collection of anchored vessels over to their left. Each was marked with one lamp on their mast and another above their anchor. The hulls, however, seemed as dark as the sea; and there was no sign of Kryk and his craft.

'He must be moving quicker than us,' said Elaria.

'Stupid great lump,' said Dawin, sounding truly angry for the first time. 'When we get closer, we'll be able to work out which are the fishing ships. He'll be heading for one of them.'

'Dawin, the closest of them is at least a quarter-mile.'

'The wind will help us.'

'It's coming straight over the harbour heading east. We're going more to the north.'

'Don't worry, I'll adjust.'

With that, Dawin returned to his rowing. Staying low, Elaria soon became used to the spray striking her and the salty taste in her mouth. In order to keep track of their position, she alternated her gaze between the ships and the harbour. She could see that Dawin was trying to stay parallel with the land to compensate for the wind's effect; but they had already been pushed a long way out.

'Can I turn yet?'

'No. As you are. We're sliding right all the time.'

'Might be the current as well.'

'The what?'

'The current – I heard there's one on this coast.'

Elaria shook her head, eyes still fixed on the lights of the anchored ships. They did at least seem closer but every yard of forward progress north through the choppy water was accompanied by one to the side.

'Dawin, I think we should turn back. It'll be doubly hard to row into it.'

'We've just got to stay upwind – keep ourselves between the ships and the shore.'

But after five more minutes, Elaria became unsure if that was even possible. The ships seemed no closer and they were being pushed ever further out to sea.

'Dawin, we're in trouble.'

Now breathing quickly, he stopped. 'Hell, I'd thought we'd made progress there.'

'I'll lend a hand.' Elaria moved back and sat beside him.

With an oar each, and Dawin calling out each stroke, they worked hard for another five minutes; then another five. By then, the closest of the ships was no more than a hundred feet away – but they were already sliding past it.

'Come on!' yelled Dawin. 'One last effort.'

They heaved, sucking in breaths of cold, salty air. Everything from Elaria's shoulders to her fingers ached.

'And ... pull, and .... pull, and ... pull.'

She couldn't fault Dawin's energy but it was clear his judgement had been way off.

Another fifty strokes and they stopped again, now able to see the angular prow and glittering anchor chain of the nearest ship. But the vessel had been directly in front of their bow; now it was alarmingly far to their left. There was another boat seaward of this one but it was too distant for them to even get close.

'We have to call for help.'

'What will we say?'

'Who cares?' shouted Elaria. 'There's nothing between us and the open sea! We need help.'

'One last go.'

Dawin returned to his oar, forcing her to do the same. But at the third stroke, Elaria heard a crack, then a vicious stream of curses.

'Hell, rowlock's gone. Can't use the bloody thing now.'

That was enough for Elaria. She got off the bench and crawled to the bow.

'Help! Please help!'

Dawin joined her and the two of them took turns to bellow at the shadowy ship. Elaria knew they would get no closer to it; no closer to safety. She also belatedly realised the wind was blowing their voices away.

The little boat drifted on. The two recruits shouted until they were hoarse.

'Did you hear something?' said Dawin at one point. 'I think I heard something?'

Elaria reckoned he'd imagined it. She kept shouting until her throat ached and nothing would come out of her mouth. With Dawin still trying, a pitch of emotion now in his voice, she slumped down into the boat. She had only a tunic on over her under-shirt and – now she had stopped moving – she was shivering. She looked to the east and could not even make out where sea ended and sky began. All was black.

***

It was to be the worst night of her life. With the damaged rowlock there was no way to use the oars and there could be no doubt that their fate was out of their hands. Regardless of the current, the wind was pushing them offshore and when cloud covered the moon, they even lost sight of the land.

Dawin had already apologised more times than Elaria could count. They lay at opposite ends of the boat, as low as possible to get out of the wind. There was at least a little wooden jug for baling. Dawin took this on as his responsibility so at the very least they didn't have to lie in the freezing water. Elaria didn't understand much about sailing or currents or winds but she knew that Shya and the Madlands were directly east of Heartsong; and that was the direction they were being blown.

At what they agreed was roughly half way through the night, the wind eased off. Elaria held onto Dawin's legs while he stood up and looked around but he spied nothing that could help them.

'How far do you think we've gone?' she asked as he settled back into his end of the boat.

'No idea. Elaria, again-'

'Yes, yes – you're sorry. So am I. I should have listened to Sharlee.'

'We survived those Beastkin, didn't we? We'll survive this.'

Elaria thought, *we can't guide ourselves, we have no food and no fresh water.* But she said nothing.

'Sharlee will raise the alarm when we don't come back,' added Dawin. 'They'll send someone.'

'They have bigger things to worry about than us.'

With that, Elaria pulled her sleeves down to cover her frozen fingers and tucked her hands under her armpits. She didn't want to look up for they were surrounded by darkness. The sky was bad enough, but the black depths below were what truly terrified her. Elaria was a fair swimmer but if anything happened to the boat, she knew she wouldn't last long in open water. And what of the creatures lurking there? Shredders and sharp-fins and grabbers. Though it was all so horribly real, some small part of her wondered if she wasn't still tucked up safe in the barracks, enduring a terrible dream.

***

Somehow, she slept; and awoke to hear Dawin shouting. 'Kryk! Kryk!'

Elaria sat up. The sun had just risen, spilling pink light into the sky. Dawin was gazing at a strange metal structure floating atop the waves. It had a wide base but narrowed to a point about ten feet above the water. It had clearly been painted green at some point but was mostly rust now. Roped to the bottom of it was a small boat, very much like their own, but apparently unoccupied. But then someone sat up, and there was no mistaking the chiselled features and broad shoulders.

Kryk seemed unable to believe what was happening. 'Dawin? What? How?'

'Hang on, we'll come to you. Elaria!'

She picked up her oar and by positioning themselves on either side of the boat they were able to paddle over to Kryk. Dawin threw him the rope and Kryk tied them to his boat.

The big recruit let out a long breath. 'Don't tell me…you came after me?'

Though glad that the situation had improved a little, Elaria wasn't really in the mood for conversation, especially with Kryk.

'We thought we could stop you,' replied Dawin. 'From making a mistake.'

'I couldn't stop myself – literally.' Kryk shook his head. 'Must have set off too quickly. By the time I realised I was in trouble, I was too far out. With that wind I guess they couldn't hear me calling for help.'

Elaria was examining the metal structure. 'What is that thing? How does it float?'

'Hollow at the bottom there,' said Dawin. 'You get enough air in something, it'll float. It's called a buoy. Used for navigation.'

'Really?' said Kryk. 'I was wondering.'

'Then the fleet might use it,' suggested Elaria. 'They might come close. Maybe we have a chance.'

***

They sighted the first of the ships around midday. By this time the wind had risen again and there was quite a chop on the water. The constant motion made all three of them feel sick and both boats had needed some baling out. Thankfully, the wind was still offshore and before long they could see more dark hulls and pale sails. The southernmost of the vessels appeared to be aiming straight for the buoy until it – and the rest of the fleet – abruptly changed course, heading more to the north. This development was harder to bear as they could actually make out the sigil of Heartsong on the foresail; the vessel was no more than half a mile away.

'No!' yelled Dawin. 'Why are they turning?'

Kryk was bellowing at the top of his voice.

Elaria looked on; scarcely able to believe that they would so narrowly avoid rescue again.

The young men were now both standing up, waving their arms.

'Sit down,' she said. 'Both of you.'

'What?' replied Kryk, 'we have to-'

'Sit down!'

There was such venom and force in her words that they did so. Elaria stepped up to the bow. She grabbed the rope holding both boats and pulled them towards the buoy. Seeing what she was up to, Kryk came forward and held them close as Elaria clambered onto the buoy. The bars of the metal structure provided well-spaced steps and – despite the movement of the water beneath – she was able to climb up. Once atop the buoy and with her feet set, she told Kryk to throw her an oar. His aim was true and she snatched it out of the air one-handed. She then raised the oar as high as she could and began to wave it from side to side.

'Why didn't I think of that?' said Kryk.

'I can see them,' said Dawin. 'I can actually see the sailors. Please someone look this way. *Please*.'

'They will,' said Elaria. She was sure that the fleet had turned because of their proximity to the buoy. In the great expanses of the sea, a mile or two was nothing. There had to be scores of men on that ship; surely one of them would look back.

Yet the other vessels were all further away and the Heartsong ship was moving at some speed.

Look! Look!

'Oh no,' wailed Dawin. 'They're so close.'

The ship sailed on, sails full. Beyond it, they could see eight other vessels, all headed north-east.

Elaria kept at it, swinging the oar until her arm ached. When she eventually stopped and looked down at the water, she felt a little faint.

Look this way! Please!

They had spied no other vessels other than the fleet since dawn. If they weren't seen now, she thought it possible – probable – that they would perish.

'Ha!' cried Dawin. 'Ha, look!'

The three of them had been so focused on the ship that they had not turned towards the shore for some time. To the west, propelled by several banks of oars, was a low, broad vessel bearing a huge Heartsong standard from the stern.

'The mayor's ship!' yelled Kryk, 'must be slower because they've got no sails.'

The ship was no more than a quarter-mile away and headed directly for them.

Elaria was so relieved that she seemed to lose all her strength and dropped the oar into the water. She couldn't help laughing as Kryk and Dawin embraced, almost turning both boats over in the process.

***

By the time they were aboard, any remaining relief had been replaced by shame. The ship was packed with Heartsong Militiamen, all of whom glared at the young trio as they were sent to the stern and the ship's commander. As soon as they'd climbed aboard, their little boats were cast adrift.

A large drum struck up a beat and soon the sixty or so oarsmen were again pulling hard. They were sitting in pairs on benches but along the middle of the vessel was a raised platform. Here were the soldiers and their gear – a hundred men at least, all equipped with armour, helmets, shields, lances and swords. There was barely enough room to pass and Elaria felt her face glowing as they finally reached the commanding officer. She did not recognise him and he did not introduce himself. He was a short, sturdy man clad in an impressive breastplate that also bore the Heartsong sigil.

'Explain yourselves – quickly.'

Elaria thought it only right that Kryk answer and for once Dawin kept his mouth shut.

'My fault, sir. I wanted to join the fleet. These two came after me – to stop me – and we were all blown out to sea. If not for the buoy, we'd still be out there.'

Not for the first time, Elaria was struck by how Kryk's rather high, youthful voice did not match his impressive frame.

'Frankly, that might have been better all round,' said the commander. 'This ship was already lagging – thanks to you three dolts we're even further behind.'

'I apologise.'

'You're Pathfinders?' asked the officer, brow furrowing.

'Recruits, sir. Just recruits.'

'You disobeyed orders, then?'

Kryk simply hung his head. Elaria realised how pitiful they must have looked. Kryk had his uniform and weapons with him but she and Dawin looked like commoners; bedraggled commoners at that.

Kryk mumbled something.

'What's that?' barked the commander.

'Just wanted to fight, sir,' replied Kryk. Though he towered over the commander, he was reluctant to meet his gaze.

The Militiaman shook his head. 'You may well get your wish, lad. There's nothing but sea between here and Remmar. Corporal.'

A younger man hurried over.

'Put them on cleaning duty for now.'

'Yes, sir.'

The commander turned back to the three Pathfinders. 'If we're stuck with you, you may as well do something useful.'

CHAPTER 10

The ship was named *Defender* and she was one of Heartsong's coastal patrol craft, apparently also used for fishing. Slender and a hundred and twenty feet long, she was an impressive ship. Malcanoth found the crew equally impressive; there were only thirty-five of them but they maintained and operated the vessel with great skill and enthusiasm. There were two masts and currently two vast sails raised, propelling them eastward at quite a rate. The only covered section was a wooden shelter built over the wheel and the captain's station nearby. All of the military equipment was below – as were the sleeping quarters – but the soldiers had been invited up on deck to enjoy the clement weather.

The Pathfinder contingent on this vessel was divided into two platoons, each of forty soldiers. One was led by Sergeant Haskey, one by Malcanoth. The patrol craft could not take as many passengers as the two bulkier transport ships but was evidently quicker. The *Defender* was leading the way towards Remmar, and indeed this seemed to be a point of pride for the skipper, a stern fellow named Serkeen. Captain Kano was aboard one of the transports, *Heartsong Conveyer,* and the other officers and men were scattered across the fleet.

To Malcanoth, the attack plan remained disturbingly vague. Even so, Serkeen was evidently experienced and apparently knew the approach to Remmar well. He had told the Pathfinder sergeants that the Bay of Brakken, just south of Remmar, was suitable for a swift, large-scale landing. Assuming the weather remained favourable and they could approach the coast under the cover of darkness, there was surely a chance of catching the enemy unaware. Even if King Flint's army had already counter-attacked by land, the occupiers would surely not expect Whispvale to come to his aid.

'What is that thing anyway?' asked Haskey, who was sitting with Malcanoth, repairing a hole in his cloak with needle and thread. The sergeant nodded at a short wooden tower close to the bow.

'Mounting for a weapon,' said Malcanoth, who had asked the same question of the captain. 'Basically, a large crossbow – it fires heavy bolts. One per minute, I'm told.'

'Useful.'

'Half of the sailors are trained archers too. Let's hope we don't need them.'

'Don't fancy a naval engagement?' asked Haskey with a slight grin.

'We can't be of much use in such a battle. If we're going to fight, let's fight on solid ground.'

'I'm with you there.' Haskey nodded down at the weathered book in his fellow sergeant's lap.

'Sorry. I suppose I should let you study.'

'Can't really practice properly on here. Too cramped.'

'You think it's too late for me to learn?' asked Haskey.

'Probably. They say it's best to start in adolescence.'

'I wonder if Kano will pull out one of his tricks. I heard he once set a wooden tower aflame but I've never seen him do much in an actual fight. It hurts, right? Afterward?'

'It does. And it drains your energy for hours after, sometimes days.'

'You think they use the Way? These Madlanders?'

'Who knows?'

Captain Kano had asked Malcanoth and the others not to disclose what they'd heard from Craggy Kingthyme. Malcanoth gathered that the strange old man was travelling north, though he knew not why. He recalled what Kingthyme had said about the Haar Dari leader – the "demi-god". If it was all true, there could be no doubt that he was a Waymaker. Malcanoth wondered if the leader was in Remmar. There were so many stories about the terrors that lurked in the Madlands; it seemed they were about to find out how much of it was true.

'Might try and sleep,' said Haskey, having finished his sewing.

'Don't know how you can.' Malcanoth had always envied Haskey's cheerful nature. Even now, he maintained his air of calm and optimism.

'We have right on our side,' said the sergeant. 'We'll send those devils back where they came from. They'll write songs about us.'

Within a few minutes, Haskey was sound asleep. Malcanoth glanced over at the soldiers gathered in small groups around the ship. He wondered how many would survive, how many would be killed. He wondered how many good decisions he would make, how many bad. Then he resolved not to indulge in such harmful rumination. All he could do now was prepare. He picked up his book.

***

The man who gave them their orders was called Corporal Layt. At first, he was very strict but by the second day it was obvious to Elaria that he actually felt a little sorry for the youngsters. They had spent much of their time doling out bread, dried meat and water to the Militiamen. Some of the soldiers made fun of them (one cretin in particular kept calling her 'buoy-strous'); others were curious about how they had ended up in such a mess. Elaria has lost count of the times she'd recounted the story. When not distributing food, they cleaned the decks with brushes and rags and buckets of seawater. None of the three complained and Elaria was actually glad to have something to do.

As usual, the gregarious Dawin had managed to make a few friends and deduced what he could. The Militiamen didn't seem to know a great deal but Layt was well-informed. He was a kind of assistant for the skipper – whose name was Gerrik – and had revealed that the journey east was proceeding well. This became obvious at dusk, when a distant landscape came into view. While the crew ate, the trio had a few moments to themselves. The *Spirit of Heartsong* had just about kept pace and now the entire fleet had halted. A nearby oarsman had left his post so Elaria, Dawin and Kryk gathered at his bench and gazed out through the porthole.

'See the other ships all have their sails down?' remarked Dawin. 'That's so we're not spotted. I can't see it yet but apparently there's a headland out there somewhere which marks the northern end of the Bay of Brakken. We'll head south then come up to get a direct run in. They'll time it so that we land as close to dawn as possible.'

Elaria looked around. 'So, who'll stay aboard?'

'Enough men to run the ship, I suppose.' Dawin ran a hand through his auburn hair, his expression intense. 'When we secure the shore, everyone else can land and then attack Remmar.'

'*When?*'

The new speaker was a bald, muscular man of around fifty. Like most of the oarsmen he wore a sleeveless tunic while rowing. He swigged some water from a flask but kept his eyes on the youngsters.

'Don't you mean *if?*'

Not even Dawin had an answer for that.

'You three would have been safer taking your chances in those little boats.'

Elaria turned to him. 'Will you go ashore?'

Another man, younger, on the next bench along spoke up.

'He'll be one of the first. This here is Narg Neckbreaker. He's fought Madlanders before.'

'Really?' asked Dawin, fixated by the aged warrior.

Narg nodded and drank more water.

'When?'

'Did you see the islands we passed yesterday?'

'The Kerradaes,' said Elaria, who'd paid close attention to everything discussed by Gerrik and his officers.

'There's iron there.' replied Narg. 'Lots of it. We used to control the trade. Few years back some Madlanders decided they wanted it for themselves.'

'Few years,' said the young man, who despite his break was still covered in sweat. 'About twenty-five, wasn't it?'

Narg nodded again. Kryk and Dawin sat down with Elaria on the bench. She noted how battered Narg's head and arms were. The worst of the marks was a livid pink scar across one cheek which looked like a burn. His chin had been sliced open at some point and didn't appear to have healed well. His voice was a rasping rumble.

'The mayor – it was Elator back then – sent a hundred of us to guard the iron mine on Kerrada. The Madlanders must have landed in some quiet cove because we never saw them approach. First attack was swordsmen – big, tough bastards but we stopped them. Then came a lone man, just walking up the slope towards us. Long black cloak, couldn't see much of his face. We had the high ground. Archers shot at him, everything missed. Lances too – not a single one hit. By then he was within fifty feet. He was laughing, aiming his staff at us. We only realised why when we turned around. There was a rock face above. Whole bits of it just fell off, hit the ground and rolled on to us. Great big boulder missed me by an inch. When it was over, there were only a few of us left. The warlock just walked away, still laughing. Then more swordsmen came – not many but too many for us. We grabbed the miners, got down to our ship and cast off. We were the last Heartsong folk to ever set foot on the Kerradaes.'

'The Madlanders know more of the Way than anyone in Whispvale or Skornland,' said the younger man. 'Expect the unexpected.'

***

The wind came from the south and remained steady, allowing the fleet to sail slowly on through the night. The ships stayed as close together as they could but no lanterns were allowed and lookouts were posted to avoid collisions. As the first smudges of light appeared on the horizon, sails were lowered and oars deployed. They had even been favoured by a low mist that would obscure their approach. Visibility was therefore not good but – from what Malcanoth could gather – Serkeen had a bearing on the headland. The *Defender* remained the lead ship and they were now aiming straight for the Bay of Brakken.

Just behind them was the *Conveyor*, one of the two bulky transport vessels. Malcanoth could see Captain Kano at the bow with several other officers. Serkeen had earlier observed that the *Spirit of Heartsong* was lagging again but even she had now caught up. Malcanoth turned to his right and watched one of the converted fishing ships cut through the water. Divided between this vessel and another were the men of Slate; they had arrived less than hour before departure.

Haskey joined Malcanoth at the stern. Just in front of them, Serkeen himself had his hands on the wheel. Beside him on a raised platform was his navigator, who alternated his gaze between a paper chart and the deep green seascape ahead.

'The Gods approve of our mission,' said Haskey. 'Conditions could not be better.'

'Always the optimist.'

'Someone has to be.' Haskey gave his fellow sergeant an affectionate shove.

Malcanoth glanced at the large group of soldiers sitting nearby. With the oars in use, the passengers had to remain in the middle of the narrow craft. Some of the Pathfinders seemed to find solace in talking: exchanging views on what they faced, trying to lighten the mood when they could.

Others stared down at the weathered timbers of the deck or up at the pale blue sky.

'What do you think?' said Haskey. 'Should we start briefing them? Get their gear on?'

Malcanoth shook his head. 'Serkeen said there's at least two hours to go. We start building them up now, they'll be exhausted by the time we hit the beach.'

'I was listening in. Some of them are as worried about the water as they are the enemy.'

'Serkeen says he can get us in close.'

'And if we're under fire?'

Malcanoth nodded forward. 'It's up to the sailors to give us some cover.'

'If we had a few Waymakers we could summon more mist. Maybe Kano's got something up his sleeve.'

'The key is that we all land at the same time and get ashore,' said Malcanoth. 'Once we've secured the bay, we can head inland, then to Remmar.'

Haskey turned to the bow and the area north of the headland. 'Wonder if old Flint's boys have drawn blood yet.'

'They were to strike at dawn; or close to it. Let's hope so.'

'To think we're relying on *them*.'

'And they on us,' countered Malcanoth. 'It's their city. They'll fight hard to retake it.'

Haskey lowered his voice. 'Orders are orders, of course. But I have to wonder, if things don't go our way…'

'I thought you were the optimist.'

Haskey gave a grin but it soon vanished when a young female Pathfinder ran past. She leaned over the stern and could soon be heard vomiting.

Haskey laughed. 'Poor Tamia, she always suffers with nerves.'

Before he could finish, another soldier had joined her.

'Could be seasickness,' said Malcanoth.

'Could be both,' added Haskey.

Malcanoth felt his own stomach turn over. He looked out at the sea, then at the land ahead. It all looked so calm and peaceful.

***

The Bay of Brakken was long and curved, enclosed at both ends by headlands that also sheltered the approach. There were no obvious obstacles such as rocks or sandbanks; in fact, the beach seemed to be composed entirely of pebbles. Now only half a mile off the shore, the fleet ploughed on. The bay was easily wide enough to allow them all to land simultaneously. But it was surely only a matter of time before they were sighted, especially as the earlier mist had lifted.

'Looks deserted,' said Dawin. The three recruits had been earlier tasked with cleaning the deck but had now been sent to the stern, ordered to stay out of the way. Those oarsmen who would also fight had their gear within easy reach. Even the drummer whose rhythm guided his fellow sailors was oiling a sword. The Militiamen were sitting, all now clad in gleaming helmets and armour. The mayor's ship had a special ramp at the bow for ease of access which would enable the soldiers to disembark at speed. Most were leaving their lances behind for ease of movement but every man was armed with sword and dagger. For once, the *Spirit of Heartsong* would be leading the way.

'Are you sure?' asked Elaria.

'I can't see a single person. Couple of caves but no sign of life there either.'

The trio watched as Gerrik and Orrsen, the ranking Militia officer, each spoke a final few words. A tall, broad man with spiky hair, Orrsen's helmet and chest-plate were lined with silver. He cut an impressive figure but his expression and manner suggested uncertainty. Elaria didn't blame him but she wondered why someone like Narg Neckbreaker wasn't in charge.

She wasn't sure if she wanted to miss the fight, but it seemed now that they might not even see the enemy. Would the recruits simply wait around in the bay with the sailors for word of what had happened?

'The *Defender*'s right in the bay now,' said Dawin, 'she can't be more than a quarter-mile off the shore.'

***

Malcanoth and Haskey stood together, close to the bow. Malcanoth wore only a thick leather jerkin under his tunic; it was comparatively light and would save him from most arrows, though it would do little against a strong stab of lance or sword.

Just ahead of the two Pathfinders, a trio of crewmen were manning the giant crossbow, which had been fitted to the mounting and was now loaded and ready to fire. The huge bolts were five feet long, fletched with glittering blue feathers. Serkeen also had a dozen of his archers crouching close to the bow. The captain himself was standing nearby, gaze fixed on the beach. The sun was bright now and Malcanoth had to shield his eyes.

'By all the great gods,' breathed Haskey.

Shouts went up. The archers stood to see what had caused such alarm.

Malcanoth looked out beyond the prow and then he saw it too.

Halfway between the *Defender* and the shore, a great mass of silvery blue tentacles rose from the waves. As the slithering limbs spread out in every direction, an oval head appeared. The creature seemed to have no eyes, only a black maw containing dozens of shard-like teeth. The vast, glistening beast was bigger than the ship and still rising.

Malcanoth felt a jolt of fear surge down his spine. Looking around, he realised that every single person aboard was now staring at the creature. The crossbow crew hadn't even bothered to aim their weapon; which would surely have done nothing against the behemoth. The oarsmen had stopped rowing.

Malcanoth was the first to say anything other than an oath or a prayer. 'Captain?'

Serkeen slowly turned around, eyes bulging.

'Starboard! Starboard, now! Hard over!'

At least the helmsman seemed in control of himself. As he turned the ship to the right, Serkeen bellowed at the oarsmen. Another officer called out a stroke and soon had his crew back at work. Even then, the men turned and strained to keep their eyes on the creature. Malcanoth saw that most of the other ships had altered course too, including the *Conveyor*. He looked back at the creature. The head seemed to have sunk a little but the tentacles were flailing towards the fleet. Each great limb looked capable of tipping the *Defender* over.

Haskey planted a hand on Malcanoth's shoulder. 'Could it... are they... controlling it?'

Ignoring him, Malcanoth stalked across the deck, having to push many of the soldiers aside because they couldn't drag their eyes off the sea creature. When he reached the left side, he had a good view of the *Conveyor*. All the other ships had now turned away from the bay. Like him, Captain Kano was one of the few not still staring in that direction. Kano was at the side-rail, eyes moving from ship to ship.

Malcanoth raised his hand and eventually caught Kano's attention. The captain pointed to the north. Malcanoth nodded. The reserve plan had been communicated to all the officers before departure. Between the Bay of Brakken and the city itself was a marshy inlet. Serkeen and the other sailors had confirmed it was the best spot to land after the bay; but it was close to the city walls and the enemy would now spot them easily.

Malcanoth's thoughts turned to the creature. He had heard of such beasts but how could the enemy manipulate it? Use it for their own means? Could this be the work of their leader? Was he in Remmar? Malcanoth could not see how their meagre force could possibly match such power. Nor could he avoid the feeling that none of them would leave Remmar alive.

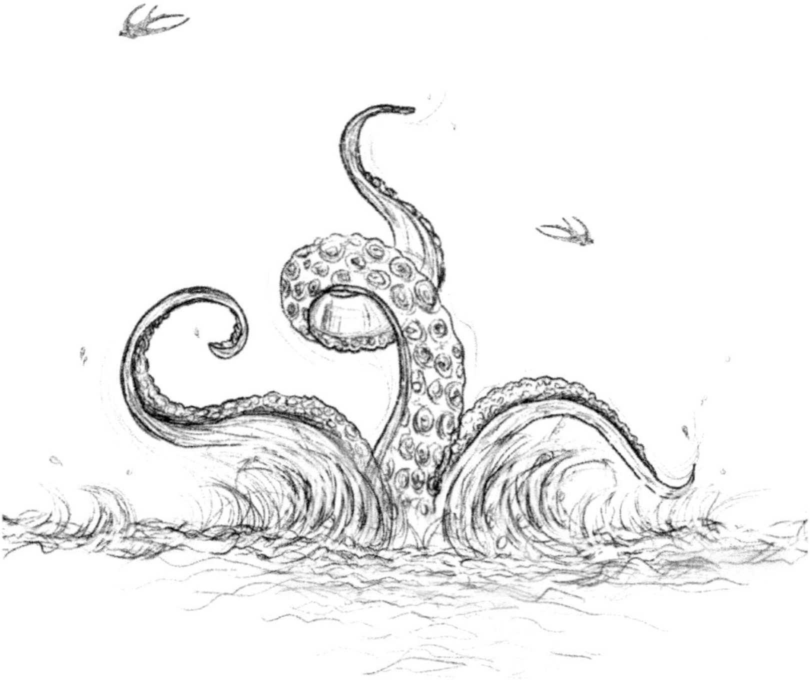

CHAPTER 11

'One hundred,' said Lisahra, who had been counting since the last of the enemy ships turned away.

Xalius stepped forward and put a hand on the backs of the two sisters. 'No more.'

He looked out from the cave and watched the apparition disappear. The sisters both collapsed from the effort and were caught by Ogon and Darian, then lowered into waiting stretchers. When he saw their ashen, contorted faces, Xalius decided to leave his congratulations until later.

'Take them. And treat them well, Darian, we owe them a great debt.'

'Of course, sir.'

Darian directed some waiting attendants to lift the stretchers, then he, Ogon and a squad of Siad's men trooped towards the narrow tunnel that led out of the cave. A second squad remained behind with Xalius.

Lisahra joined him as leaned against his staff, standing over the flat piece of rock where the eyeless squid had been placed. The creature was no more than a foot long; plucked from a rock pool the previous day. The twins – Lisl and Tysa – had been with him for some years. Xalius considered it essential to maintain a band of warlocks with a great variety of talents and he'd always insisted that the twins focus on their peerless ability for projection. Though spectacular, their apparitions could never last long, required a reference point in reality, and cost them a great deal of energy. Xalius used the twins sparingly, but he imagined their contribution today might save hundreds of warriors' lives.

The conquest of Remmar had cost the Haar Dari six hundred – and as many wounded – but, overall, he'd been surprised by the lack of resistance. Small pockets of loyal troops were still active in the surrounding countryside but the city was theirs.

When Carli had given him news of her vision of the ships attacking a wide bay three days ago, he and his warlocks had been mystified. Xalius had disregarded it but his memory was triggered upon learning of the Bay of Brakken. He now took his spyglass from his cloak, raised it to his good eye and looked out at the bay. Not one of the vessels had a sail up but he could make out the Heartsong sigil on several hulls.

'Even Carli did not predict that King Blythe might come to the aid of King Flint.'

'There must be hundreds of men aboard, maybe thousands.' Lisahra observed.

'I should think so,' replied Xalius, watching as the first of the ships passed out of sight behind the northern headland.

'Are you not concerned?' said Lisahra, 'they're heading for the city.'

'Not particularly. Now that this ruse has succeeded, they have no choice but to attack directly. Unless they're foolhardy enough to make for the harbour, there is only one alternative for a landing. Preparations have been made.'

He noted that Lisahra was still staring at the sea, not the ships. 'The creature. It looked completely real.'

'Remarkable, eh? I myself am not capable of anything quite so spectacular.'

'*I* will be,' said the girl, stroking her hair. 'One day, I will do even better.'

'Time will tell,' replied Xalius. 'Come, girl, let us see how Siad is getting on.'

Scouts had reported the appearance of Flint's army two hours earlier. They'd had some information about Skornland gangsters also coming to his aid and this seemed to be accurate. Xalius was not overly concerned. Flint's troops had already been defeated once and if he was recruiting criminals, he clearly didn't have much faith in the rest of his army. The city was not walled but the Haar Dari had established effective defensive positions and taken most crucial areas intact. Siad had swiftly directed the Sand Lions and the Irregulars to the northern edge of Remmar and he could reinforce with the Ironhands if necessary. Xalius hoped to be able to oversee both sides of the battle from the Sea Tower, the highest structure in the city.

Turning around, he once again noted the soldiers' interest in Lisahra. It was not only her hair: she had a pretty face and a fine figure. The girl was utterly oblivious; she seemed only concerned with the Way and those who could help her progress.

'What now, sir?' asked the senior bodyguard.

'Back to the city. Send someone ahead to bring that carriage up to the path.'

A man was dispatched. Lisahra and the soldiers waited for Xalius to lead the way. He sighed then plodded across the sand. By the time he was struggling up the murky, uneven path, he was wishing he'd brought a stretcher for himself.

***

The *Spirit of Heartsong* was quiet. The oarsmen had plenty to occupy them as the ship again tried to keep up but there was hardly a word said between the soldiers either. Each of them seemed lost in thought, even though they would soon face battle. Elaria had heard a sailor comment that he'd seen a large squid before but nothing of that immense size. The fact that the creature was clearly protecting the bay seemed almost impossible to accept. She felt sure that such a thing could only be achieved by use of the Way; if their foes could do this, what else were they capable of?

She couldn't help thinking about all those hours in the tiny boat before she, Dawin and Kryk had been rescued. The creature or something like it could have been below them and they would not have known. Suddenly she longed to be back on dry land, somewhere where such terrors only existed in stories and nightmares.

'We should go home,' murmured Dawin. Like the other two he was standing at the rear of the oar deck. 'Something like that…it's… we shouldn't be here.'

Even the usually bullish Kryk couldn't summon an encouraging response. Elaria glanced over at Captain Gerrick, who was just behind the helmsman, again deep in conversation with Orrsen.

Leaving the others, she went to look out through the closest oar-hole on the right side. They were past the headland now. Ahead was the strip of coast south of Remmar. Elaria could make out a road that led down from the headland, through a hamlet to the outskirts of the city itself. Remmar boasted many large buildings – most constructed of a pale stone

– and high arches, some topped by gleaming statues. Further inland was a cluster of high, square towers, each containing dozens of windows and decorated by colourful, ornate patterns. Close to the water were numerous quays and pontoons though she could see only small vessels. If there were usually any banners or standards flying over the city, they had been taken down.

'Still no sign of the Remmari ships,' observed Orrsen.

Elaria hadn't even realised that King Flint had ships. With the noise of the creaking oars and puffing sailors, she couldn't hear very well so subtly moved closer to the two senior officers.

Gerrick kept his voice low. 'If we're lucky, they scuttled them before the enemy could take control. The central harbour can't be seen from here.'

'Flint has four war-boats, correct? Would they all fit in the harbour?'

Gerrick didn't seem impressed by Orrsen's obvious lack of knowledge. 'That's what they built it. The ships are old but we couldn't hope to match them.'

'Would the Madlanders know how to sail them?'

Gerrick glared at the younger man. 'How should I know? I suggest you prepare your men, Orrsen – the inlet is no more than a mile away.'

***

'It's quiet,' said Haskey.

'Too quiet,' replied Malcanoth.

Serkeen had just arrived behind them, a spyglass in his hand. 'I think I know why. The lookouts report fighting to the north of the city. The standards of King Flint.'

'Then we may have achieved surprise after all,' said Haskey.

As usual, the speedy *Defender* had pulled ahead of the other vessels. Captain Kano had waved his approval; it seemed wise not to risk the larger *Conveyor*. Serkeen raised a hand and aimed it to the right. Moments later, the *Defender* turned inland towards the shore. Between the edge of the city and the headland was a long strip of marsh, mostly high grass and the odd windblown tree.

Directly ahead was an inlet. The mouth was no more than fifty feet across but it was clearly navigable; small wooden jetties had been constructed on either side and several boats were tied up. Yet – as with what they could see of Remmar – there seemed not to be a single person present. The nearest dwellings were close enough for Malcanoth to spy a pile of firewood beside a door, tunics hanging from a washing line, even smoke rising from a chimney – but not a single man or woman.

Serkeen pointed forward. 'We'll make for the third jetty on the left, give the others space to come in behind us.'

Haskey also pointed – at a muddy path that led up to the main road, which would give them access into the south of the city. There were no walls, just a gap in the angular houses marked by an arch.

'There, we can secure the gate. Wait for the others to land.'

Malcanoth said nothing. It was possible that the enemy were indeed occupied with Flint's forces to the north but why did the southern edge of the city seem abandoned?

Commander Serkeen ordered the oarsmen to slow as the *Defender* entered the inlet. Malcanoth turned and saw the masts of the fleet lined up neatly behind them.

Haskey addressed the troops. 'Get yourselves off quickly but safely. Clear the way for those behind you. Fan and out and watch for hostiles.'

Malcanoth knew something was wrong. His abilities with the Way were limited to combat but he sometimes felt that his training had given him a heightened awareness. Yet it had done nothing to warn him of the Beastkin attack. Doubt gripped him. He thought perhaps he should speak and yet what exactly could he say?

The *Defender* passed the first of the jetties.

'Sir, I saw something.' The speaker was a Pathfinder, gazing at the marshy ground to the right of the ramshackle jetty.

Malcanoth had only been looking there for a moment when he heard a shout from the far side of the *Defender*. Something clattered against the side of the ship. Then came another shout, this one in a language Malcanoth did not recognise.

Suddenly arrows and spears were flying from the bank towards the *Defender*. Wild-haired, dark-skinned figures could be seen pressing forward through the reeds, each of them carrying bundles of spears or quivers for their bows.

'Down!' yelled Haskey. 'Down!'

He and Malcanoth sought cover with the rest of the Pathfinders. Then came the screams. Malcanoth saw a male Pathfinder writhing on the deck, a four-foot spear embedded in his shoulder, blood already colouring his white tunic. An oarsman on the far side of the boat was groaning, a gory wound in his flank. While many of the arrows were whistling harmlessly over their heads, the enemy had already adjusted to curve their spears over the side-rail and into the massed occupants of the ship. The projectiles lacked power but were doing plenty of damage. The first two victims were soon joined by others.

'To the near side!' shouted Serkeen, now crawling across the deck.

Leaving Haskey to care for another casualty, Malcanoth ran to Serkeen in a low crouch. 'Captain, your archers!'

Serkeen called out to the men and ordered them to fire. Though it was awkward, most chose to shoot through the oar-holes rather than expose themselves. Malcanoth stood and peered over the top of the side-rail. Whoever the warriors in the reeds were, there were hundreds of them. Most were gathered at the bank, many of them whooping and shouting. They clearly loved battle.

Serkeen sprang up next to him. The captain opened his mouth but no words came. He staggered into Malcanoth, already coughing up blood. As he helped him down onto his knees, Malcanoth saw the spear sticking out of his back – the projectile had come from the other side of the inlet. Serkeen pawed at him, eyes begging for help, his body spasming. More blood issued from his mouth then he became still. Another spear sunk into his lower back, and another thudded into the side-rail, no more than a foot from Malcanoth's head. Everywhere he looked he saw terrified faces. Another man was hit, then a female Pathfinder, somehow not screaming though she had been skewered through the knee.

Malcanoth ran across to the other side of the ship and peered out at the far bank. There were at least another two hundred of the barbarian warriors there. He and all the others aboard were like fish in a barrel: vulnerable to fire and without a method of escape or counter. Even the giant crossbow was useless – it had a narrow field of fire for targets in front of the ship. Suddenly the *Defender* lurched forward, almost knocking Malcanoth off his feet.

He looked to the stern and saw that the *Conveyor* had struck them. In fact, something had become entangled because the ships seemed to be locked together. Then a volley of arrows flew towards the shore: at least Captain Kano was fighting back. It seemed that the attack had taken some of the pressure off the *Defender* because the number of projectiles lessened.

Malcanoth could see no way of getting the ship moving again but he could at least ensure the remaining soldiers and sailors had some protection – the small covered area above the wheel.

'To the stern! All of you, to the stern!'

The spears and arrows kept coming but he repeated his shouts and pushed dozens of soldiers and sailors in the right direction. As they congregated under the wooden roof, Malcanoth found himself next to young Tamia. She was caring for a man who had been struck in the stomach. The wound was bleeding profusely.

Haskey arrived, dragging another wounded Pathfinder by both arms. Others were pulling injured under the shelter but Malcanoth could see at least thirty prone figures that would never move again.

'What now?' said Haskey.

Above them, spears and bolts thudded into the wooden roof.

'We're not going to get this thing moving again. We could move everyone onto the *Conveyor* but they'll pick us off as soon as we show ourselves. Any archers left?'

'A few,' replied Haskey.

'Use them and round up any spare bows. Return fire as best you can.'

Though they shared the same rank, Malcanoth held superiority because of his extra years of service.

'What are you going to do?'

'Try to find Kano. And a way out of this.'

***

The *Spirit of Heartsong* drifted up alongside the other ships of the fleet, all of which had stopped once the attack began. The three vessels ambushed in the inlet were stationary. The remaining Militia transport, the *Conveyor II,* was currently turning away from the shore to join the other five ships.

'A trap,' said Orrsen, rather unnecessarily. 'They were waiting for us.'

'So were *they*,' said Captain Gerrick, looking to the north. 'Elaria, what do you see?'

She had continued to follow their conversation and now returned to her viewing position at the oar-hole. Curiosity drew Kryk and Dawin to the same location.

'What's going on?' asked Kryk.

'I'm not sure.'

Then she saw it: a high, red prow emerging from the hidden harbour of Remmar. The ship moved at remarkable speed, massed ranks of oars thrashing. Another ship immediately appeared behind it, also with a red prow, the rest painted black. These vessels had no masts. They had to be war-boats the captain had spoken of.

'That's one question answered,' said Gerrick.

Corporal Layt approached him and pointed west, out to sea. 'Sir.'

'By all the gods,' said Gerrick. 'There other two.'

Orrsen's face turned pale. 'What...how...'

'They must have been standing off the coast, waiting for us to approach. They knew we'd come from the south to avoid being sighted.' Gerrick turned to Layt. 'Inform the other ships.'

'Yes, sir.'

Layt had four coloured flags which were used to relay signals. Elaria wondered if he'd be able to attract the attention of the other vessels with the battle still unfolding at the inlet. She wondered about Tamia and Malcanoth and all the others. Were they under attack? Were they injured? Alive?

'What can we do?' asked Orrsen.

'This fleet was despatched to transport men from one place to another, captain. We haven't a single war-boat among us. Frankly, there isn't a great deal we can do.' After a few moments, a grim smile appeared on Gerrick's face. 'Except ram them.'

Despite his anxiety, Orrsen seemed to at least appreciate a definitive decision. 'I don't suppose the mayor would approve much of that.'

'Oh, I don't know.' Gerrick nodded to his drummer, whose efforts returned the oarsmen instantly to their duties. As he struck up a slower beat to start the stroke, the *Spirit of Heartsong* began to move once more.

***

Malcanoth was still at the stern and glad to see that Haskey's archers were at least returning fire. But what next? The bow of the *Conveyor* had likely broken the rudder of the *Defender* and, in any case, they no longer had enough fit men aboard to man the oars. And anyone who tried to get onto the *Conveyor* would be vulnerable. Malcanoth risked a quick look over the stern rail but could see little; clearly the occupants of the transport ship were also taking cover.

'Captain Kano! Captain Kano!'

No answer.

'Anyone aboard the *Conveyor*!'

'Who's there?'

He didn't recognise the voice. 'Malcanoth, Pathfinders.'

'Alkrin, Militia. The *Guardsman* is heading to the far bank to help us out.'

Malcanoth could see that the mast of the third ship was moving. Soon after, he heard a loud metallic clang then cries from the bank. Evidently, they had been able to bring their crossbow to bear on the enemy.

'Alkrin, where's Kano?'

'He's here but he's working on something. Malcanoth, get everyone to the stern, get them ready to move.'

'Very well.'

Malcanoth picked his way through the dead, injured and terrified. He could not imagine what Kano was "working on" but he hoped he was doing it quickly. Haskey and his archers were still retaliating when they could but the sheer weight of fire kept their heads down. The deck of the ship was now littered with arrows and spears.

'What's going on?' asked the sergeant.

Before Malcanoth could answer, a shout went up from the bow.

He hadn't realised anyone was still up there but a lone sailor was now fleeing towards them. Something flashed behind him and he fell forward, killed by a single blow. Standing where he had been only a moment before was one of the wild-haired warriors. The man was dark and lean, his robe of animal skin still dripping water. In one hand was a bloodied hand-axe. Two more warriors climbed over the side-rail and dropped down beside him, also holding axes.

Malcanoth and Haskey drew their swords and charged.

***

The Remmari war-boat was no more than two hundred yards away. The red prow stood high above the water; the ship was at least twice the size of *Spirit of Heartsong*. Captain Gerrick was manning the wheel himself, eyes fixed on the dark ship now heading towards them.

'Full speed!'

At this command, the drummer increased his pace. Elaria, Dawin and Kryk looked on as the sweating oarsmen hauled at their oars, powering the ship onwards.

'This is insane,' said Dawin. 'We don't stand a chance against that thing.'

'Look,' said Kryk. 'It's turning.'

The war-boat was dead ahead and had indeed turned away from the shore. The banks of oars were now still.

'Ha!' cried Gerrick.' We will strike his flank.'

Orrsen seemed to have lost a good deal of his enthusiasm and said nothing. Elaria couldn't see much sense in it either, though they were at least drawing attention from the three vulnerable ships in the inlet. The rest of the fleet seemed undecided. Some were not moving; others had hesitantly followed Gerrick's lead.

'The second one's turning too,' observed Kryk, whose height allowed him to see more than the others.

Orrsen approached the captain. 'What armament do they have?'

Gerrick ignored him. 'We'll be on them before they can do anything!'

Despite the efforts of the oarsmen, it seemed to Elaria that it would still take them a long time to cover the distance. Even the sides of the war-boat were protected by angled slats; they couldn't see a single person.

Nor did they hear the weapons being launched. The first Elaria knew of the attack was Dawin pointing at something in the sky.

'What is it?'

Some of the soldiers had seen it too. One of them called back to Orrsen but Elaria couldn't make out his words over the drum.

'Dawin?'

He didn't answer but kept his eyes fixed on the skies above.

Corporal Layt ran up to his captain. 'Sir, they must have catapults. I saw a great stone hit the water. It was a yard across, at least. If-'

The impact was loud: a sharp, splintering crack.

'We're holed!' yelled one.

'It just missed me,' cried another.

'Keep at your oars,' bellowed the captain. He altered course slightly.

'A hundred feet,' said Kryk.

The *Spirit of Heartsong* would get no closer. Elaria had no idea which of the enemy boats fired the second stone but it smashed into a rank of oarsmen and sent shattered timbers flying. As cries went up, the sailors let go of their oars. The captain continued to yell but then seemed to realise just how much damage had been done. Water was coming up through the two holes and lapping at the feet of those on the low rowing deck. Gerrick still had his hand on the wheel, even though his ship was drifting.

As if dropped from the sky by an invisible hand, the third stone ploughed into the bow, splitting the boarding ramp in two. The soldiers looked on helplessly as the sailors used sheets of hide to try and stem the influx of water but it was clearly not a fight they could win. Worse still, one of the war-boats was turning towards them, oars once more in the water.

Dawin gripped Elaria's arm, his face rigid with fear. She glanced at Kryk, whose expression was different.

'I'm sorry,' he told his friends. 'I'm so sorry.'

***

Bones crunched as Malcanoth hammered the hilt of his sword into a warrior's nose. Somehow the man fought on, swinging his axe with arm outstretched. Malcanoth threw his head back and watched the axe head fly past. He swept two-handed at his unbalanced foe's neck. The blow sliced a long rent in the warrior's flesh and he fell, choking on his own blood.

'More of them!' cried Haskey.

The two sergeants had already accounted for five of the warriors. Malcanoth had forced himself to ignore their war cries and undisciplined method. He and Haskey had used the longer range of their swords to good effect. Haskey had been cut high on his arm but they were otherwise unharmed.

'Come on.'

The two sergeants ran back along the deck. The only soldiers and sailors not at the stern were the dead and those too injured to move.

'Cover us!' instructed Malcanoth as he and Haskey reached the archers. A mixed group of Pathfinders and sailors had armed themselves and were able to hold the attackers at bay, even though yet more of them had scrambled aboard.

Just as Malcanoth neared the stern he saw several lanterns thrown from the *Conveyor*. He watched them sail over the attackers and land in the reeds. Some simply smashed but two spread enough burning oil to ignite a small fire. Malcanoth's confusion ended when he saw Captain Kano stand high and aim both hands at the flames.

In seconds, a thin tongue of fire flew at the warriors. Kano swept his hands to the right and the flames engulfed more than a dozen of them. Agonised screams went up as they collapsed: clothes, skin and hair burning. Some threw themselves into the water to escape.

After seeing so much death and injury on their side, Malcanoth couldn't help cheering. He turned towards the far side of the inlet. The *Guardsman* was still doing enough to keep the remaining warriors occupied. This opportunity had to be taken.

***

'Most ingenious,' said Xalius, stepping out of the elevator onto the narrow balcony. As Lisahra and the two soldiers followed, he examined what he could see of the elaborate system of cables and weights. 'This may not be their time but one has to admire such achievements. There was a time when these people led the way.'

Despite the easy passage to the top of the Sea Tower, he was weary from the morning's exertions. He hoped neither of the unfolding battles would require any further intervention on his part.

'Sir.' One of the soldiers was pointing down at the inlet where the Irregulars had just ambushed the enemy ships. Xalius joined him at the surround.

'How's that fire moving so quickly?' asked the other soldier. 'Can't be natural.'

Lisahra arrived, the breeze blowing her hair into Xalius's face.

'Indeed not,' he said, peering through his spyglass.

'Do you have a warlock down there?' she asked.

'No. You three leave me alone. I must concentrate.'

The two soldiers moved away at once.

'What are-'

He cut Lisahra off immediately. 'Leave me. Now.'

Xalius closed his eyes and began the chant.

***

The war-boats passed either side of the sinking *Spirit of Heartsong*, paying them little attention. Up close, the black ships looked even more fearsome: prows reinforced with metal, rowing positions protected by wooden grilles. Suddenly, a white-haired man appeared above the shielding, gazing down curiously at the smaller vessel.

Captain Gerrick raised a fist and shouted curses at him.

'That's Remmari naval uniform,' observed Corporal Layt. 'They're fighting for the enemy!'

Gerrick ceased his swearing and watched as the war-boat cruised past. Then he stood still, idly observing the sailors vainly struggling to plug the holes. There was now two feet of water in the ship and it seemed to be getting higher with every passing minute.

'What do we do?' asked Elaria.

For once Dawin seemed unable to speak. He was standing with his head bowed, watching the cold water rise up past his knees. Kryk sloshed his way forward and swiftly returned with three oars. He handed one each to Dawin and Elaria.

'These will help us keep afloat. It's not far to the shore.'

'But what then?' she asked. Elaria moved to the nearest oar-hole and looked to the south. The ships of the fleet were facing in different directions and appeared to be in utter disarray. The four Remmari war-boats closed in.

***

Thanks to Captain Kano, there was no longer a threat from the near bank. The archers had taken care of the warriors attacking from the bow and now turned their attention to the far bank. The *Guardsman* had backed out of the inlet; presumably to give the *Conveyor* space to move. The last of the injured had been moved off the *Defender*.

Satisfied that there was no one left to help, Malcanoth sent Haskey first then climbed up after him. Dropping down onto the deck of the *Conveyer*, he was surprised to see how ordered the transport ship was. There were many injured but the sailors were now back at their oars and preparing to heave the ship out of the inlet. Kano seemed confident that the bow was not badly damaged and that the oarsmen could pull it clear of the crippled *Defender*.

Still protected by two shield-bearers, the captain stood ahead of the mast, his long, fair hair almost as pale as his tunic. He continued to direct the flames at any foe still moving, face impassive as he incinerated the enemy. To Malcanoth, the screams of the dying warriors were no less awful than his allies. He wondered how Shai Kano could shut them out.

Picking his way towards the stern, he soon found himself with Haskey and a group of the injured. Tamia was there, now holding a bandage to her own head.

'You all right?' he asked.

'Yes, sir. Thank you.'

Malcanoth placed a hand on her shoulder then moved on. Haskey was on his knees, trying to lever an arrow out of a soldier's thigh. The man had another arrow clamped in his mouth for something to bite down on. Leaving his fellow sergeant to his work, Malcanoth continued, looking for the commander and hoping they could get moving immediately.

He had taken only two steps when he heard a noise that sounded like a sudden gust of wind. He turned and watched in horror as a wall of flame spewed onto the ship, engulfing the entire front half. Malcanoth recoiled as the heat hit him. Throat burning, eyes stinging, he fell to his knees.

Flaming figures collapsed. Everything seemed to be alight. Malcanoth saw a man lurch across the deck, his hands high. Somehow, he seemed to have resisted the inferno. There seemed to be a halo of golden light around him; protecting him.

Kano.

He was being pushed backward by the force of the flames and their unnatural shape showed a Waymaster was at work. All Malcnaoth could do was watch: this clash was far beyond him.

Just as Captain Shai Kano seemed to steady himself, he let out a great yell and his halo disintegrated. Instantly the flames surged into him. A great orange flare went up and when it receded, the captain was simply not there.

Malcanoth could feel the hair on his arms burning. Knowing he couldn't stay a moment longer, he ran to the side-rail and threw himself over it.

***

Nothing could have prepared Elaria for the speed at which the *Spirit of Heartsong* disappeared from under them. No more than ten minutes after the ship had first been holed, she found herself swimming away from the foundering vessel, both hands gripping the oar Kryk had given her. He and Dawin were close by and they were surrounded by dozens of sailors and Militiamen, all of whom had been forced to abandon their weapons. Elaria was already shivering; she had never been in water this cold. In fact, it was so intense that she barely spared a thought for the mysterious creature that had deterred the fleet.

Some of the sailors and soldiers were already swimming towards the shore, which was at least three hundred feet away. The closest area was a long quay that seemed to be deserted. Elaria had not seen either of the senior officers since jumping off the ship but Corporal Layt was close by.

'There's no choice,' he told the youngsters. 'We can't stay out here.'

'The ships?' said Dawin, sodden hair plastered across his brow.

'They don't stand a chance. Not against those war-boats. We may be able to slip away. Come on.'

Layt set off for the quay, as most others had now done.

'He's right,' said Kryk. 'We've no choice.'

Dawin nodded; Elaria too.

The three of them kicked for the shore.

***

Xalius felt a hand on his arm. He had slumped against the surround and still felt rather faint. His hands throbbed. All his concentration had been required to recite the chant correctly but it was the sheer distances involved that had really drained him. He tried to stay away from such labours if possible; that's what his warlocks were for.

'Are you all right, sir?' asked Lisahra.

'I'm fine,' he croaked.

'I saw it,' said Lisahra. 'What you did. You defeated them.'

Xalius drew in some deep breaths then straightened up. 'Good. To be honest, I couldn't see exactly what I was doing.'

He could, however, see the two ships now aflame in the inlet.

'Another one has just sunk,' said Lisahra. 'The war-boats destroyed it. Now they're going after the others. Sir, how did you persuade the Remmari sailors to fight for us?'

'Oh, that was Siad's doing. He had the families rounded up. Standard tactics. By the ancients, my throat. Does anyone have any water?'

CHAPTER 12

There were few survivors. As he floated in the water, watching the *Conveyor* and *Defender* burn, Malcanoth could see only a few heads bobbing in the water. Around him were dozens of bodies, most charred beyond recognition. The smell in the air was horribly reminiscent of burned meat. Someone somewhere was coughing: an awful, agonized wheeze. Malcanoth turned to see a sailor only a few yards away. Much of his hair had been incinerated and skin had peeled from his forehead. Grabbing a nearby wooden shield, Malcanoth swam over to him.

'Here, let me help.'

The sailor's face was black and he seemed unable to open his eyes.

'Hold this.'

Malcanoth planted the man's hands on the shield, which at least helped keep his head up.

'Hey!'

The shout came from behind him. Malcanoth turned to see a small, twenty-foot tender manned by three sailors. Not far behind it was the *Guardsman.* The patrol ship had not been struck by the flames and several officers were standing at the bow.

'Am I alive?' asked the injured man. 'Am I alive?'

***

Elaria already felt weak from swimming. She had both hands on the oar and was resting her chin on it. Dawin was a little way ahead but she and Kryk were the furthest back. She had glimpsed soldiers and sailors pulling themselves up onto the quay but had concentrated on staying afloat.

'Only a hundred feet or so now,' said Kryk. 'Looks like almost everyone got off. We might be all right. We might-'

'What is it? Kryk?'

'Oh no,' he breathed.

'What-'

Then she saw them. Dozens of dark-skinned warriors were sprinting onto the quay. Shouting and whooping, they launched spears and fired arrows, downing several of the already-exhausted survivors. The sailors and soldiers had nowhere to go. Those not killed by the initial onslaught were set upon with daggers and axes. The warriors then began to pick off the defenceless survivors in the water.

Dawin had already turned. 'Go! Go!'

Kryk grabbed the oar and helped Elaria; soon they were kicking away from the shore as fast as they could. She did not allow herself to think of anything other than escaping the enemy. She had survived all the trials of recent days since that fateful decision to follow Kryk: she could survive this.

'Keep going!' he yelled.

Something landed in the water just ahead of them. Only when her hand touched it did Elaria realise it was an arrow.

Kryk cried Dawin's name.

Elaria stopped and looked over her left shoulder. Dawin was only twenty feet away but something had happened to him. He dipped below the waves, arms flailing.

More arrows struck the water, several where Dawin had just been.

Kryk let go of the oar and took a stroke back towards the shore but Elaria threw herself forward and grabbed his arm. 'No. Don't!'

Dawin surfaced once more, his face contorted in pain, then disappeared again below the surface.

'Come on!' She hauled on Kryk's arm and now it was her task to turn *him* around. 'He's gone, Kryk. We have to move. We *have* to.'

There was no further trace of Dawin, just arrows splashing into the water.

Face frozen by rage, Kryk put his hands on the oar and they both kicked for their lives once more. The cries of dying men drifted across the water but neither of them looked back.

When they eventually stopped, they were puffing so hard that neither of them could speak. Elaria eventually managed to look at the shore. She saw dozens of bodies in the water, many floating with arrows and spears sticking out of them. On the quay, the pale stone was streaked with red. An enthusiastic archer tried a shot at them. When it landed well short, he dropped his bow and joined his compatriots as they tipped the dead men off the quay.

Kryk rested his face against the oar and sobbed.

Elaria turned to the south. It seemed that the remainder of the fleet must have tried to escape because the four war-boats were pursuing them. Only a single ship was left near the inlet. One man at the bow was pointing at what looked like a small group of survivors in the water. They weren't all that far away.

Elaria grabbed Kryk's arm. 'There's a ship. It's our only chance.'

When he opened his eyes, she saw there was still some hope there.

'One last effort, Kryk. We can do it.'

***

Malcanoth did what he could do to help the injured man up into the boat but he suddenly felt incredibly tired. Once he'd been dragged aboard, he lay back and just sat there; gazing down at his torn, blackened clothing and the blistered skin on his legs and chest. Strangely, it didn't hurt all that much. He imagined the water had helped. He didn't recall being on fire but he reckoned he must have been. The man he had helped was whimpering; and he continued to do so as the sailors recovered four others.

Kano consumed his mind: how much pain had his captain and mentor felt? What were his last thoughts? Had he known it was the end?

This was too much; Malcanoth leaned over the edge of the boat and vomited. When he'd recovered himself, he realised he had no idea what had become of Haskey. He tried to shout his compatriot's name but his parched throat couldn't produce any words.

'Mate, save your strength,' advised one of the sailors.

The *Guardsman* was close by and other survivors were climbing up a net hanging from the side-rail. Malcanoth couldn't understand why the ship wasn't being attacked. The sailors in the smaller boat plucked two more people from the water then headed for the *Guardsman*. They were all busy and didn't seem to notice what Malcanoth saw.

***

Elaria simply could not move her legs anymore. She and Kryk clung to the oar but only he could summon the strength to wave at the ship. Thankfully the battle to the south had kept the war-boats occupied and there seemed a good chance of escape. But the little tender was now heading back to the ship and there were no other survivors visible. It was no more than two hundred feet away yet no one had turned back to see them. *The Spirit of Heartsong* was now deep beneath the waves and everyone else was dead. Why would they look back?

But then the little boat veered away from the ship and turned to the north. It seemed packed with people but the sailors were rowing right towards them. Somebody was waving.

'They've seen us,' said Kryk. 'They've seen us!'

'Actually, I think they saw me.'

Hearing the growling voice, Elaria turned and saw the hairless head and battered face of the Militia veteran, Narg. He was holding a torn red and white striped flag which he ditched before swimming over to them.

'Found it just now. Gods must be watching over me. And you two, I reckon.'

***

Xalius had never seen so many prisoners gathered in one place. Remmar's centre was a huge rectangular space enclosed by grand public buildings. At one end was the royal castle, which was connected to the square by a broad set of steps. It was not a huge building, but made more impressive by three voluminous domes and four slender towers now casting elongated shadows across the square. At the top of the steps stood the victorious Siad Borshan and his commanders. Still rather drained from the trials of the day, Xalius joined him there and looked down upon the thousands gathered below.

Fighting had halted in the early afternoon. Though the defenders had lost hundreds, King Flint's rag-tag army had been no match for the Haar Dari. Siad's troops had met the attackers beyond the walls to avoid a chaotic, unpredictable street battle. The open ground had also suited the Sand Lions and the desert dogs when they launched their counter-attack. A second offensive by the Ironhands had routed the Skornish. Some had fled to the north, more than a thousand had been killed and now at least two thousand were gathered in the square, unarmed and on their knees.

Their commanders – identifiable by red cloaks – were in a small group at the base of the steps, surrounded by the giant Graggs. Other than a few scouts and guards, the entire Haar Dari force was also present. Siad had removed his armour and seemed to be enjoying the sight before him.

'Any more from the ships?' he asked Xalius, having been too busy with Flint's force to concern himself with the attempted landing.

'The war-boats have sunk or captured all but one of the enemy vessels,' replied Xalius, who had remained up in the Sea Tower to observe the slow-moving battle.

'And what about that one?'

'Escaping to the west. One war-boat in pursuit. I must say I'm rather impressed that the two kings managed to coordinate an attack. Not that it did them much good.' Xalius nodded down at the enemy commanders. 'Got anything out of them?'

'Haven't tried yet. I'm sure we can obtain what we need out of the junior officers. See the fellow with the white hair?'

'Yes.'

'Lord Amos.'

'Ah.' This name was known even in the Madlands. Amos was no nobleman; he had lowly origins but had won his position as King Flint's most trusted general by repeated success over a number of years. Even during the recent troubled times, Amos had maintained his reputation as a formidable foe.

'He's sixty-five,' said Siad. 'Old bastard still killed three of mine.'

Xalius knew the commander meant Ironhands.

'We could interrogate him, I suppose,' added Siad. 'Even use him as a hostage.'

'Or? It sounds like you have another alternative in mind?'

'Personally, I would like to chop his head off. Right here. Right now.'

Siad's axe was hanging over his shoulder. The blade was clean.

'Only some of the men down there are soldiers. The rest are criminals. But they all know Amos. Killing him will crush their spirit, make it easier for us to recruit. They won't all turn, of course, but–'

'I understand,' said Xalius. 'You plan to do this yourself?'

'On the steps,' said Siad with a sly smile. 'This stone is almost white – they'll see the blood right at the back, perhaps even the head rolling down.'

Xalius would have thought that a man who had seen and inflicted so much violence might have tired of it by now.

'The Imperator gave no specific instructions regarding prisoners,' he replied. 'But it does seem like a good idea.'

'Glad you agree.' Siad took the axe from his shoulder and strode down the steps.

***

If death was coming, it was coming slowly. The *Guardsman* –sole surviving vessel of the disastrous attack on Remmar – sailed west under a middling breeze. The enemy war-boat was still following them, and they seemed to gain a few yards with every passing hour. As dusk approached, they were no more than half a mile away. The captain had decided to head south along the Skornish coast, hoping to lose the war-boat in the darkness.

In order to gain every possible fraction of speed, he had ordered that everything not essential be thrown over the side. This had included military weaponry and equipment, some personal belongings and also the bodies of three injured soldiers who had died since being brought aboard. A bearded, composed fellow named Kyrax, the captain was often in discussion with a fisherman who knew the waters well and seemed convinced they could outwit their pursuers.

Those aboard were a mix of crew, Militiamen, Pathfinders and even a couple of soldiers from Slate. During the initial moments of their flight from Remmar, there had seemed an optimistic air amongst the survivors; but this had been swiftly replaced by a communal disbelief that the force had been repelled so easily. And now, as the sun set, almost all seemed preoccupied by their struggle to escape. Many times, the sailors cursed the Remmari fleet; unable to comprehend how these men could abandon their former allies and fight for their conquerors.

When the last of the sun's light had gone, the captain put his crew to work once more and altered course. The aged fisherman hurried up to the bow and began issuing instructions that were passed back to Kyrax, who had taken the helm himself.

Elaria had been sitting in the same place for hours. Once aboard, she'd been taken below and helped out of her clothes by the only other female Pathfinder aboard, a woman named Treyda. Once dry, she had been given some spare clothes found on the deck. Elaria didn't like the idea of using the trousers and tunic of someone who might be dead but she had to wear something. After a fortifying mug of wine, she'd spent some time with Kryk, who she found in another cabin. Elaria hadn't felt much like talking herself but she felt she at least had to try. Kryk said nothing, instead pouring himself a large mug of wine. Elaria had then taken herself up on deck and sat with Treyda, a blanket wrapped around her shoulders. The Pathfinders had found a spot in the middle of the ship, well out of the sailors' way.

Various people had come and gone during the evening and she was glad of company to occupy her. Without it, she risked more thoughts of the attack from the shore and poor Dawin. She couldn't help wondering if his lifeless body was still floating in the cold water or if it had sunk into the cold depths. It was no way for such a good young man to die.

After observing the comings and goings all day, Elaria now knew exactly who was on the *Guardsman* and who was not. Tamia, Sergeant Haskey, Captain Kano and many others – all missing or captured or dead.

She had not seen Sergeant Malcanoth since the little boat had rescued them. Though it was he who had noticed the three survivors of the *Spirit of Heartsong*, he hadn't said a word and seemed to be in a bad way. His clothes had been partly burned and though his face had been spared, he'd sustained damage to his chest and arms. He too had been taken below and only now did he reappear.

Walking slowly back from the bow, he sat beside Elaria and Treyda, grimacing as he lowered himself to the deck. He wore only trousers and held a cup of wine. Much of his chest and his left upper arm were covered in bandages.

'Are you cold, sir?' asked Elaria, offering him her blanket.

Malcanoth shook his head.

She couldn't see much of his face; the captain had ordered that no lanterns be lit.

'Any idea what's happening, sergeant?' asked Treyda. She was an older woman, forty at least, but as tall and muscular as many of the men. She had a kind way about her.

'We're close to a small bay called the Sinking Hole,' said Malcanoth, his voice quiet. 'The fisherman seems to think he can get in there. Apparently, there are several reefs and they reckon the war-boat won't follow.'

'What then?' asked Treyda.

'I don't know.' Malcanoth leant his head back against a barrel.

'Sir, do you know what happened to Sergeant Haskey?' asked a passing male Pathfinder. 'And the captain? I'm not sure there are any other survivors from the *Defender* and the *Conveyor*.'

'You have your answer then,' Malcanoth replied, impassive. The man moved on without a word.

A bottle of wine was handed around. Elaria felt she had drunk enough but kept drinking anyway as quiet chat resumed. It was a surreal, almost dreamlike occasion, a moment unlike any she had ever experienced. The soldiers had all endured something terrible, and yet this was what united them.

She thought Malcanoth might have fallen asleep but he spoke up some time later.

'Hold on. You're a recruit, Elaria.'

She was surprised he hadn't said anything earlier.

'And didn't I see Kryk?' added Malcanoth. 'What the hell are you two doing here?'

***

Not long after Elaria finished recounting her tale, the captain ordered silence. This was to allow he and his fisherman guide to devote all their energies to the perilous passage through the reef. Along with the rest of the passengers, Elaria and Malcanoth stood to observe the approach. The pursuing war-boat also had no lights on and had disappeared into the darkness. Ahead, the land was only a shade murkier than the sky. Elaria could not conceive how the fisherman might know his way; it seemed impossible to make out a landmark of any kind.

As she gazed towards the shore, messages were passed back from the bow and adjustments made. Eventually, the onlookers began to whisper in urgent tones. It was Treyda who pointed the surf out to Elaria; the vaguest hint of breaking waves perhaps a hundred feet to the right of the *Guardsman*'s bow. She commented that the gods had finally shown them some mercy; the light southerly breeze was sufficient to propel them forward but kept the sea calm, making the hidden dangers easier to see.

A minute later, the messages from the bow suddenly grew more desperate. The crew made some hasty alterations to the sails and the ship turned sharply until she was following a reverse course. It soon emerged that the guide was unhappy with the angle of their approach. Everyone seemed concerned that they might now possibly be sailing back towards the enemy and Elaria was glad when they spun around and made for the shore again.

Relief finally came when they passed between two reefs made clear by churning white water and the noise of it lapping against solid rock. The jubilation only lasted until the sailors informed the passengers that this was simply the entrance and that worse was to come. As the captain reduced his sails, the ship eased slowly forward, the reefs and the breaking water drawing ever closer. Twice the guide ordered a halt and it seemed that there was now not even space to turn back. The sails were lowered and oars deployed; and observers posted all over the ship. Calls were made constantly to inform the guide and the captain of angles and distances. Elaria was beginning to wonder if this trial would ever end when the passengers sighted a line of surf and the pale tones of a sandy beach.

Not long afterward, the fisherman announced that they had reached the precious anchorage. There were no cheers but many words and prayers of thanks. Elaria didn't need expert advice to conclude that the much larger and less agile war-boat would have no chance of negotiating the reef. For the moment, they were safe.

***

Xalius had taken a wing at the castle, where he had also installed Darian, Ogon, Carli, Lisahra and the twins as thanks for their efforts in the bay. He had hoped for a quiet night but Siad had indulged his troops with celebratory handouts from the Remmar stores. The Ironhands had occupied the square and sung long into the night with the Sand Lions. By late morning, Xalius had not yet heard from Siad so he despatched Lisahra and Ogon to ride around the city and check that all was well. A further attack by Flint or a local insurgency hardly seemed likely but he didn't want to take any risks.

Ideally, he would have liked to continue his study of the Shyan tomes or begin an inventory of what had been claimed within the city. He at least didn't have to worry about the treasury, which was housed in a basement accessible by a discrete passage within his wing. Siad had a squad of reliable men on duty which Xalius had supplemented with three of his warlocks. He hadn't yet had time to investigate fully though it was clear that Flint had left little of monetary value behind.

'Any more from the war-boats?' he asked as Darian opened the shutters of a spacious dining room.

'Not that I know of, sir,' replied the attendant.

'I wonder if they caught that last ship.' Xalius reached into a nearby bowl and grabbed a handful of berries. He was being looked after well; a few of the female castle staff had been retained to keep the grounds and attend to the new residents.

All the male staff had been sent to join the other prisoners captured during the occupation and Flint's counter-attack. Siad was keeping them inside the city's circular arena. His plan was to feed them almost nothing, let conditions deteriorate and wait for them to volunteer for the Haar Dari. Apparently, dozens of the criminals who had fought under Flint's banner had already done so.

Overall, Siad's method seemed sensible to Xalius. They had to be careful with recruitment, both to the Haar Dari itself, but also their army. Discipline was relatively easy to maintain while all went well but if reverses came, large-scale mutinies were a danger. Volunteers were always preferable to conscripts and any determined to resist had to be crushed. They also needed plenty of wives to reward their most successful warriors; it suited them to execute a few hundred soldiers and create a few widows.

'I'd like some milk.'

'Of course, sir.' With a cordial bow, Darian departed.

Xalius cast an eye around the dining room. On one wall was a large painting of the very war-boats they had earlier discussed. On another were several portraits, presumably relatives or antecedents of King Flint.

When Darian returned with the mug of milk, he also had news of two visitors. Xalius agreed to meet the first of them in the adjoining room. He was determined to not get drawn into another administrative quagmire and that meant using locals – carefully chosen locals – to shoulder most of the work. The mayor of Remmar had surrendered early on during the attack and, from their meetings so far, seemed like the realist Xalius needed him to be.

Mayor Brayber was a slender man with snowy white hair and a matching beard. He was brought in by two guards who remained close, even when he sat down opposite Xalius.

'Morning, mayor.'

Brayber sat in his seat, hands clasped, apparently unwilling to meet his host's gaze.

'Something wrong?' asked Xalius, not that he particularly cared.

'This business at the arena, sir. It really is intolerable. The smell is spreading through the city. And I do wish you'd reconsider allowing us to deliver some food.'

'Not possible, I'm afraid. Those men can halt their suffering by joining us. You yourself have agreed to undergo the Ceremony of Acceptance.'

Brayber took a long breath. 'You must understand – I am not a religious man but many within this city are. We have worshipped the Espheral Gods here for-'

He stared at the gloved hand Xalius now held up.

'Do not speak of such matters here. I will not tell you again.'

'My apologies.'

'I understand how difficult this must be,' said Xalius, who in truth had little sympathy for the man. 'You could not have foreseen a change such as this in your lifetime. But we are here and we are not going anywhere. There are really only two choices open to you and your people – obey us or face the consequences. If some wish to martyr themselves for their false gods, then it will be so. I must tell you, it will not be the first time.'

The mayor wiped sweat from his brow and gazed down at the ornate tiles beneath his feet.

'The first Ceremony of Acceptance is in five days,' added Xalius. 'I will, of course, expect you to attend. Every adult member of your family too. At times like this, it's essential that influential men such as yourself set a good example.'

Mayor Brayber glanced over at another portrait. Xalius recognised the subject as King Corin Flint, the present king's grandfather.

'Did he not enjoy the longest reign of any Skornland king?'

'Yes, sir. And he lived to ninety-two.'

'Ah. I myself am one hundred and fifty-one. And you will have no doubt heard that I set the Heartsong ships ablaze with my own hand while watching from the Sea Tower.'

Brayber gulped before nodding.

'You must understand then that you, your king and your people have not faced anything like us before. I encourage you to propagate this notion – it will make both our lives considerably easier.'

***

Xalius's second interview of the morning was with Vikter Aggor. As Remmar was now secure, the time had come to arrange a meeting with this Sawfang Mawraze character. Xalius considered it unlikely that King Flint would be able to mount an attack any time soon but the Haar Dari had sustained significant losses in recent weeks. He felt the time was right to recruit allies that could share the load. Having sent the enthusiastic Aggor north with an invitation, he summoned two of his warlocks and met them in the castle's gardens. It was a pleasant day - the flowers looked spectacular in the sun, which was noticeably less blistering than in Shya – and he managed to walk some distance. By the time his underlings arrived, he had settled on a bench under a tree.

'I have a job for you,' he said when they stood before him.

Izilis had developed both hearing and sight to a remarkable degree. As these abilities were fortified by a calculating character and impressive blade skills, he was exceptionally qualified to function as spy or assassin. He carried only a dagger but Xalius knew he needed no greater weapon to despatch a foe. Izilis was no more than thirty but his hair had prematurely turned grey.

Xalius took a moment to enjoy Lisahra before continuing. Where some fair faces lost their appeal in bright sunshine, hers was only enhanced.

'I have no doubt that both of you would prefer to work alone but you will do this together. Lisahra, Izilis – Vikter Aggor has just left to arrange a meeting between myself and Mawraze. The pair of you will follow him, learn what you can about both individuals – and their relationship – and return to me before the meeting. Is that clear?'

Xalius was pleased that neither raised a protest; both were incredibly wilful in their own way. He pointed at Lisahra.

'Do not neglect your practice, girl; we will continue your instruction upon your return. Izilis here has proved himself to me a hundred times.

Here is a chance for you to do the same. But be in no doubt – he is in charge. Understood?'

She bowed.

'Good.' Xalius used his staff as he lifted his aged frame from the bench. Upon straightening up, he realised the pair hadn't moved.

'Why are you still here? Go!'

CHAPTER 13

The soldiers disembarked at dawn. It was possible that enemy reinforcements would arrive either by sea or land so it had been decided that the survivors should make their way west along the coast. The captain and crew would wait to see if the war-boat was still in the vicinity and, if not, attempt to sail back to Slate, the nearest Whispvale town. All agreed it was essential that King Blythe and the leaders of Whispvale learn immediately of the defeat.

The *Guardsman* was anchored as close in as it could get, about sixty feet off the beach. Malcanoth looked on as the last of the soldiers swam ashore. The only Militiaman present of any rank was a corporal. One of the two Slate men was a captain but he had suffered horrific burns to his face. He could walk but was in no fit state to lead.

And so Malcanoth found himself in charge of this disparate, depleted force. Four seriously injured men had been left aboard the ship but those now under his command were as weary and shattered a group as he'd seen. Malcanoth didn't feel all that different himself; but there were fifty-four people in need of direction, and he intended to give it. He'd ensured that everyone at least had a sword or a bow; they could protect themselves if need be.

Once the last of the soldiers reached the shore, others handed them blankets to dry off. Clothes and packs had been safely transported aboard a make-shift raft constructed by the sailors. Malcanoth gave a final wave to Captain Kyrax, then walked up a sandy slope though high, pale green grass. His burns ached but Elaria had located some salve to ease the pain and there was a good supply of bandages. At the top of the slope, he found Jinn – the lower-ranking Slate man – who knew the land between his city and Remmar better than anyone present.

'They should be ready to move in a quarter-hour,' said Malcanoth.

'Sir.'

Malcanoth guessed Jinn was around his age; a short, stout man who wore a belt bearing the sigil of his city. He looked anxious.

'Sir, you must understand, I've never actually been here, though I do know the main routes once we're inland.'

'We should probably aim to avoid them.'

'Good point.'

'How far to the border?' asked Malcanoth.

'About fifty miles. We'll be safe once we get there. But I reckon we're only about thirty miles from Remmar, which means the enemy could get to us-'

'-Any time.'

'Exactly, sir. But we also have to consider the Beastkin. I know I don't have to tell you how far they've spread and we've had numerous skirmishes on the border. From what we've heard, a lot of the Skornish have headed north. There was never much on this stretch of coast anyway. It's pretty bleak, we may not see many people.'

'That could work in our favour. Staying in sight of the coast reduces the chances of getting lost. Agreed?'

'Sounds right to me, sir.'

Malcanoth looked inland. The strip of sand was not very wide and soon gave way to marsh that then became a low, grassy plain dotted with patches of scrub and stands of trees. They would at least have some cover.

'There's no coastal path that I can see,' added Jinn. 'I'll head directly inland and see what I can find.'

'Very well.'

With that, Jinn bounded down the far side of the slope.

Malcanoth set off in the other direction. As he walked across the beach, numerous faces turned towards him. He guessed they expected him to say a few words.

***

Elaria didn't think much of Malcanoth's speech and, from her observations of the other soldiers, neither did they. She did not care; the sergeant would be judged by his actions and leadership over the next few days and she, for one, was glad to have him in charge.

Once through the sand and the marshy ground, the column headed north-west across terrain that turned out to be less comfortable than it appeared. There was high grass to contend with, hidden holes and mounds, and insects that simply would not give up. Within an hour, Elaria had numerous little bites across her exposed hands and face. They itched only mildly but the insects clearly enjoyed human prey and drove everyone mad. Only when the column finally struck higher ground did the accursed creatures disappear.

To avoid heading too far inland, they had to traverse a large headland with little cover. Here they encountered some grazing wild ponies, most of them coloured white and brown. Elaria thought of Stripe; it cheered her to know he was safe and sound back in Heartsong. The ponies seemed unconcerned by the soldiers' presence and only a few interrupted their munching to look up. As the line neared the top of the headland, Elaria noted many nervous glances to the rear. Even though Malcanoth had posted scouts a mile ahead and behind the main column, an air of fear pervaded the whole group. They were not far from Remmar and it was widely assumed that the Skornish army had also failed. After all, if the enemy could conquer the city and prevent the landing so easily, it seemed likely that they would also have defeated King Flint's counter-attack.

Elaria was close to the centre of the column and had walked for the most of the day alongside Treyda, who spoke solemnly about the comrades she had lost at Remmar. Elaria appreciated her kindness and honesty but she was wary of growing close to fellow soldiers again. Most of those she had previously befriended were now either dead or in enemy hands. She could not be certain that poor Tamia had lost her life but few had escaped that inlet alive. As for Kryk, he was further back in the column and had shown little interest in talking to Elaria. It was guilt, of course, and a part of her wanted him to feel it. There was no getting away from the fact that he had – indirectly – caused Dawin's death. That was something he would have to live with.

Less than two months had passed since Elaria had left Clearwater. What had she expected? Adventure? Excitement. Undeniably, she had experienced both. But there had been so much fear since the day of the Beastkin attack. And since that fateful decision to take the boat, dread had never been far away. She wanted to protect Whispvale and she wanted to fight alongside her fellow Pathfinders. But the fear was exhausting; and she didn't want to die at the hands of some horrible creature or Madlander. She was young and she wanted to live.

Head down, lost in thought, she walked across the far side of the headland. If they made it to safety, she wasn't sure she even wanted to stay in the Pathfinders. Would she really want to join the inevitable counter-attack? Every sword would be needed, that much was clear. Elaria had lived with fear for most of her seventeen years. Did she really want to remain in its grip for the rest of her life? Forever?

***

That night they camped in a hollow not far from a low set of cliffs, in earshot of the water below. They had seen no one all day and passed only two isolated farmhouses, both apparently long abandoned. Malcanoth realised now just how quickly the Haar Dari invasion had affected so many. Just before dusk, the keen-eyed Jinn had caught sight of something that cheered the whole party. The *Guardsman* had escaped the Sinking Hole and the attentions of the Remmari war-boat and was flying west under full sail. Malcanoth saw relieved tears from many of his fellow soldiers and felt a surge of optimism himself. The ship looked quite beautiful; and at least some of them had survived the disaster of Remmar. It was easy to get drawn into thoughts of how the remaining Pathfinders and King Blythe would respond to such terrible news but he forced himself to concentrate on the here and now.

Having posted sentries in three directions, he visited them all before settling down himself. No one had anything more than a cloak or blanket to lie on and Malcanoth was no exception. He slept fitfully; his burns were less painful but finding a comfortable lying position was simply not possible. He woke early and roused the column for a swift start.

As the second day drew to a close, he reckoned they'd covered at least twenty miles. They stayed close to the coast and only emerged from a stretch of thorny bushes and dense undergrowth in the late afternoon. Navigation was difficult but Jinn had performed well and even seemed to be enjoying the opportunity. They also passed through a hamlet with a population of no more than a dozen. The inhabitants seemed to live off several herds of sheep and were blissfully unaware of events to the east. Malcanoth guessed – and hoped – that they were too few in number to attract the attention of the enemy. They were happy to sell some meat to the soldiers and cook it for them before they left. One of the shepherds directed them to a good spot for the night, which appeared to be part of an ancient network of mines. Once the soldiers had all eaten and found shelter in caves and tunnels, Malcanoth went to check on his sentries.

It didn't seem sensible to go alone, especially in his weakened state. As Jinn was exhausted from the day's exertions, Malcanoth collared one of the Militiaman. He had already exchanged a few words with Narg, who was clearly very well-respected by his younger compatriots. The battered warrior agreed readily and strode out of the temporary camp.

Malcanoth's four sentries were posted to the north, south, east and west. On this occasion, each were five hundred paces out and – as Pathfinder training dictated – had used the stars to guide them. All was quiet to the north, so they moved on, heading for the man to the west. Upon reaching the area where the sentry was supposed to be, they could find no one. Even after ten minutes of widening the search, the man could not be located.

'Back to the camp?' growled Narg.

'We need to know what happened to him.'

'Nothing good, I'll wager. Ah, perhaps that's him?'

There was enough moon and starlight to make out the figure walking towards them from the west. Pathfinder and Militiaman drew their swords.

'Not sure yet.'

But soon he could clearly see the lanky Pathfinder with long hair and a distinctive profile.

'Orvent?'

'Who's there?'

'Sergeant Malcanoth.'

Orvent hurried across the grass and hunched close. 'Sir, sorry for leaving my position but I saw a light. They're camped out around a fire. I didn't dare get too close.'

'You did the right thing. Stay here. We'll take a look.'

'You can't miss the lane, sir. The camp is on the far side of it, behind a wall. That's why the fire can't easily be seen from here.'

'See anything of the men?' enquired Narg.

'No.'

'How many?'

'Not sure. Quite a few.'

Malcanoth and Narg moved carefully and reached the lane without incident. The paved route was muddy and overgrown but wide enough for two horses to pass. They looked carefully in both directions before crossing swiftly, hunched and alert. Once over a ditch and through a stand of trees, they saw the wall. Malcanoth smelt smoke and tracked in that direction. The stone barrier was in some disrepair and at one of the many gaps they spied the bloom of flame.

Malcanoth could see four figures sitting on stone blocks, close to the fire. Behind them, several tethered horses were grazing.

Narg gripped his shoulder and whispered in his ear. 'See the badges on their tunics? Always worn just above the heart. Land Patrol – regional Militia. They operate under a royal commission.'

'Allies.'

'Unless we're really unlucky – yes.'

***

There was a tense moment when the pair stepped over the rubble and introduced themselves but they were soon gathered around the fire with the Land Patrol men. Narg eased their fears by mentioning a couple of individuals he'd met while on joint manoeuvres many years before. There were seven men in all and they hailed from the closest town, Longfield. The senior soldier was named Tarmik: a big fellow with a round, ruddy face.

As Narg related what had occurred at Remmar – with occasional contributions from Malcanoth – Tarmik and his men listened intently. When he finished, the Skornish men shook their heads or stared thoughtfully at the fire.

'We would have gone too,' said the leader eventually. 'But the Land Patrol was ordered to remain here. We're supposed to be guarding against Beastkin attack, not that there's a lot we can do with so few of us.'

'The bloody things are everywhere,' added another man, 'the coast, north as far as Tickwood. We were trying to return to Longfield but we couldn't get through.'

'There *were* ten of us,' said Tarmik, gravely.

'Sorry to hear that,' said Malcanoth. 'We were going to continue west along the coast. Sounds like we may have to change plans.'

'Lucky we came across you lot,' observed Narg, 'or we would have walked straight into them.'

'We're staying well clear of the coast,' said Tarmik. 'Better to head north-west through the Crystal Mountains.'

'What about the dragons?' asked Malcanoth.

'They keep to the high peaks,' replied Tarmik. 'At this time of year, the Low Gorge is passable. Trust me, if you'd seen what we have, you'd do the same. It will add a few days to the trip but it's better than being chomped to death by oversize vermin.'

'You know the way?' asked Narg.

'Aye,' said Tarmik. 'South end of the Low Gorge is only three days from here.'

'Can we join you?' asked Malcanoth.

'By all means. How many others survived the battle?'

'About fifty.'

Tarmik grinned. 'Sounds more like *we'll* be joining you.'

CHAPTER 14

There was an elegant simplicity to the Ceremony of Acceptance. Five hundred of Remmar's most important administrators, military officers, merchants and priests bowed before the Eye of Rael and pledged allegiance to the Haar Dari.

From this day forth, I follow the will of Rael and his earthly agents.
I reject the authority of all false gods and prophets.
All I have is his; my health, my wealth, my family, my head, and my hands.
I kneel before him, I bow before him, I accept him.
There is only Rael.

Xalius and Siad stood outside the castle once more, clad in ceremonial cloaks. Once the five hundred had repeated the pledge three times, they were ordered to their feet. Each was given a tunic bearing the Sign, which all donned swiftly. They were all now *haar dari* – "eternal followers" in ancient Ilerian.

Looking on from the edges of the square were thousands of city-folk ordered to attend: men, women; young and old. One fool gave a shout, cursing the invaders. His protest was cut short by the sword of an Ironhand.

Mayor Brayber was summoned to the top of the steps and obediently read the script given to him. He announced the disbandment of Remmar's city constabulary and further details of the new regime. Brayber also explained that the opportunity for the prisoners within the arena to join the Haar Dari had passed. Eight hundred of them would be publicly executed over the next few days. Xalius admired the will of these men and women but killing them was a small price to pay for the widespread obedience it would achieve.

Siad then spoke, announcing that all curfews had been lifted. The citizens of Remmar were now free to go about their business, though leaving the city's environs was still forbidden without special permission. Schools, stores, smithies, workshops and other workplaces would now reopen. However, the numerous chapels and churches within the city that honoured the Espheral gods were barred shut. Xalius had decided there was no sense in destroying them just yet. The Imperator might feel differently but it seemed early to risk enraging the entire city. As Siad finished and his troops broke up the crowd, Xalius was amused to see a few dozen locals offering themselves for the next ceremony; there were always a few pragmatists.

He and the marshal walked back towards the castle together. Xalius imagined it was only a matter of time before the commander rounded up some of the local women but, for the moment, he remained focused on military matters.

'I've patrols out as far north as Hardwater and Littlewick. No serious resistance encountered. I see no reason why we cannot strike Bruj within a matter of weeks. I hope the Imperator will allow us to press our advantage. We should not give Flint and Blythe time to regroup. What of this Mawraze character?'

'I had a message from Aggor this morning. We will meet in two days' time on the Remmari Downs just outside the city. Would you like to be present?'

'Do you need me there?'

'No.'

'Then I leave it in your capable hands.'

Xalius had also received a message from Izilis. The spy and Lisahra had gathered considerable intelligence and expected to return the following day. Xalius was interested to learn what they had discovered. When he met with Mawraze, he wanted to know exactly what and who he was dealing with.

***

Sergeant Malcanoth had explained why they needed to turn east and avoid the coast. Elaria accepted this, especially when she heard the stories that Tarmik and the other Skornish had to tell. But it was only when they came to the village that everyone understood why it had been the correct – and only – decision.

Even before they'd reached it, the column could smell death. Malcanoth took a small scout party forward then the others followed. The village consisted of about thirty houses clustered around a small square with a well and a sign that announced it as Lesser Trailton. Most of the houses had been gutted by fire and everything of value had been stripped and removed. All they found was bodies: decaying, maggot-infested bodies left to rot in the sun. The Beastkin clearly had no regard for gender, age or infirmity. Every occupant of the village had been slain, and the bite and claw marks were visible upon every corpse.

Some of the soldiers had seen enough after a few minutes and withdrew. Elaria elected to walk around, take it all in. She realised then that many of her questions had been answered.

No decent person could stand by and allow this. Regardless of her own fear, it was now her duty to remain with the Pathfinders and resist any who did harm to such innocent people simply living their lives. Whether that be the Beastkin or this new enemy, it mattered not.

Later, she remembered that their column was equipped with a few spades. Returning to the village's tiny and now ruined chapel, she began to dig. Soon almost a dozen of her compatriots had joined her. From the village's single sundial, Elaria knew they spent only two hours there. But by working swiftly, they buried every man, woman and child and marked each grave with fresh flowers.

Though physically tired and with her arms in immense pain from all the digging, Elaria felt strangely renewed when they set off once more.

***

Five days after landing, they were in sight of the Low Gorge. The Crystal Mountains loomed high above, with only the tallest peaks covered by snow in the summer months. But the unique minerals held within the pale rock still sparkled, a breath-taking sight that seemed to herald a change in fortune. The far end of Low Gorge was only forty miles from Laketon, one of the safest and easily-defended of all the settlements in Whispvale. But the gorge was open and exposed, and immensely long, cutting straight through the mountains. They would be easily traceable by any Beastkin that might have picked up their scent.

As the sun descended, Sergeant Malcanoth ordered a halt. Tarmik and Jinn went forward to scout a suitable place to camp and the others sat down on the sides of a track they had been following. Malcanoth chose his sentries quickly and – as they happened to be standing together – Elaria was sent south with Narg.

'Mind if I come along?' asked Kryk as they passed him.

'Why not?' said Narg, as usual stripped down to the sleeveless tunic that displayed his stringy muscles and countless scars. The Militiaman set off first, shouldering his way through a patchy hedge and striding across the dry, sandy soil that seemed prevalent near the mountains.

To Elaria, who had never before beheld the peaks, the Crystal Mountains could only be a creation of the gods. There was nothing to prepare an observer for the endless slopes and towering peaks that seemed to reach as high as the heavens. It was said that only one adventurer had ever reached the summit of the biggest mountain, which was known as Emperor. Cian Wayfoot, the greatest of all Lyther explorers, claimed the mountain stood fully five miles above the sea. Elaria could hardly believe that she was about to walk through the range to the other side.

Narg came to a stop beside a dead tree and leant against it, eyes fixed on the forest to the south. He picked up a stick, drew his knife and began whittling.

Elaria and Kryk stood on the other side of the tree. They had barely exchanged two words since coming ashore. As she looked at the big recruit, Elaria couldn't help thinking back to the first time they had met – in battle at the Tournament. It seemed a lifetime ago.

'Do you hate me?' Kryk said quietly.

'No,' she replied honestly. 'I just thought you might want to be left alone.'

'All this walking. Lot of time to think. A couple of times…I've considered just stopping somewhere or going my own way.'

'Why?'

'Because…what will I say to them? What *can* I say?'

'To who?'

'Dawin's parents.'

'I've had plenty of time to think too,' said Elaria. 'All three of us made mistakes that night. There was no way you could have predicted Dawin would follow you. You knew it wasn't for him; that's why you went off alone.'

'He was such a good friend.'

'Kryk, hundreds of people died at Remmar. I'm sure they were all good friends to someone. Or good sons or daughters, or brothers or sisters. Dawin's parents will know that he died fighting the enemy. He joined the Pathfinders. They must have known what could happen. Dawin would want us to stay. Stay and fight. You know that, don't you?'

Elaria gripped his arm. 'We can avenge him. And Haskey and Kano and Remy. And those poor people at the village. We can fight for *them*.'

Kryk managed a nod.

Elaria found she had to look away and wipe her eyes. 'Those mountains are really something, eh?'

Suddenly, Narg threw his half-whittled spear to one side and dropped to the ground.

'Down,' he hissed. 'Now!'

Elaria glimpsed men moving out of the treeline before she ducked down. Before she could think what to do, Narg had scuttled around the rear of the stump to her and Kryk.

'Lots of them. I'll see if I can get a count. Warn Malcanoth. Stay low until you're through the hedge.'

They did exactly that but Elaria had to force herself not to look back. Once through the hedge, they sprinted to the track. When the other soldiers saw the panicked looks on their faces, many sprang up and grabbed their weapons.

Malcanoth also noticed them. 'You two, what is it?'

'Soldiers, sir,' said Elaria. 'Coming out of the trees to the south. Narg stayed to get a count.'

By now, everyone was on their feet. Weapons in hand, the rag-tag force congregated around the sergeant as he waved them in. The archers all drew arrows from their quivers and those few with helmets and armour hastily pulled them on.

Malcanoth pointed to his right. 'Everyone withdraw to the trees there. Go.'

The soldiers set off towards the only nearby location they might be able to defend. The trees would provide cover and were surrounded by open ground. Elaria was about to follow when Narg barrelled straight through another section of the hedge. He had not lost his composure but Elaria found herself frightened by the look in his eyes.

'Broad line of advance, curving at both ends to surround us. They wear the same sign as those at Remmar – Madlanders.'

'How many?' asked Malcanoth.

'A hundred, maybe more. The trees?'

'No other choice.' Malcanoth bodily pushed Elaria and Kryk in that direction. As the pair ran after the others, Elaria could hear the shouts of the attackers from beyond the hedge. She was about sixty feet from the trees when she realised those ahead of her were already firing arrows back at the enemy.

Drawing her sword, she turned and saw a small group of warriors only yards behind Narg and Malcanoth. The enemy soldiers were armed with swords and axes. None wore armour but all were clad in a red tunic with a symbol painted roughly in black.

Seeming to sense that they were vulnerable, Malcanoth and Narg had also stopped to face their pursuers. Two of the enemy warriors were struck by arrows and fell, closely followed by two more. Realising that they were safer with their foes between them and the archers, the remaining four warriors flew at Malcanoth and Narg.

The gleaming axe-blade of the quickest man slid harmlessly past Narg, who had twisted nimbly and now drove his short sword two-handed up through the warrior's chin. The man could only issue a weak groan as his body went limp. The veteran Militiaman retracted his sword and the warrior collapsed. Sparks flew as Malcanoth parried the blade of another warrior.

Kryk rushed past Elaria and swung wildly at one of them, distracting the enemy long enough for Malcanoth to slash across his foe's throat. Blood coloured the air as the remaining two warriors fought on. In his eagerness to help his superior, Kryk had neglected his own flank. Elaria saw what was happening and ran at the man now attacking him. Knowing she wouldn't make it in time, she simply screamed.

The noise stopped the lank-haired warrior in his tracks. Kryk drove at him but the man recovered quickly enough to bat the attack away with his own sword. Elaria heaved at his shoulder and was stunned to see the blade sink two inches into the flesh. Kryk attacked again, this time slicing across the tunic and into the man's chest.

As the warrior staggered backwards, Elaria saw that someone must have landed a blow on the fourth enemy soldier. He was holding his wrist, staring dumbly at a thick gout of blood.

'Come on!' Narg grabbed her by the arm and suddenly she was running towards the trees once more.

'Kryk?'

'Right behind you!'

The archers were kneeling in the gaps between the trees but two moved aside to let Elaria through. She was relieved to see Kryk, Narg and the sergeant close behind. Malcanoth's face was stained by blood but he seemed unhurt.

Suddenly the air came alive with the sound of snapping bowstrings. More of the enemy fell. Several injured men scrambled backwards and at a shouted order, the forty or so visible warriors retreated.

'You all right?' asked Treyda, her hand on Elaria's shoulder.

'I think so.'

***

The copse of trees was perhaps a hundred feet across. Trying to ignore his aching burns and still holding his bloodied sword, Malcanoth withdrew to the centre of the space and surveyed the position. The enemy – who did indeed bear the same sigil as the defenders of Remmar – had swiftly surrounded them. They remained at around three hundred feet, gathered in an uneven circle. There were indeed at least a hundred of them; his force was outnumbered two to one. Yet the trees provided decent cover and he had at least thirty bowmen with plenty of arrows. A concerted charge might prove decisive but the enemy would pay a heavy price on the open ground.

'Every archer to a protected position!' he ordered. 'Check your field of fire, arrows at the ready. Everyone else find cover where you can.'

Tarmik was standing close by, knuckles white on his sword-hilt. Despite the circumstances, the Skornish man found a grin. 'Maybe we should have stayed on our own.'

Malcanoth made sure he kept turning to check the enemy hadn't advanced.

'Then again,' added Tarmik. 'I'd rather fight this lot than the Beastkin.'

Narg was there too, calmly sipping water from a flask as if the last few minutes hadn't happened. Malcanoth had already realised how valuable the battle-hardened veteran might be to him.

Narg nodded at three of the enemy gathered on the track, all clad in grey cloaks. 'Officers – planning something, by the looks.'

'At least they don't have many bows,' added Tarmik.

Malcanoth leaned close to Narg. 'Stay here. Watch them for me.'

'Sir.'

Malcanoth completed a circuit of the wooded area, relocating archers where necessary to ensure every angle was covered. On the opposite side of the trees to the officers, some of the enemy were jeering and spitting insults in some foreign tongue, inviting their foes to come and fight. Malcanoth had little doubt that if he took the battle to them, not one of his subordinates would survive. The sky was already beginning to darken; there was no more than two hours of daylight left. It seemed to him that their best bet was to wait for nightfall, then split up and run; divide the attacking force. At least that way some of them might make it.

***

But it soon became clear that the enemy officers weren't prepared to take that risk. Not long after Malcanoth returned to the middle of the copse, Narg informed him that a fire had been lit. And before long, the purpose for it became clear. The survivors of Remmar and Tarmik's men looked on as the enemy troops wrapped arrow-heads in oiled skin then set them alight. The flaming bolts were then handed to six archers who drew their bows and took careful aim.

Malcanoth glanced up. The trees were covered in thick foliage and dry enough to burn. Only two arrows from the first volley lodged above but one of them set leaves aflame almost immediately. Of the next two volleys, three bolts struck home and soon four separate fires were alight. Within minutes, burning leaves and branches were falling onto the defenders. They had no way to extinguish the flames.

'Good thinking,' said Narg, grimly.

The defenders were already beginning to move positions to avoid the dangers from above. Malcanoth considered telling them to keep their eyes on the enemy but that was hardly fair.

'Any ideas?' he asked the veteran quietly.

'One. Round up a dozen volunteers and charge the officers. That might draw in enough of them to give the others a chance. Tarmik knows the country and we'll have the darkness soon. I heard you're a Waymaker – can't you do anything about the fire?'

'I'm afraid not.' Malcanoth had practiced such things in his early years but since becoming a Pathfinder he'd focused solely on skills useful in combat. He knew there was another mage within the column's ranks but couldn't remember the man's name.

A flaming twig dropped to the ground close by. He stood on it, extinguishing the flame. More twigs fell, then a large branch. The fires were generating quite a bit of smoke but it was too high to aid the defenders. Malcanoth doubted they could remain within the trees for more than five or ten minutes. He had to make a decision.

Narg spoke up again. 'Happy to lead the charge, sergeant. And I know a few who'll join me.'

'No, I'll do it.'

Narg shook his head. 'That makes no sense, young man, and you know it. You've commanded us well.'

Malcanoth wasn't sure of that; it seemed to him that he'd drawn his people into a trap.

'You'll keep leading the way,' added Narg. 'Talk to Tarmik.'

Without the time to argue and with no better options, Malcanoth nodded and hurried away to do so. He had just reached the Skornish man when a cry went up. He turned to see a big clump of burning foliage strike three Pathfinders. As they hurriedly brushed the flaming leaves off, Narg shouted.

'Sergeant!'

The Militiaman was pointing to the rear, towards the voluble attackers. The entire line on that side was now charging the copse.

'Archers, fire!'

They got their shots away quickly. Three of the enemy fell, one man writhing in the grass, trying to pull a bolt from his chest.

The young recruits, Elaria and Kryk, were nearby. Elaria ran over to him. 'Sir, that noise – do you hear it?'

'Look!' yelled one of the archers.

From what Malcanoth reckoned to be the north-east, scores of horses had crested a low ridge and were now galloping towards the enemy. The first rank of riders intercepted the soldiers just before they reached the trees. Some were simply struck by the horses, others cut down by scything blades. Those missed by the first rank were caught by the second. Not a single enemy warrior reached the copse or laid a blade on the defenders.

With the attack nullified, those still alive fled, scattering in every direction. Now Malcanoth realised who the rescuers were. The riders were clad in blue and white tunics: these were fellow Pathfinders.

One of the interlopers raised his sword. Once the others had gathered behind him, he set his horse away, circling around the trees, cutting a swathe through the enemy ranks. A third and a fourth line of horses appeared over the crest and joined the effort, then a fifth and a sixth. Soon there were more than a hundred riders in view and nothing could be heard other than the rumble of hooves and the cries of dying men.

The enemy warriors were simply not prepared for this threat. Dozens were slashed across the head and neck as they retreated; only a few mounted any form of resistance. Malcanoth saw the enemy officers fleeing and before long the only remaining warriors were surrounded and finished off. The leader raised his sword once more and ordered his riders after the vanquished attackers.

But he himself wheeled his horse around and cantered over to the trees. He was met by great cheers of appreciation as he reined in.

Only now did Malcanoth feel a surge of relief as he ran over to meet him. The Pathfinder wore a striking set of armour and carried the badge of a captain. He was a noble-looking fellow with a streak of silver in his wavy black hair.

'Are you in charge?' he asked Malcanoth.

'I am.'

'Captain Quentius Farrow, Fifth Regiment, Pathfinders. And you are?'

Malcanoth had heard of Farrow; his regiment currently operated in the remote north of Whispvale so the two had never crossed paths.

'Sergeant Malcanoth Islorath, with men of the Fourth and Second Regiments.'

'Well, well. No uniform, sergeant?'

'Long story, sir. We're a mixed group. We've got Heartsong, Slate and Skornish people here too.'

Farrow nodded at the trees, which were now well aflame. 'You seemed to be in a bit of a fix. Happy to help out. We're on our way to the mountains but my scouts sighted these bastards yesterday – all with that sign on them. Any idea what it means? Who they are?'

'Not really, sir, but they're from the Madlands. We fought them at Remmar.'

Farrow's eyes widened. 'Remmar? By the gods.' He dismounted, dropping neatly to the ground. 'Sergeant, I think we need to talk.'

CHAPTER 15

The meeting took place on the Remmari Downs, an area of rolling hills north of the city. Though he had notified Siad, Xalius wanted it held in a remote location in case anything went wrong; it wouldn't do for the newly-conquered city-folk to witness a reverse for their conquerors. Izilis and Lisahra had reported back with some interesting information and their primary conclusion seemed to be that Sawfang Mawraze was fairly intelligent, highly ambitious and quite unpredictable. This did not fill Xalius with hope but he still felt an alliance might be worthwhile. Mawraze's Beastkin followers were apparently very numerous and he'd rather use them to weaken the Haar Dari's foes than Siad's valuable, battle-hardened warriors. And, despite his doubts, Vikter Aggor still seemed convinced that an agreement was achievable.

'I do wonder what exactly you think you're going to get out of this.'

Aggor was standing next to the chair in which Xalius sat. Ogon, Lisahra and Captain Verris were also close by. The shelter was open on one side, offering a fine view of the downs. The meeting was set for midday but Xalius had ensured he was there first. Mawraze's column was currently making its way up towards the plateau where the Haar Dari waited. According to Ogon, this had once been some holy site, though now there was nothing but thick grass.

'That is not a concern for today, sir,' replied Aggor.

'I would have thought it's your *only* concern.'

'I simply wish to facilitate progress between two great factions.'

Verris mumbled something.

Xalius turned to him. 'Something to add, captain?'

'One, sir. One *great* faction. And a criminal leading a bunch of man-rats.'

Aggor turned to the captain with an obsequious smile. 'Please, captain, I would ask you to keep such thoughts to yourself, at least for today. Now that they are organised, the Beastkin are a very effective fighting force. I know for a fact that the Pathfinders are terrified of them.'

'The Pathfinders are terrified of everything,' countered Verris, drawing chuckles from his two officers.

'I think of the children, the women,' said Xalius. 'They will come to fear *us*, of course, but imagine it – the very thought of these creatures turns the stomach. People do so loathe an infestation.'

When Xalius stood to stretch his aching legs, young Lisahra handed him his walking stick. Darian was absent, ill with a stomach sickness that was rife in the city and had also accounted for Izilis. Xalius had no idea of the cause but it seemed to him that it might be something the Madlanders were not used to as they seemed particularly badly affected. He hoped it would pass soon; it was surely only a matter of weeks before the Imperator reappeared or sent his next order.

As usual, Lisahra gave him the sweetest of smiles. Xalius was beginning to feel almost embarrassed by the effect she had on him. He considered his attachment to be one quarter desire, three parts admiration. That delightful hair and comely face would have turned the head of any man but it was her naked ambition that really set her apart. During the briefing with her and Izilis, the veteran spy had spoken first, but Lisahra finished the stronger, relating some very insightful comments for one so inexperienced. No day passed without her making some enquiry about the Way and Xalius knew she spent every spare hour studying. He was not the only one she drew knowledge from. Izilis, Carli and several others had complained about her incessant questioning. But not Ogon. Xalius imagined that the young warlock would have happily spent every waking moment with her. But for now, as protector of Xalius, he had to follow him as he paced across the grass. The minutes passed. The only noise came from the horses tethered behind the troops.

Xalius was about to return to his chair when one of Verris' men rode up and dismounted. The captain joined Xalius to hear his report.

'No more than a mile away, sir. Two hundred at least.'

'Two *hundred*?' Verris shot a glare at Aggor, who trotted over immediately.

'Is that not acceptable?'

'It is to me,' said Xalius calmly. 'We said he could bring his personal guard. If that's two hundred, so be it.'

Verris's expression became grave. 'I have only sixty soldiers.'

'Not worried about a few *man-rats*, are you, captain?'

Verris ignored the comment and turned to his officer. 'He's the only man?'

'Yes, sir – rest are Beastkin. Not sure I'd call him a man though. Looks like a Gragg.'

'He's no Gragg,' said Lisahra quietly, 'and I would advise against calling him one. He's just a very big Skornish man.'

'No one is going to be calling anyone anything,' said Xalius, who'd made it clear that he and Mawraze alone would conduct the talks. However, as agreed by both sides, Aggor would also be present to aid the negotiations. Xalius considered this circumspect; he knew little of the Beastkin and not enough about the Skornlands.

When Mawraze and his guard trooped up onto the other end of the plateau, Xalius allowed Verris to move his guards forward. Then, as the newcomers approached, Xalius led his three companions through the middle of the soldiers.

Sawfang marched towards him at the head of his host. The man was a similar height to Siad though it was obvious that he lacked the broad features and frame of a gragg. He did, however, cut an impressive figure. His robes were modest but over them he wore a cloak of vivid red. Arranged across his shoulders was a thick, golden chain that must have weighed as much as a small child. Hanging from Mawraze's belt was a broadsword at least five feet in length. Upon his head was a sturdy silver helm, which reached down to his brow and protected ears and neck.

'By Rael,' breathed Verris. 'Look at those…*things*.'

Directly behind Mawraze were five Beastkin, each with their own, smaller gold chain around their necks.

'The brood chiefs?' said Xalius.

'Quite so, sir,' replied Aggor.

During his travels as a young man, Xalius had seen such creatures but the sight of them remained startling. It seemed odd for them to stand upright and they retained the plump hind-quarters of their rodent cousins. Their arms were thin but all muscle and sinew, their legs bulky and powerful. Xalius knew that they leapt well and sometimes ran on all fours.

The brood chiefs carried swords and also wore red cloaks. The ranks of warriors behind them were armed with spears and shields, each of which had been decorated with a red boss. The equipment looked rudimentary but strong. Clearly those clawed hands did not prevent them fashioning weapons.

Sawfang Mawraze came to a halt, some twenty feet from the Haar Dari.

'Good day to you.' His voice was a gritty rasp. 'I hail noble Xalius and the forces of the Haar Dari.'

Xalius was quite impressed with the pronunciation. He decided to echo the sentiment.

'Good day. I hail noble Sawfang Mawraze and the Beastkin host. Shall I have the chairs brought forward so that the two of us may speak?'

Mawraze nodded.

Verris had men ready and – though both were simple wooden chairs – they'd made sure that one was sufficiently large for Mawraze. A table was also brought forward and Vikter Aggor trotted alongside it, greeting Mawraze as he placed paper and writing equipment on the table. If the discussion went well, the preliminary agreement would be recorded. Both sides acknowledged that this was only a first step.

Once the table and chairs had been arranged, Mawraze sat down, his manner measured and calm. Xalius gestured for Aggor to join him there and he stood to one side, head level with the seated giant's shoulder.

Before Xalius could join them, Verris spoke up: 'Sir, are you sure you want to let him keep that sword?'

'Yes, captain. It's not as if I am defenceless.' With that, Xalius exchanged a brief glance with Ogon. From this point, the young mage would drop into a near-trance, ready at any moment to summon a shield of wayforce to protect his superior. Though he continued to work on other abilities, Ogon had perfected this skill.

Xalius walked across the grass. The Beastkin brood chiefs were not far away and now he could better see their snouts, whiskers and eyes. He found it difficult to discern if what he saw in them was wit or simply alertness. He had often pondered the example of birds, many of which looked intelligent though they were clearly just creatures of instinct.

Feeling rather as if he was too old for occasions like this, Xalius took his seat and regarded the man opposite. He was indeed no gragg and certainly no more than forty years old. Xalius supposed females might consider him handsome in a brutish way but there was also a sharpness in his pale green eyes. He was evidently no stranger to battle; his nose was a misshapen mess, his chin heavily scarred.

Xalius spoke first. 'Please feel free to remove your helmet. It can't be comfortable and – as you can see – I carry no weapons.'

'It is perfectly comfortable, thank you. I have been wounded in the head several times and it…makes me feel at ease. A sign of weakness, I suppose.'

Xalius was surprised by his polite, almost humble tone. 'Not at all. I understand you have come quite a long way.'

'Not as far as you, I think.'

'What do you know of the Madlands?'

'Not much. I certainly didn't expect an army to come out of it and defeat King Flint in a matter of weeks.'

'I doubt you're the only one.'

'What do you want?' asked Mawraze, somehow still polite.

'What exactly do you mean?'

'I know there is one above you – the Imperator – but what is the aim of the Haar Dari?'

'If he was here, I suspect the Imperator would say "enlightenment". We follow the will of Rael, god of gods.'

'I don't hold with the idea of gods,' replied Mawraze before tilting his head towards the Beastkin. 'Neither do they.'

'Do they understand the concept?'

'They do.'

'I must say I'm intrigued by how you've managed to take them over. As I understand it, they were no more than an unruly mob before you established yourself.'

'I saw the potential, took the time to understand them.'

'And you speak their language.'

'Not well, but better than any other man. What they do understand is power.'

Xalius grinned. 'I'm sure. And what do they get in return for fighting with you?'

'Safety. We are clearing whole swathes of the country of men so that they can live in peace. Men have hunted them for centuries, driven them into forests. I have brought them organisation, strength in numbers. I give them weapons, food, building materials. I am *civilising* them.'

'And what have they brought you?'

'An army. A loyal army. Master Xalius, you did not answer my question.'

'Ah, yes. Well, in order for the rest of the world to follow the will of Rael, they must be conquered, then enlightened.'

Xalius differed from his master on this point. He could not help admiring the man who had made himself a god – after all, who better to follow? – but he did not share Atavius' zeal to ensure that the rest of the world worship Rael. However, this was his master's goal, and so it must be his own. If he gathered wealth, status and knowledge while spreading Rael's word, all the better.

For the first time, Mawraze glanced at Aggor, who was following every word.

'Everyone?'

'Some allowances can be made,' said Xalius. 'But only for our most important allies.'

'How would that work? If we agreed to cooperate?'

Xalius had already decided on his requirements. If the Imperator chose to change the approach later on, there was little he could do.

'You would have to demonstrate your devotion to the Haar Dari and to Rael.'

Sawfang Mawraze scratched his mangled nose. 'How? Would I have to wear the sign of the eye as you and your men do?'

'No.'

'Would I have to pray to Rael?'

'No. What we would require is that you and your... commanders undergo the Ceremony of Acceptance. It's quite short. Only a few words.'

'You're saying it's symbolic. I wouldn't have to mean what I said.'

'I can see that you're a man who understands the importance of how things appear.'

'I am.'

Nothing was said for some time. One of the soldiers coughed. Xalius watched one of the brood leaders stick his snout in the air, as if sniffing something. Wind cut shapes in the grass around them.

'If I may,' ventured Aggor in his high voice. 'Perhaps we should move onto specifics.'

'Quite so,' said Xalius. 'Military matters first?'

Mawraze had been looking over Xalius' shoulder for some time. 'Would I have to *kneel*?'

Xalius was growing rather tired of the man. Who did he think he was? Didn't he understand the balance of power here? That he could either ally with the Haar Dari or be crushed by them?

'You would. As do I. As do we all.'

Mawraze glanced at Aggor and sighed deeply.

'I'm leaving. I was not told I would have to kneel.'

'You're not serious?' said Xalius.

'I am.' Mawraze stood. 'Good day to you.'

Xalius was not unused to such swift reverses and he made his decision quickly; he would turn the man. Mind control was not his speciality but he reckoned he could handle Mawraze until one of his specialist mages back in Remmar took over. He recalled the incantation and recited it swiftly without opening his mouth. He tried to keep his movements to a minimum but Mawraze noted his outstretched fingers.

'That won't work.'

Xalius felt embarrassed that he had not realised sooner. 'Ah. Your helmet. Ilerian silver.'

'I see now that if I am not with you, I am against you.'

Xalius stood. 'I fear that is how it shall be.'

'If there is to be a fight, I may as well strike the first blow.'

Until he spoke these words, Xalius had not thought it possible that Mawraze would attack. As the sword was pulled from its sheathe and swung at him, he knew his life was in Ogon's hands.

The air around him changed. He felt something tug at his throat, pull at his body. To the uninitiated, it would have been an unpleasant feeling; Xalius welcomed it. As the sword clanged off the invisible field of Wayforce, Mawraze staggered. Xalius turned and tried to run but one of his feet caught in his robes and he soon found himself face down on the ground. The impact knocked the wind out of him and he looked on helplessly as one the brood chiefs scuttled around the table and straight at him, clawed hands outstretched.

Before Xalius could react, the creature crashed head-first into the ground, rolling over onto its back and sliding to a halt only feet away. A sword swung down, slicing deep into its neck and leaving the creature bloodied and writhing. Xalius looked up to see Verris standing there. The captain had just raised his sword once more when Mawraze ran around the field of wayforce and heaved the mighty broadsword down at him. The blade cleaved through Verris' shoulder, almost severing his arm.

Face frozen by agony, Verris dropped to his knees. As Mawraze tried to free his blade, Xalius felt a hand on his shoulder and turned to find Lisahra behind him.

Verris' men were there too. In swift succession, three arrows thumped into Sawfang's chest, two of them pinning the red cloak to his body. Mawraze's sword fell from his grasp and the giant's head lolled as the wounds took their toll. Two more arrows struck. The golden chain crashed to the ground yet he somehow stayed on his feet.

Lisahara helped Xalius up. He heard the soldiers on the move and saw the Beastkin brood chiefs charge, their warriors with them.

'Enough!'

Channelling all his power, Xalius lifted the giant into the air, only halting him when he was ten feet from the ground.

The soldiers stopped. The Beastkin stopped.

The crouching Vikter Aggor looked up as Sawfang Mawraze's body began to rotate in the air. Blood dripped onto the grass. The dying man moaned. The brood chiefs watched, whiskers trembling, as their leader continued to turn until his head faced the turf.

Xalius resisted the temptation to enjoy the moment. He let go. The giant struck the ground with a sickening thud. Neck broken, his ruined form fell onto the grass.

Xalius took two steps forward and aimed a hand at the remaining brood chiefs. Even though he felt exhausted, he shouted as loudly as he could: 'You will kneel! Aggor, show them.'

With a frantic nod, Aggor turned to the Beastkin and knelt. The brood chiefs didn't even look at each other. They knelt and bowed their heads. The hundreds of other warriors followed instantly.

Xalius cast a look at Verris, who had already lost pints of blood. 'Bring up the surgeon.' They had to try, even though the chances were slim.

'Yes, sir,' said one of the officers.

'Are you all right, sir?' asked Lisahra, her hand on his shoulder.

'Yes, girl.' Xalius was watching the Beastkin. 'Our newly-departed friend Mawraze was right. They do understand power.'

CHAPTER 16

The bodies were still burning. When she turned back the way they had come, Elaria could see the black smoke drifting up from the site of battle. Some had clearly escaped but Elaria reckoned at least sixty corpses had been piled up and set ablaze. She wasn't sure it was right that the enemy dead be treated in this way but after they'd buried their own in a large grave, there'd been little time. Captain Farrow made it very clear that they had to get away swiftly to avoid reprisals.

Sitting on a white-barked log with Treyda, Kryk and Narg, Elaria looked out at the temporary encampment. Sergeant Malcanoth was making his way through the second regiment, heading towards Farrow, who was unsaddling his horse. Though still full of relief that they'd been spared, Elaria wondered how this fortuitous meeting would change things.

'Someone must be watching over us,' remarked Treyda. 'I honestly thought that was the end.'

Narg grunted his approval.

'What do you know of him?' asked Kryk before tucking into a strip of dried meat.

Treyda stretched out her legs. 'Farrow? Very good reputation. The Fifth have had a difficult time of it what with all the sellswords and the Beastkin. Wouldn't have expected to find them all the way over here though.'

'They're on some special mission,' said Narg, drawing curious looks from the other three.

'What mission?' said Kryk. 'And how do you know?'

'Overheard some of them while we were digging. That's why we're heading to the mountains. Farrow was sent this way about the same time we were sent to Remmar.'

'We're heading to Low Gorge, aren't we?' Kryk looked concerned. 'Like the sergeant said.'

'We're heading for the mountains,' replied the Militiaman. 'After that, who knows?'

Kryk chewed his meat morosely.

'What's wrong with you, lad?' asked Narg. 'Thought you wanted nothing but scrap after scrap.'

Kryk just looked at the ground.

'I can't believe you two are recruits,' said Treyda. 'I didn't see a sword drawn in anger for my first four years.'

'Is it true?' asked Elaria. 'What they say – about the dragons?'

Narg sniffed noisily. 'Never seen one myself. But I've met men who have.'

Kryk looked up. 'They're real?'

Elaria turned and looked towards the Crystal Mountains. Much of the range was wreathed by cloud but the vast peaks still glittered; as dangerously seductive as any jewel.

'I hope we don't find out.'

***

Malcanoth handed the flask of wine back to Farrow.

'Thank you. As good as you said.' In truth, he preferred cheaper, sweeter stuff but Farrow was a nobleman, and such people had their own ways.

'Damn right. Bloody good stuff.'

Farrow dumped his saddle and gear on the ground. 'Used to have a man to take care of all this. He had some kind of seizure so I had to leave him back in Slate. Inconvenient.'

Running his hand through his hair, Farrow eyed the soldiers gathered in the clearing. 'An hour only. We can't know how many more enemies might be in the area. Come, we should keep this discussion between ourselves.'

He led Malcanoth over to the bank of a nearby stream. Malcanoth noted how remarkably neat and well-presented the captain was, despite the fact he had lost his servant. Only a few specks of dirt and blood upon his trousers betrayed the fact that he had been in a battle only hours before.

'Sergeant, you only gave me the basics earlier. It might be best if I have the whole story now.'

Malcanoth reckoned it was about time *he* found out something but he couldn't refuse the senior man. Though it at first seemed odd to be taking orders again, he was actually relieved to share the burden. Malcanoth knew that Farrow's distinguished background hadn't made him universally popular within the Pathfinders but Captain Kano had always spoken well of him; and that was more than good enough for Malcanoth.

Though Farrow had indeed heard some of it already, his expression spoke volumes as he learned just how many had been lost at Remmar and how easily their enemy had triumphed. He listened patiently, asking only a few questions before Malcanoth concluded his summary with events since their landing at the Sinking Hole.

'The loss of so many only makes our job all the more important.'

'And that is?'

'Do you know of a man named Kals Rycliff?'

Malcanoth shook his head.

'He was a Pathfinder, probably before your time. Proved himself very adept at operating alone in dangerous locations. He was recruited to the palace several years back to serve as a spy. I gather he performed very well, often working amongst the Skornish and even heading north to keep an eye on the Lyther. Several months ago, the king's advisers sent him to the mountains. There had been several incidents between the dragons and Pathfinder patrols and the king wanted to put an end to it. Generally, they keep themselves to themselves but they're very territorial. I have to tell you – nobody even uses the Low Gorge these days.'

'Ah.' Malcanoth already understood that the captain expected his rag-tag mob to join the fifth regiment. He was sure most of the beleaguered soldiers would have preferred the peace and safety of Laketon but every one owed their lives to Farrow and his people. He didn't expect to hear any complaints.

'Anyway, Rycliff was tasked with opening a line of communication with the dragons, seeing what could be done to avoid any more confrontations.'

'How ... would ... they can communicate?'

'The larger ones – the Cave Kings – understand human tongue. Some can even say a few words. They're far more intelligent than most people understand – not like a man – but with as much wit as the Beastkin, possibly more. In any case, Rycliff got a couple of messages out that confirmed he had made contact but the last of them was months ago. When the seriousness of the threat from the east became clear, I received orders – directly from the king – to enter the mountains. Whether – we can locate Rycliff or not, I am to try and open a dialogue with the creatures – see if we can win them over to our side.'

'How? What can we offer them?'

'Contrary to popular belief, they care nothing for gold or treasure of any kind. Their food source is secure: they live off the wild horses in the mountains. But after centuries of skirmishes with our people and those that came before us, the king believes they crave security. In return for meeting this new threat alongside us, he is offering to create an enclave – the entirety of the mountains and the territory for ten miles around. We could even bestow a title on the closest thing they have to a monarch – a Caveking named Zikaza. Apparently, he's more than three hundred years old and rules over all of them, even the Wingborne.'

'What's the difference?'

'It's said that there was once a single, great race – all could fly, all a similar size. But over time, two species developed – one small and agile, able to fly great distances. These are the ones occasionally spotted over our lands. Most are no more than fifteen feet in length. The Cavekings, as the name suggests, spend much of their time underground. They're bigger – so big that some can barely fly.'

'This may be a stupid question, sir, but can they breathe fire?'

Farrow seemed faintly amused by the idea. 'Frankly, they don't need to. The Wingborne can fly quicker than a yellow condor, the Cavekings are stronger than ten mammuths. It's lucky for us that they rarely stray far from the mountains.'

'Do we know how many there are?'

'Rycliff estimated no more than fifty Wingborne, perhaps half as many Cavekings. This may be another reason why they're so reclusive and protective – they're dying out. I've heard it said that there were once thousands of them, in the days when they roamed over the whole world.'

'Do you think Rycliff is still alive?'

'Who knows? But either way we have to try and make contact with Zikaza. From what you've told me, these Madlanders won't be happy to settle for Remmar.'

'We need allies.'

Farrow nodded. 'Or one less enemy, at the very least.'

***

Though offered a horse by several of the fifth regiment Pathfinders, Elaria chose to walk with her friends. For most of the day, not much was said. She put this down to the effects of the battle but realised also that Kryk was still very much preoccupied by deeper thoughts. As for Narg, he never said all that much.

Elaria had tried to recall the horror of the battle several times but she could summon only feelings and images, even becoming confused about the order in which things had happened. She knew she would not forget the murderous faces of the enemy warriors; the desperate feeling of being trapped amid the flaming trees; the deadly charge of Farrow and his men. When she thought about Remmar and all she had seen since, she almost began to long for the peace and quiet of Whispvale, even Serenity. She felt as if she had been chasing life for many years. Now it was rushing towards her.

'You all right?' asked Treyda. Despite her age, she was a formidable marcher and Elaria found it easier to keep her feet moving while beside her.

'Not sure.'

'Thinking of home?'

'A bit.'

'Me too,' said Treyda.

'You have a family?'

'Mother, father and sister.'

Treyda was at least as old as Elaria's mother, one of the few female Pathfinders over thirty.

'I couldn't have children,' she explained with a sudden frankness. 'Husband went off to find a wife who could give him more hands to work the farm. Didn't join up until I was twenty-seven. No one thought I would get through the Tournament. By then I'd had that many fights with my husband, I knew I had a good chance.'

'Fights? Fist fights?'

'Oh, not just fists. Sticks, plates, chairs, even the odd frying pan.'

Elaria could stop herself giggling. 'Sorry.'

'Don't be. Made me who I am.' Treyda rubbed her stomach. 'And right now, I am seriously hungry. Hope we stop soon.'

'Mmm,' grunted Narg.

The sky was growing dark. To the north, the red hues of the fading sun were reflected back by the immense flanks of the Crystal Mountains. The ground, the trees, even the faces of the soldiers had acquired a pinkish hue.

When the conversation died down, Elaria could hear only the unrelenting beat of boots and hooves on the sandy track. Sometimes she thought of Dawin, and how she missed his boundless energy and curiosity. It was hard to believe he was truly gone. But here – now – she was so very glad to be among her friends and fellow warriors. Now she really understood what poor Tamia had been talking about that day at the blacksmith; this sense of fellowship and togetherness was something unique. She glanced at Kryk, at Treyda, at Narg. She liked and respected them all. But she reminded herself not to grow too close. Because she might have to watch them die.

***

'What is it today?'

Lisahra looked up from her book. 'Ah, morning, sir-'

'Don't get up,' said Xalius.

She stayed on the stool and tapped the page of writing before her. 'Maeskens.'

'Ah yes. The section on hypnosis is particularly informative. Please, keep at it.'

Xalius was disappointed to see the girl's hair tied up but – as always – just seeing her gave him a little boost. On their way back from the fateful meeting with Mawraze, he'd learned that it was Lisahra who'd downed the attacking brood chief at the crucial moment, allowing Verris to finish the job. The captain was expected to survive though it would be months before he was fit to return to duty. Lisahra had reacted quicker than all the soldiers and perhaps even saved Xalius's life, though he liked to think he would have recovered in time to do something. When he thanked her later, the girl seemed immensely proud. She had learned the skill from one of the other warlocks, knowing that it might help protect her master. Xalius was in no doubt now that hers was a precocious talent. In return for her efforts, he'd promised to tutor her personally as often as he could. He found that he actually felt younger around her, able to momentarily forget the burdens of age and responsibility.

'See you tomorrow for your exercises.'

'Yes, sir. Thank you, sir.'

Xalius continued through the anteroom and into what had been King Flint's dining room, a cavernous space with tall, narrow windows. He had now invited all of his warlocks into the castle and put aside this entire wing for study and research. Ogon and several others had colonised one end and collated books and equipment related to the experimentation tomes unearthed in Shya. The young warlock hurried over to his master and bowed unnecessarily. Three days had passed since the meeting on the downs but Ogon still seemed ashamed that his shield had not fully protected his master.

'Morning, sir.'

'Morning. How are you faring?'

'We've completed the initial review of the main library and found a good deal of relevant material. I believe it will help us fill in some of the gaps in our understanding.'

'Good, good. But we must move to live experimentation as soon as possible if any of this is to actually be of use. For now, we will focus solely on bodily augmentation. We can use animals to start with, then perhaps prisoners. Make a list of proposed experiments, increasing in complexity and scale. Can you have it ready for me by tomorrow?'

'Of course, sir.'

Xalius surveyed the others present: Carli and several other warlocks were studying texts, while a number of Remmari clerks arranged the books and unloaded boxes. Xalius also noted a frail figure studying a piece of equipment with a magnifying glass.

'Who's the old fellow?'

'Professor Skeltine, sir. Carli asked Mayor Brayber for a list of notable scientists and his name came up. Darian sent a couple of guards to bring him in yesterday. His credentials are very impressive – he was chief surgeon and has developed several effective medicines. His wife is ailing. I told him that he could use any supplies and equipment for her treatment as long as he works for us here during the day. He says he can bring in other specialists if necessary. They are all proving much more cooperative as the ceremonies continue, sir.'

'It's partly that, partly the number of heads Siad has chopped off.'

Ogon conceded the point with a nod. Perhaps assuming that Xalius was occupied with the new arrival, the young man looked through to the anteroom where Lisahra studied alone. Xalius didn't begrudge his interest in the girl but he doubted Ogon would ever catch her eye. For all his ability and intellect, he was a tad dull.

The morning light illuminated clouds of dust within the chamber that even Xalius could see. 'A cleaner or two wouldn't go amiss.'

'Yes, sir. It's all the old tomes.'

'Do those windows face north?'

'They do, sir.'

'Continue with your work, bring me that list tomorrow. I want progress. *Swift* progress.'

'Of course, sir.'

Xalius walked up to the window. He did not look down at the sunlit city, but to the encampment to the north-east. It grew every day, and already accommodated several hundred Beastkin warriors. Xalius had ordered Mayor Brayber to send ten of the city's best linguists to the camp, where they were to learn the creatures' tongue as quickly as possible. He had insisted that the four brood chiefs accompany his party back to the city and Vikter Aggor had been able to explain to them that he eventually wanted at least three thousand warriors at his command. They would be supplied with food of their choosing in return for complete obedience. When they had served their purpose, they would be allowed to return to their homeland. This area would be guaranteed to them in perpetuity as long as they supplied any warriors requested by the Haar Dari.

They were to expect swift deployment and any failure to comply with his instructions would result in executions. Xalius had struggled not to laugh as the Beastkin had followed dolefully behind his column, even the brood chiefs as fearful as errant children.

Sensibly, Vikter Aggor had also kept his head down after offering profuse apologies for his part in the disastrous meeting. For the moment, he was useful, but once the linguists could take over his role, Xalius intended to deal with him. Something unpleasant.

Knowing that Siad probably wouldn't approve of these new recruits, Xalius was using a regiment of the Remmari army to watch over the encampment. These were men who had already sworn allegiance to the Haar Dari; they were even being paid half their previous wage as an incentive to others. With all provisions within the city prioritised first for the Haar Dari, then the converts, Xalius knew the message would soon hit home. Their convert commander hadn't seemed overly enamoured with his task but had dutifully created a cordon between the encampment and the city walls.

Xalius had neither seen nor heard from Siad since his return. The marshal seemed preoccupied with spreading their reach westward, scouting routes of advance and crushing any centres of resistance before they could establish themselves. Rumour had it that he spent his nights with whichever of the local whores had taken his fancy.

Hearing swift footsteps, Xalius turned to see a messenger boy run into the room. Ogon intercepted him, took the piece of paper and delivered it to his master.

'Read it, would you? I don't have my eyeglass with me.'

'It is from Marshal Siad, sir.'

'No matter. Go ahead.'

'It's very brief: Irregular patrol attacked and routed fifty miles to the north-east. More than a hundred dead. Pathfinders.'

CHAPTER 17

Even the lowest peaks of the Crystal Mountains seemed impossibly high. Having spent three days negotiating the rolling foothills, Captain Farrow's force had reached a narrow valley between two of those peaks. The sheer, imposing flanks were dotted with crevices and gullies but little life was seen save for high-flying condors and the occasional goat. Sunlight had already been lost for the day, casting the valley into gloom and allowing the cold of the rock to radiate outward.

There was no clear path but sufficient turf for the column to travel swiftly, the infantry bookended by the cavalry. Since entering the mountains, they had seen not a single person to question about Kals Rycliff. Two anxious nights had been spent there already and Malcanoth was not looking forward to a third. It seemed to him that they simply did not belong here and he could not avoid the feeling that Rycliff was dead and that this was a fool's errand. Captain Farrow clearly didn't know if this route would take them all the way through the mountains; he was simply searching for the king's agent or some trace of the dragons. The veteran was at least taking careful note of defensive positions, including several caves large enough to shelter the whole column. They'd passed another only half an hour earlier and seen a number of ancient paintings; clearly men had resided here at some point.

At a noise from above, several heads turned left and looked up but Malcanoth swiftly saw that it was just another fall of scree upon the slopes. He estimated that both mountains were at least ten thousand feet high and that the snow began at around six thousand feet.

'I can't say I like it here much.'

Malcanoth had noticed young Elaria come up alongside him but had said nothing. Talking to those under his command – especially the recruits

– simply reminded him of his responsibilities. Even so, he admired the way the girl had acquitted herself since Remmar. He and most of the others had at least previously seen action, while she had found herself thrown into the middle of a war. If nothing else, he was desperate that she and the lad Kryk reach safety. He felt it crucial that some markers of hope were salvaged from the defeat. It was at least reassuring to see that she had fallen in with veterans like Treyda and Narg.

Malcanoth forced a smile. 'Can't say I do either.'

'I feel better now that we're with so many other Pathfinders.'

Malcanoth nodded.

'I expect you wish Captain Kano was still with us.'

He wished she'd move on. If they were walking through the streets of Laketon or at a table in a tavern somewhere, Malcanoth would have liked to chat to a fair girl like Elaria. But here – now – it was simply awkward. He was an officer, she was a recruit and that was that. This was not the time or place for idle talk.

But as they trudged on across the grass, she kept with him, stride for stride. He told himself to consider how she might be feeling. Perhaps he could reassure her and then she'd go and talk to someone else.

'Quite some adventure you've had. I think I can already say that we'll pass you for the first year.'

She smiled. 'Really?'

'It'll have to be made official, of course, but I can't see anyone raising an objection. You and Kryk have been through more action than a lot of Pathfinders see in a lifetime.'

'Everyone will see action now, won't they, sergeant?'

'I fear they will. You're from Lower Saxan, is that right?'

'Yes. A place called Clearwell. It's very quiet. Nothing interesting ever happens.'

'Ah. Well, I was born in Riverton. Not a lot happens there either.'

'Was your father a Pathfinder?'

Malcanoth was surprised by how forthcoming the girl was but there was some space between the ranks in front and behind; no-one else seemed to be listening in. He generally didn't speak about his past with his fellow soldiers but, on this occasion, it didn't seem to bother him.

'No. He was a fisherman.'

'That can be a dangerous job too.'

'It can. It … well … it cost him his life. My older brother as well.'

Elaria averted her eyes and didn't seem to know what to say.

'He would usually stick to the estuary but there was a good run of weather so they went further out. The last sighting of them was from a lighthouse keeper at Wildsteel point. We never found out what happened. That's the sea. It could have been one of a dozen things.'

'You were young?'

'Eight. I'm fortunate in a way, though. My grandmother was quite wealthy – she paid for a portrait of my parents and my brother and I just the previous year. The artist was very skilled, the likenesses are excellent. When I go home, I can see their faces as they truly were. I always feel sorry for people who have no such thing to look at. Memories fade with time.'

'I wish I had a painting like that,' said Elaria. 'My father died not so long ago, but I find it hard to remember him.'

'What happened?'

'Illness. Some growth in his stomach. He was in a lot of pain towards the end. "There's nothing can be done" – that's what he used to say. And he was right. I do have this though.'

Elaria reached inside her tunic and showed Malcanoth a gem on a string around her neck.

'By all the gods,' he said. 'Is that a Night's Eye?'

She nodded and hid it once more.

'Elaria, don't show it around. There are mages – and thieves – who would kill for that. How did your father come by such a gem?'

'He was a trader – usually in cheaper stones – but he gave me this before he passed on.'

'A fine keepsake. But you-'

Suddenly several people were hailing him. Malcanoth looked up to see Farrow beckoning him forward. Without another word, he steadied his sword and ran around the marching troops up ahead. By the time he reached the captain, Farrow had dismounted and was pointing along the valley.

'What do you make of that, Islorath?'

On the right side of the valley, some three or four miles ahead, smoke was rising from a small fire. The smoke itself was white, which meant it stood out from the grey rock behind it. A moment's observation showed that the puffs were being controlled.

Before Malcanoth could reply, Farrow answered his own question. 'Longs and shorts. That's Pathfinder code.'

There was no swifter method of conveying a message than various combinations of short and long puffs to denote single letters. These could then form words and sentences. The entire column had by now stopped and Farrow was not the only one to call out the letters.

'G ... O'

A pause.

'B ... A ...C'

Farrow turned to his two sergeants. 'Fetch firewood. We will answer. We must know who it is.'

'No time, sir,' answered one of them. 'Look there!'

***

For several moments, Elaria simply could not move. Even when she saw the five moving shapes stark against the high snows, the sight was almost impossible to take in. But a glimpse of the elegant, fast-moving wings told her that the dragons were closer than she thought. Not only were they real, they were flying straight for the column. And she was still watching when the graceful creatures pushed back their wings and dived towards the valley floor.

A shout went up: 'To the last cave!'

'Come on,' shouted Kryk, suddenly beside her. Together they turned and charged back the way they had come. While some of Farrow's riders were alongside them, those with bows moved away from the column and nocked arrows. Concentrating on her footing, Elaria pumped her legs hard to try and keep up with Kryk. She reckoned it was at least two miles back to the cave where they had seen the paintings.

'Look out!'

Something smashed into a pile of scree about fifty feet away, sending shards of rock into the air. A male Pathfinder was struck in the head and fell. Several went to his aid but most kept moving, Elaria and Kryk among them.

The chilling shrieks of the dragons seemed to echo along the entire valley.

'Rocks,' said Treyda as she caught up. 'They're bombarding us.'

Barely able to believe what she was hearing, Elaria looked up in time to glimpse a dragon swoop overhead, a flash of power and grace. She actually heard its wings cutting through the air before another rock thudded into the ground and several screams were heard.

'Keep going,' said Treyda. 'If we stop, none of us will make it.'

***

Malcanoth hadn't got far. The mount of one of Farrow's sergeants had been struck on its head and fallen on the rider, trapping him. A nearby impact sent a shard of rock slicing across Malcanoth's calf. Ignoring the pain, he knelt beside the sergeant and grabbed his arms. Try as he might, he could not shift him. Then he realised that the man was limp and no longer breathing.

'Islorath!'

He turned to see Captain Farrow, knuckles white as he gripped his reins.

'With me! We cannot stay out in the open.'

Realising there was no more he could do, Malcanoth let go of the sergeant.

Farrow offered his hand. His mount was a tall, strong horse; fully capable of carrying two men. Malcanoth was about to jump up when he spied a bow and quiver lying on the ground nearby. He grabbed both and threw them over his shoulders.

'Hurry, man!' bawled Farrow. They were alone, now separated from the fleeing riders and infantry.

Both men knew the correct technique. Farrow urged his mount towards Malcanoth who reached up and gripped his hand. Using the momentum of the moving animal, he swung up and onto the mount behind the captain.

Farrow set off after the others, already yelling orders. 'Spread out! Don't bunch up!'

Though he was gripping the horse with his thighs, Malcanoth couldn't steady himself enough to even try a shot.

'What are you doing, man?'

'We can fire at them – at least force them higher.'

Farrow said nothing more until they'd caught up with the stragglers. His surviving sergeant had ridden ahead to take charge at the cave.

'All right, Islorath, try it.' The captain looked up.' Oh, hang on.'

With calmness and consummate skill, Farrow sent his horse shuffling sideways, ensuring that the next rock struck only grass.

'Bloody unfriendly, aren't they? There's one of the bastards reloading.'

As he nocked an arrow, Malcanoth saw one of the five dragons land on the slopes far above. In seconds, it had gripped a suitable rock with its talons then launched itself back into the air. Ignoring another agonised scream, Malcanoth kept his aim on the creature as it spun itself around and flapped towards the fleeing column. He estimated its current height at four hundred feet but it was already gliding and losing altitude, legs fully extended as it prepared to release its load.

Malcanoth retracted the string. Unused to bows of late, his fingers were already shaking.

'Got the range?' asked Farrow, doing his best to keep the mount steady.

'Hope so.'

The dragon swooped lower, now almost over the column.

Malcanoth adjusted his aim for the speed of the creature and let go. The bowstring pinged loudly and he lost sight of the bolt in the sky.

But it must have been close. The dragon's long neck jerked upwards and it lost its grip on the rock.

'Ha!' cried Farrow. 'Didn't hit but you gave him something to think ab-'

Malcanoth and the captain watched the rock fall towards the column.

He couldn't stop himself yelling. 'Look out!'

The rock hit the ground just behind a speeding rider who didn't even notice.

Farrow set his horse away once more. Before drawing another arrow, Malcanoth watched the dragon. It was circling now, moving higher. Of the others, two were heading for the slopes to arm themselves, two were on their way back.

'That did some good,' said Farrow. 'But we need reinforcements.'

Urging the horse into a gallop, the captain soon caught up with some of the riders and halted them. He then swiftly picked out men armed with bows and in a minute had formed eight more pairs.

'Target all of them. If we can't drive them off, we can at least keep them higher up.'

His prediction soon proved correct. As Malcanoth had suspected, the dragons were not slow to learn. One was struck in the wing by a brilliant shot from a Miltiaman. Though it seemed to have little effect on the creature, all five were forced to gain altitude. This reduced accuracy and gave those on the ground more time to take evasive action.

In between loosing arrows, Malcanoth saw that at least ten warriors had been killed and several badly maimed. Farrow insisted on ordering others not to risk their own lives by going to their aid.

'Captain, look there!'

One of the other bowmen pointed to the opposite side of the valley. Clear against the blue sky, more dragons were speeding towards their location. Malcanoth counted six.

'On to the cave,' ordered Farrow. 'Cover as best you can.'

***

Elaria struggled up the slope, feet slipping constantly on pebbles and loose soil. Kryk and Treyda were not as nimble as her but had kept pace.

'Keep moving!' yelled Sergeant Norik, who had now dismounted and was dragging his horse upward. The very quickest of the soldiers had reached the cave. There was no need to actually enter it; a thick shelf of rock above provided sufficient protection from the dragons. Elaria had already resolved not to waste time looking ahead or at what was going on behind her. Dying in direct battle with your foes was one thing, being crushed by a rock was another. Though every breath burned and every inch of her legs ached, she powered up the slope. Close to the shelf, the angle steepened and she used her hands to negotiate the final few yards. Once there and safe, she collapsed onto her knees. By the time she'd recovered herself, Treyda and Kryk were beside her.

Looking down the slope, she saw that the column was very strung out, with the last of the stragglers still several hundred yards below. At least the archers were returning fire but the bombardment of rocks was becoming heavier. One missile hit a steep section of the slope and caused a miniature landslide that sent four warriors sprawling. The retreat was little short of chaos but Elaria couldn't see what other choice there had been for Captain Farrow.

Almost all the horses had been abandoned and, once free of their riders, every last one bolted back down the valley. Elaria watched one accelerate past the others, eyes bulging, foam flying from its mouth.

She had lost track of Narg but now saw him emerge from behind a boulder. He had a man over his shoulder but was still ascending with remarkable speed. An impact showered him with rock but he pressed on with predictable courage.

Elaria was on the verge of running to help when Sergeant Norik hurried along the lip of the shelf, waving them towards the cave. 'Captain's orders. Stay back. It'll be dark soon – we can recover the wounded then. Stay back!'

Elaria couldn't watch any more. She walked into the dank shadows below the shelf towards the cave. There she found dozens of exhausted Pathfinders and Militiamen. Also present were Tarmik and his fellows. The warriors stared out in disbelief as the rocks continued to rain down upon their compatriots. Elaria turned and gazed into the depthless black of the cave. The entrance was a hundred feet wide and thirty high.

'Those out there are the Wingborne,' said Tarmik before nodding over his shoulder. 'We supposed to go in there and introduce ourselves to the Cavekings too?'

***

Malcanoth was the last soldier up the slope. By that point, he had survived three near-misses, two of them by actually watching the dragon release the rock in order to avoid it. Farrow – now also on foot – pointed to his right and issued instructions between panting breaths. 'There. We must do what we can to protect the wounded.'

Below the far corner of the shelf, a number of archers had gathered.

'Sir.' Picking up the bow and quiver he had only just deposited, Malcanoth ran to them. Several more were close behind, taking their numbers beyond twenty. From what he could see, they didn't have a vast supply of arrows, yet those fired might be recovered later and it was an ideal position to strike back from.

'Fire at will,' he ordered. 'But don't waste a single arrow.'

The soldiers took time with their shots and on a couple of occasions almost struck the dragons. Malcanoth sent one bolt close to a tail but they all desisted when the creatures were clearly out of range. Before long, all eleven of them had flown high enough to be safe. A few more rocks were aimed at the defenders, some striking the slope, others thumping harmlessly into the shelf above. The dragons soon gave up and thankfully left the injured alone. The exhausted soldiers watched as the creatures departed, flapping their wings to gain altitude then gliding onward.

Malcanoth lowered the bow. His gaze shifted to the broken bodies scattered across at least a mile. The Militiaman next to him had made a count. 'Forty at least. And not many of them are moving.'

***

Elaria waited at the edge of the shelf along with Narg and Kryk. Treyda had turned an ankle and was currently helping out with the walking wounded close to the cave. They could hear the cries from the stricken below but Captain Farrow insisted on waiting until the sky was dark. Elaria had a grudging respect for his discipline in trying to retain as many fit fighters as possible but saved her true admiration for Sergeant Islorath, who was already pressing his superior to assist the wounded. Only now did she think back to their discussion just prior to the attack. She'd been both surprised and delighted that the usually gruff sergeant had opened up to her; and to find that they had a good deal in common.

Kryk claimed he could still hear the dragons above but Elaria wasn't convinced. After another hushed conversation between the two officers, the sergeant spoke up.

'Any volunteers – gather here.'

Elaria, Kryk and Narg joined him, along with about fifty others.

'Groups of three. Two to carry the wounded, one to look out. Only move those we can help.'

'What about the others?' said Narg, too quietly for Sergeant Islorath to hear.

'Sergeant Norik will equip each group with a lantern. Do not expose the light unless you have to. Gather what medical kit you can. Prepare yourselves and be ready to leave as soon as possible.'

'Medical kit?' said Kryk quietly. 'What are we going to do with broken arms and legs?'

'Whatever we can,' said Elaria.

'I'll see what I can scrounge.'

'And I'll fetch the lantern,' offered Narg.

Elaria stayed where she was, looking on as the sergeant boldly made his way down the slope. He was soon lost to the gloom but she could hear him, moving slowly at first, then quickly; almost as if to make a target of himself. He came back unharmed a few minutes later and announced that it was safe to begin the rescue operation. Elaria waited impatiently for Narg and Kryk to return and was by then eager to get started.

'Stay together, stay as quiet as you can,' said the sergeant. 'Bring back one casualty at a time and note the location of anyone not being helped.' In the darkness he couldn't see their faces. 'Who do we have here?'

'Me, sergeant – Elaria. Kryk's with me and Narg of the Militia too.'

When the sergeant hesitated, she feared he might insist that the young recruits split up.

'All right. Get to it.'

***

With the moons veiled by cloud, the descent was difficult. Narg immediately told the youngsters to slow down, reminding them that they were to rescue the injured; not add to the list. They passed two Pathfinders who were already being tended to and then encountered a stoic Militiaman who Narg knew by name. The warrior was not actually badly injured but a rolling rock had trapped his foot. Unable to shift it himself, the man had patiently waited for help to come. It didn't take Narg and Kryk long to push the rock away. Elaria opened the lantern shutter for a moment and was relieved to see only a few scratches upon the Militiaman's ankle. She was touched by his offer to help the rescue effort but Narg insisted that he head up to safety.

They passed another trio helping a man whimpering with pain and then found themselves the most advanced search party. The retreating warriors had not followed a single path so they had to range left and right to ensure no one was missed.

After ten minutes of searching to no avail, Narg decided to call out. He reasoned that some might need to be roused and that others might be too frightened to draw attention to themselves. His efforts soon yielded a result and when they approached the casualty, Elaria knew it was bad.

The rock that had caused so much damage lay on the grass beside the injured soldier. Made a weapon by the dragons, it now seemed to belong in that place; as if it had been there since the dawn of time.

'I cannot move,' breathed the man.

Having already opened the lantern-shutter, Elaria knelt beside him and placed a hand on his shoulder. She did not know him so assumed he was one of Farrow's men. He was lying face down in the turf, arms stretched out, head turned to one side.

'Where is the pain?' asked Narg.

'Back,' hissed the man through gritted teeth.

'What about your legs?'

'Can't feel them. Cold.'

Among the items Kryk had placed in their pack was a blanket. Once she'd given the man some water, Elaria took it out.

'Wait,' said Narg. 'We can use it as a stretcher. Friend, we have to try and move you.'

The man summoned a nod.

Narg took the blanket and lay it out on the ground beside the casualty.

'First we'll turn you over.'

'Do what you must. But I warn you – I will cry out. I can feel the bones moving. I'll not walk again. I know it.'

Elaria could feel tears coming but she told herself not to be so weak. If the man was not crying, how could she? As Narg and Kryk positioned themselves to turn him, she backed away.

'You all right?' asked Kryk.

She nodded and moved the lantern over them. Narg would move the man's body, Kryk his legs. The pair placed their hands on the casualty.

'Ready, friend?' said Narg.

'As I'll ever be.'

The two were so focused on their task that they didn't hear what Elaria did. In fact, she wasn't sure if she'd heard something or merely sensed it. But whatever it was, it was close.

'Wait,' she whispered.

Narg looked up at her. 'What?'

In one movement, Elaria drew her sword and spun around so that the lantern-light projected outwards.

A dim shape. A figure. A man.

He stepped towards the light. Hands up in surrender, the stranger gazed at Elaria and the others.

'You're Pathfinders?'

Elaria kept her sword aimed at his neck. 'What of it? Who are you?'

With a broad smile of relief, the stranger dropped to his knees. His grimy face was covered with an unruly beard and his clothes were filthy and worn.

'Thank the gods.'

Narg stood beside Elaria. 'Who are you?'

'My name is Rycliff. Kals Rycliff.'

CHAPTER 18

Xalius took the bottle from Darian and downed a quarter of the sugary liquid within. He had been suffering from a terrible headache and this medicine had been prescribed by Professor Skeltine. Though he considered an assassination attempt unlikely, Xalius had insisted that the tonic be tested on one of the castle staff. The man had not expired. According to Skeltine's instructions, the liquid was to be taken as soon as Xalius felt the headaches coming. So far, it had proved remarkably effective in nullifying the pain.

Skeltine had also proved himself exceptionally able in assisting with the practical side of Xalius' experimentation. In fact, the scientist was so knowledgeable that Xalius was considering placing him in charge of the whole project. The professor seemed very enthusiastic and had already scheduled some practical trials on animals. He had offered no moral objection to moving on to human subjects at some point. Not for the first time, Xalius was struck by the ease with which people could put aside the suffering of others if it helped the ones they loved. With access to everything he needed, Skeltine was once again able to alleviate the worst of his wife's symptoms and continue to search for a cure. Xalius had no idea what was wrong with her – not that it mattered.

'Where is Lishara? I haven't seen her for days.'

'No idea, sir,' replied Darian as the aged pair walked through the quiet castle gardens. 'Studying perhaps?'

'Probably.'

If Darian had an opinion on his master's unlikely friendship with the girl, he had not aired it.

'Have the ships returned yet?'

'No, sir, but they were sighted last evening – should be in by the afternoon. I shall have the captains' reports as soon as possible.'

Xalius had despatched the Remmari ships to reconnoitre the coast of the Skornlands and northern Whispvale to see if any moves were afoot. Though the enemy forces had been dealt a considerable blow, King Blythe would undoubtedly possess other ships stationed elsewhere. Intelligence on this matter was disturbingly vague and Xalius wanted to know if reinforcements were on the move. For the moment, the Remmari captains were being kept in line by threats to their loved ones. That was not a long-term solution.

'Good. I also want you to identify one man to promote to overall charge of the fleet. You know the type.'

'Of course, sir. There was also some correspondence from Shya this morning. I've not had a chance to read it all properly but it's clear that trade is picking up.'

'And any word on the Imperator?'

'Not that I'm aware of, sir.'

Xalius shook his head. 'One understands that he always has his own concerns but it would be nice, once in a while, to know what's going on.'

Darian did not respond, instead pretending to be interested in a sprawling plant with a red bloom at its centre.

'I sometimes wonder if he enjoys leaving the rest of us in the dark.'

Darian definitely wasn't going to respond to that, not that Xalius could blame him. They walked on before some time before the administrator spoke up again.

'Sir, there is another issue. I hesitate to mention it but I would not wish to see a minor concern turn into a major one.'

'Spit it out, man.'

'The Beastkin encampment. There have been a few small incidents.'

'I know. Nothing to concern us.'

'Which incident are you referring to, sir?'

Xalius tutted. 'Well, one of the linguists accidentally insulted one of the brood chiefs, correct? Fortunately, that Remmari captain … what's his name?'

'Yaridan, sir.'

'That's it – he restored order quickly. I don't suppose the brood chiefs like being watched over by their historic enemy but I think we've made it clear they have no choice.'

'Indeed, sir – in fact it's remarkable there haven't been any more issues. Yaridian does seem very circumspect. I believe he keeps his distance unless absolutely necessary. But that's not it, sir, there is another matter.'

Xalius stopped in the middle of the path and aimed his walking stick at Darian. 'By Rael, are you actually trying to annoy me? *What* matter?'

'Sir, the woods north-east of the city are populated by deer and some of Marshal Siad's men hunt there. Unfortunately, they are not the only ones. Beastkin have been sighted and they reportedly stole a deer already killed and claimed by an officer. The soldiers gave chase but didn't catch the culprits.'

Xalius tutted again. 'A trifling matter. What of it?'

'Sir, I only mention it because there is the potential risk of another confrontation, especially bearing in mind that the marshal seems … unconvinced about our alliance with the Beastkin.'

'Well, that's his problem. I am entirely confident that the Imperator will approve. Why that brute Siad cannot see that it is also to his advantage, I have no idea. He's probably still angry about his patrol being attacked, even though they obviously travelled too far north.'

Darian wafted a hand at a fly that was already buzzing away.

'But you are right to raise the matter,' added Xalius. 'Have Yaridian look into it. And have one of the linguists inform the brood chiefs that they are to keep their underlings out of the woods. We are providing them with sufficient food.' Xalius tapped his stick against the paving slabs. 'I would like to deploy them as soon as possible but without any idea what the Imperator intends, my hands are tied.'

'Perhaps a limited assignment of some kind, sir?' suggested Darian. 'A detachment could carry out a raid on a town or military site to the north? It could serve as a test – to see exactly how useful and biddable they are.'

'I like it. If we demonstrate how they can serve our cause, we might also win Siad over. Go ahead.'

***

The cause of Lisahra's absence was revealed later that morning. When Ogon updated his master on progress with the experimentation, the young mage also confided that he was concerned about the girl, who had apparently not left her quarters for three days. Xalius instructed him to fetch her but Ogon returned with the news that she wouldn't even open her door. After a scheduled meeting with the ever-compliant Mayor Brayber, Xalius dismissed Darian and Ogon and went to the girl's room himself.

Her chamber was in a corridor previously occupied by senior castle staff. Xalius knocked and announced himself but no answer came.

'Girl, you know full well that I can knock this door down. Then you'll be left with no privacy at all.'

A key turned in the lock and the door opened. Lisahra did not meet Xalius' gaze and was turned away from him. She wore a plain cloak over her clothes and had wrapped it tightly about herself.

'I'm sorry, master, but I'd really rather be left alone.'

'At least tell me what ails you. Perhaps I can help. The Remmari professor is an excellent physician. Why he's done wonders-'

She shook head. 'Please, sir, I'm sure I shall feel better in a few days.' She still refused to look at him.

'This is not like you, girl. Has something happened?'

When he received no response, Xalius momentarily felt utterly foolish; standing in a doorway pleading with a young girl to tell him her woes. And yet he wanted to know; so he stepped inside and shut the door behind him.

Showing no reaction, she walked over to a table covered with piles of books and writing equipment. She sat there, hands clasped together, now looking towards the room's only window – a large triangle edged with brass.

'Might an old man also have a seat?'

'Apologies, master.'

Now that she was studying under him, Lisahra used this term. Xalius did not disapprove.

She hurried to a corner, fetched a high-backed chair and brought it over to him. Though she tried her best to keep her face hidden, that was when Xalius saw the black eye. He waited until they had both sat down before mentioning it.

'I've seen it now. You might as well show me.'

She pushed her red gold hair away and did so. It was a nasty injury, a purple welt that had swollen and now obscured half her left eye. Xalius took a moment to calm his anger, once more dismayed by his feelings for her.

'Who did that?'

Lisahra looked down at one of her books. 'I'd rather not say, master.'

Xalius felt his headache returning. 'Just tell me the truth.'

'I cannot.'

'Lisahra, this city is to all intents and purposes *mine*. If I want to find out, I will.'

'It was my own fault. I should have known better.'

'Regardless, I'd like to know.'

She touched the book, running a finger along the spine as she spoke. 'It was after the last Ceremony of Acceptance. Ogon and I went to watch. Lisl was ill so Tysa was on her own. She said we needed to have some fun; that we were working too hard. I think Ogon wanted to come back here but I went along with it. We visited a tavern, the big place over near the port. It was mostly Ironhand officers. They didn't bother us at first.'

Xalius could imagine where this was going. He discouraged his warlocks from mixing with the army; largely to ensure the females were not harassed.

Lisahra looked up at him. 'You would have preferred us not to be there, I'm sure.'

'You are entitled to some free time. The army do not own the city.'

Xalius was surprised to see tears form in Lisahra's eyes. She cleared her throat and wiped them away with a force that suggested considerable shame. 'I suppose they'd had plenty of wine because just as we were about to leave, one of them approached us. He was very charming.'

Now Xalius knew *exactly* where this was going.

'Alshan.'

She nodded.

Alshan was the youngest of Siad's captains. He was also quite handsome and less 'gragg-like' than the others, presumably due to a mixed parentage. Alshan was known for voracious appetites similar to his commander and Xalius knew he had preyed on more than a few Shyan women during their brief time there.

'He asked me to go upstairs – I hadn't noticed but there was a second gathering going on up there.'

'Don't tell me you did so.'

'I didn't see the harm in it. I don't normally drink much, master, perhaps that's why my judgement was so poor. Ogon and Tysa wanted us to all go home but I – I don't know, I didn't want the night to end.'

Xalius doubted that was the whole truth. She was probably attracted to this Alshan. And why not? He was a young, striking, strong, high-ranking warrior. Perhaps Lisahra wasn't so unusual, after all.

'I am sorry, master. I have let you down.'

'Not at all.'

Xalius had already moved on to considering what he might do to Alshan. 'So, you went upstairs?'

'I did. The other two weren't happy so they left. I recognised some of the other officers. There were many Remmari women there, also. People were drinking, playing dice. It seemed all right.'

'And then?'

'Alshan said he wanted to talk to me in private about something. I didn't want to go. I refused. Then he got one of the Remmari women to come along too. I thought we'd be all right.'

For all her courage and ability, Lisahra was showing her age.

'We went to the other room. Marshal Borshan was there. We had some more drinks and after that Arshan and the woman left us alone. I think the marshal told him to leave.'

Xalius now couldn't tell where his headache ended and his anger began.

Lisahra continued without looking at him. 'The marshal tried to kiss me and ... touch me. I tried to get away but ...' Once more she had to wipe tears away. 'I got away from him and screamed. That's when he hit me. I wanted to use the Way somehow but I couldn't ... I couldn't focus. I just kept screaming so he let me out. I ran. I ran all the way back here.'

***

Captain Farrow had insisted on moving further into the cavern. Now safe, many of the injured cried out as their wounds were tended to, making it difficult for Malcanoth to concentrate on anything else. Holding a lantern, Farrow picked his way through stones and puddles and came to a stop beside a collation of boulders. He called out to a nearby guard who had been posted to warn of any danger from within the cavern. He answered that all was well.

'You needn't worry,' said Kals Rycliff. 'This isn't connected to the main system. The Cavekings cannot reach you.'

As the three of them sat on the boulders, Malcanoth noted a disapproving glance from Captain Farrow. The bearded, dirt-encrusted Rycliff gave off quite a smell.

'You've seen them?'

'Yes. But they don't show themselves very often.'

'King Blythe received your messages – that you'd made contact.'

Rycliff sighed. 'I did. I spent several weeks tracking down a man who claimed to know their movements and whereabouts. That turned out to be a dead end. Eventually, I just decided to come here alone and see what I could discover. After tracking the movements of the Wingborne, I identified several of their lairs. I imagine they are much like a bird's nest but too high for me to even attempt to reach. I continued my observations and eventually realised that the lairs are arranged strategically to cover a certain area. You have strayed into the southern end of that area. Also within it are the underground tunnels and caverns where the Cavekings dwell.'

Farrow listened keenly, eyes narrowed.

'I approached a cavern where I had occasionally seen Cavekings sunning themselves. The Wingborne bombarded me as they did you but I somehow made it. The Cavekings came at me too – a terrifying sight, let me tell you – me but when I declared myself the envoy of King Blythe they desisted. I can't blame them for not believing me at first, given my appearance.' Rycliff turned to Malcanoth. 'I have been living off the land, you see, the Wingborne snatch anything bigger than a rabbit and-'

'Please,' said Farrow. 'Stick to the pertinent facts.'

'Apologies, captain, I have not spoken to anyone in months.'

'Understood. But I need to know what we're dealing with here. I presume from what occurred today that you did not make significant progress?'

'Actually, to start with, it went reasonably well. The king had provided me with some valuable gems to offer as a gesture of goodwill. These were taken by a Caveking of some status who was also able to communicate. At first, I could not understand his speech; their voices are so very deep and they use a very simple form of the Old Tongue. But over the days our exchanges improved. I did not describe myself as a Pathfinder – after all, it was our patrols that had a couple of unpleasant encounters with the Wingborne – but I made it clear that I represented King Blythe. They seem to have at least some knowledge and respect for Whispvale, though I'm not sure they really understand the intricacies of our relationship with the Skornlands and so on. Eventually, I was introduced to Zikaza himself.'

Rycliff shook his head. 'An incredible creature. I swear the very earth trembled when he appeared. Half as big again as the others and clearly revered by them. We met only once but he listened to my proposal for a peace agreement. Then I was left alone at the cave-mouth for several days. That turned into several weeks. When I ventured into the caves, the dragon I first spoke with instructed me to leave the mountains immediately. No explanation was given.'

'When was this?' asked Farrow.

'I have been keeping track,' replied Rycliff proudly. 'Eight weeks ago.'

Another cry from some stricken soldier echoed across the cavern.

Rycliff continued his tale: 'Having learned a little more, I thought it best to withdraw and report back to the king. However, the following day I observed a remarkable sight. I had camped out under a shelf of rock and saw a figure walking towards the cavern. The Wingborne were shadowing him above but they did not attack. I got as close as I dared but saw only that the man was tall and clad in a black, hooded cloak. I don't mind admitting that there was something very … impressive about him – beyond the fact that he seemed unconcerned about the Wingborne. Hard to describe. In any case, I withdrew to a safe distance and continued to observe. The cloaked man reached the cavern and went inside. I remained for several days but saw no further sign of him and decided to leave.'

Rycliff began coughing and it took him a while to clear his throat. As the two officers waited, Farrow tapped his fists together impatiently.

'Around the same time, I noted that the Wingborne had become much more active. If I tried to move at all in the hours of daylight, they would always see me and fly towards my position. Eventually, I discovered a short cut through tunnels that led down to the Low Gorge. I was almost there when I encountered what I can only describe as … a presence. I cannot be certain that it was the cloaked man but I sensed something … malign. My every instinct told me to retreat. I'm not ashamed to say I ran. For the past few days, I have been trying to plot another route of escape. Then I saw you.'

Farrow crossed his arms as he absorbed what he'd heard. 'I suppose I should thank you for the warning.'

'I'm only sorry I couldn't do more.'

'This cloaked man – any ideas who he could be?'

Rycliff shook his head. 'None. What of the attack on Remmar? What can you tell me?'

'That can wait,' said Farrow. 'From what you've said, it's clear that we must leave the mountains as soon as possible. What is the best route?'

'You came up through what I call the Wide Pass, which is the easiest and most direct route. Frankly, I'm amazed you managed to get that far without being seen. Now they know we're here, we've no chance of getting out that way.'

'Even at night?' suggested Malcanoth.

'With all these injured?' said Farrow, rather too sharply for Malcanoth's liking.

'There is another route,' said Rycliff hesitantly. 'The short cut I mentioned. There's a good chance that … whoever or whatever I encountered has moved on.'

'Then we should take it. How long to reach Low Gorge?'

'A day or two, no more. It cuts out the Wide Pass completely.' Yet it was evident from Rycliff's tone that he was not enthusiastic about the idea.

'So, what's the problem?' demanded Farrow.

'The short cut is a system of caves and tunnels. It means going underground.'

***

Elaria wanted to make herself useful but she simply could not be around those with the most awful injuries. She knew it was wrong – and that it was an inevitable part of life as a Pathfinder – but the sight of crushed limbs and exposed bones was simply too much.

Kryk had already admitted defeat and joined those standing guard on the shelf. Narg did not seem at all perturbed and was clearly impressed by the medical skills of the more experienced Pathfinders (he'd explained that only specialists received such training in the Militia). He was currently helping one of the Pathfinders perform an amputation and it was the preparation for this that had pushed Elaria over the edge.

She was now with Treyda, who had gathered all the medical supplies together and was distributing them to where they were most needed. The Pathfinders carried stocks of a pain-numbing tonic but this had already run out. They also carried strong wine as an alternative and many of the injured were requesting it. Elaria had just carried the last flask over to one man when he began coughing up blood. Two others were trying to help but there was nothing more they could do. When it became clear that the ensuing spasms were his death throes, Elaria withdrew. Tears pouring down her cheeks, she tripped in the shadowy cavern and fell. In trying to save the precious flask of wine, she thumped down on her side and could not help crying out.

Treyda appeared out of the gloom. 'What happened, Lari?'

'Sorry. The flask is all right.'

Treyda took it from her and helped her up. 'And what about you?'

'I'm fine. Don't worry.' But in fact, her side was painful. She was worried that she might have cracked a rib.

Treyda put her arm around her and helped her back to the low, flat rock where they had assembled the supplies. She sat Elaria down and placed a blanket over her shoulders.

'What can I do?' asked Elaria, now feeling even more useless.

'Just rest a while, girl. You've not stopped all night.'

She sat there for a time and the pain seemed to lessen. Treyda continued to dole out bandages, splints and the last of the wine. When their lantern spluttered out, she had a nearby Pathfinder fetch them a replacement. After an hour or so, no further requests came and eventually Elaria realised that the cries of the stricken were lessening.

'It's quieter now.'

Treyda came and sat beside her. 'Must be the middle of the night or close to it. I've seen this before – some will be put to sleep by the pain or the wine. Some will have given up. The dying wait hours for help to come but often fade quickly when it does.'

'They don't want to die alone,' said Elaria.

Treyda put her arm around her again. Elaria placed her head against the older woman's shoulder and had almost dozed off when she heard Captain Farrow. His clear, distinguished tones filled the cavern.

'Gather around, even those out on the shelf. Quickly now! You must all hear this. You must all hear what we are going to do.'

***

From darkness into darkness. Standing at the mouth of the tunnel, Malcanoth dragged his eyes from the inky depths and looked down. Gathered upon the slope below was the entire force. Four soldiers had died in the cavern and another during the night-time journey. Five more were being carried on stretchers but the rest could walk. Fortunately, the ground was not difficult and Rycliff had been able to guide them directly to the tunnel. Captain Farrow had estimated that his Fifth Regiment was down to sixty able to fight. After the earlier battle and the dragon attack, Malcanoth could count on around thirty-five, giving them a total strength of under a hundred.

'Hide that light,' he ordered, noting that someone below had opened a lantern shutter too far. His relief that they had managed the trip in only three hours and with no contact with the dragons had swiftly evaporated upon arrival at the tunnel. Rycliff had spoken of huge caverns below but the entrance was barely wide enough for two men.

Yet there really was no choice. Taking this route would protect them from the Wingborne and swiftly get the injured to safety. Rycliff had also explained that this network was fully ten miles from the lair of Zikaza and that he had seen no traces of the dragons here. As for the cloaked man, they would have to just hope that he was long gone. Rycliff was clearly not lacking valour but there had been no mistaking the fear in his voice as he described the encounter that had caused him to flee.

Malcanoth heard the authoritative tones of Captain Farrow and those below making way for their leader. It took him some time to negotiate the narrow, uneven path just below the tunnel. Nobody in the group smelled particularly good but the distinctive odour of Rycliff was easily detectable.

'Islorath, you, I and Rycliff will lead the way. I've got ten of my best men right behind us. The injured will remain in the middle of the column, Sergeant Norik will bring up the rear. Apparently, the first of the caverns is not too far. We will rest there before continuing.'

'Sir.'

From below, the sound of stone on a fire-striker. Soon a torch was alight and passed up to Captain Farrow. The smell of burning oil and animal skin was at least stronger than poor Rycliff. Malcanoth glimpsed his bearded face in the glow of the torch, and the expression he saw did not ease his own nerves. The pitched battle that had so nearly ended in defeat had been bad enough but at least they'd fought *men*.

However good King Blythe's intentions, he had not been wise to send Rycliff and Farrow here. They were strangers in a very strange land and they now faced a foe far beyond any of them.

***

The tunnel had clearly been carved out by a flow of water at some point. None flowed now but the roof was damp and icy water dripped constantly onto the column. This left the smooth floor slippery and when the tunnel descended, progress slowed. Here, the narrow confines were actually helpful as the soldiers could reach out for holds and ease themselves down slowly. Malcanoth dropped back to oversee the lowering of the stretchers down the most treacherous area.

Thankfully the tunnel levelled out soon after. Rycliff guided the way across a low gallery strewn with shattered rock then into a narrow crevice which emerged eventually into a cavern of startling beauty. The light of the torches was magnified by a milky pool at its centre, illuminating a roof banded by remarkable blues, purples and pinks. While Rycliff went to scout the far side of the cavern, Captain Farrow called a halt.

Malcanoth knew that the spy had actually seen daylight before being forced to retreat. Rycliff estimated that they had at least ten hours travelling before that and confirmed that there were other suitable locations to stop. As Malcanoth encouraged the soldiers to keep moving around the pool to make space for those coming behind, he sensed an uplift in the mood of this rag-tag column. The early stages of the descent hadn't been much less anxious than what had come before but the chance for a rest in this attractive location offered a much-deserved fillip.

Once everyone was settled, he returned to find Rycliff again reporting back to Farrow.

'It's as I remembered – another narrow section then a descent through several caverns, some even larger than this.'

'Down *again*?' said Farrow.

The captain seemed unusually nervous, causing Malcanoth to wonder if he was afraid of enclosed spaces.

'Yes,' answered Rycliff. 'The route cuts diagonally across this side of the pass. I do not recall any serious descents beyond the caverns.'

Farrow nodded and turned to Malcanoth. 'The injured?'

'Faring as well as can be.'

'I shall check with Norik and post guards.' The captain hurried away.

'We're safe here,' said Rycliff, with some confidence.

'As long as we don't run into your cloaked friend.'

They were standing close to an outcrop of rock which Rycliff now leaned against. He wiped his brow and took off his pack.

'What do you think went on in that cave – between the cloaked man and the Cavekings?' Malcanoth had been wanting to press the spy on this point and only now had the opportunity.

'Who knows? But after his arrival – and whatever ensued – I went from potential ally to enemy. I suppose we might assume that some kind of agreement was made. Without any knowledge of who he is, we can do no more than speculate on its nature.'

'We do know that this Madland army has conquered Shya and Remmar and is now sending patrols further into our territory.'

'Given the timing, he may well be associated with those you fought, yes.'

'The Cavekings and the Wingborne might make a considerable difference, if they chose to ally themselves with one side.'

'True,' said Rycliff, 'but historically, their only concern has been to preserve their territory. Let us hope that remains the limit of their ambitions.'

***

Though he knew he should be resting, Malcanoth soon found himself standing by the pool. There was a strangely hypnotic quality to the opaque surface that also reflected the swirling bands upon the cavern roof thirty feet above. The large space magnified sound so those that were speaking did so in hushed tones. There was a church-like respect for the unusual space that now seemed a sanctuary from the denizens of the mountains. Many of the soldiers were now sleeping peacefully and Malcanoth knew it wouldn't be easy to get them up and moving again. Even Farrow was asleep, head at rest on his pack, surrounded by the men of the Fifth Regiment.

'Beautiful, isn't it?'

He turned to find young Elaria beside him. She was also gazing down at the pool.

'It is.' Malcanoth had seen her hard at work earlier at one corner of a stretcher.

'I didn't think I'd like it underground but everything seems calm here. As if all that's going on above never happened.'

'I know what you mean.'

'They had to leave them – those who passed away on the journey. On the ground up there. Alone.'

'I wish we could have done more.'

Malcanoth thought it wise to change the subject. 'That Narg is a strong fellow, I saw him shifting one stretcher practically by himself.'

'He has been a soldier for thirty years.'

'Is that right? Well, if there's any more fighting, I suggest you stay close to him.'

'I will. Or you.'

Malcanoth felt his cheeks grow hot.

'I mean … you …' Elaria stammered. 'As a leader … sorry, sergeant.'

'Nothing to be sorry for.'

'Oh,' she said after a few moments. 'You, Sanzir and Brannus.'

'Sorry?'

Elaria pointed to the left. Sanzir, a male Pathfinder, was crouching close to the pool. Beyond him was a Militiaman who stood there with his hands clasped in front of him, lost in thought.

'Sanzir is a Waymaker, so is Brannus, so are *you*. And all three of you are standing close to the pool.' Elaria turned to Malcanoth, a puzzled expression on her face. 'Can that be a coincidence?'

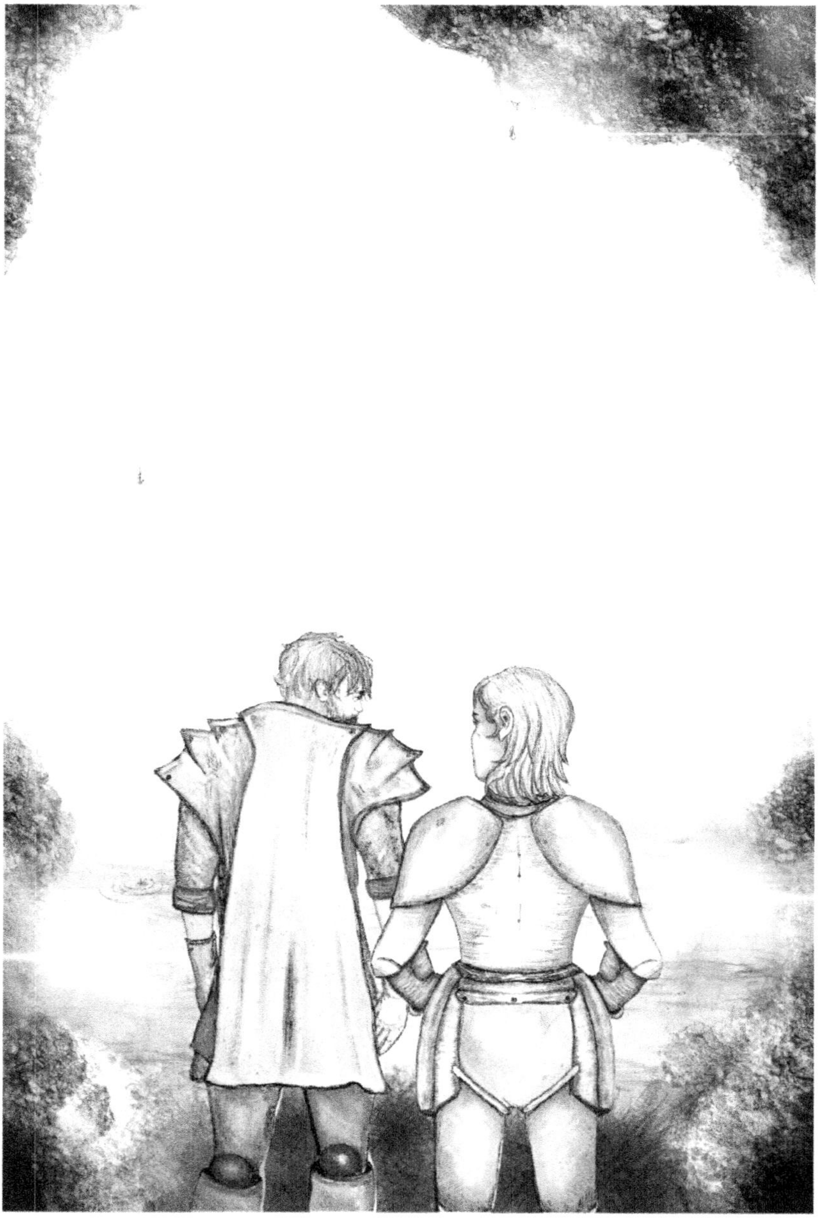

CHAPTER 19

Xalius stood upon the balcony with Professor Skeltine, Ogon and Lisahra. He had insisted that the girl join them; this was the first time she'd left the room since their discussion. The balcony overlooked a courtyard at the rear of the castle that had been specially adapted for the demonstration. Two arched exits had been barricaded by timbers and the only means of entry was by a single door. That door was now shaking under repeated impacts from within.

'Seems rather keen to get out.'

'Yes, sir,' replied Skeltine. 'The first two subjects reacted similarly. It seems this...rage is somehow connected to the augmentation. The first subject actually killed itself by repeatedly throwing itself against a wall.'

'Then perhaps we should start,' suggested Xalius, 'though you will need to address that issue at some point. A weapon that can do as much damage to its own side as the enemy is useless.'

With a cordial bow, Skeltine nodded to a guard stationed nearby. This man passed on the order and soon the watchers could hear the bolts of the door being withdrawn.

'Who is doing that?' asked Xalius. 'And why are they not being attacked?'

'One of your warlocks is assisting us, sir,' replied Skeltine.

'Ah.'

The two wolves within the courtyard were now pacing back and forth, eyes fixed on the door. They had been caught several days previously and starved to heighten their aggression.

'Sir, you will recall the dog I showed you several days ago?'

'Yes.' Xalius had in fact felt rather sorry for the black mongrel that had come and sat obediently beside him.

'I think you will notice a quite significant-'

Before the elderly professor could continue, the door flew open and a dark shape flashed across the courtyard. One of the wolves threw itself instantly at its foe. The two animals met in midair and the larger wolf was somehow knocked back by the dog. As the wolf struggled hesitantly to its feet, its companion joined the fray.

But the second wolf had barely moved when the dog darted at its throat. The jaws clamped together instantly and as the teeth worked the flesh, the wolf emitted a strangled cry. The poor beast's eyes rolled as it was ravaged and soon blood was splattering the courtyard floor. The dog continued to tear at the wolf's throat long after it had collapsed.

'That's the same animal?' asked Xalius

'Indeed it is,' answered Professor Skeltine proudly.

It certainly didn't appear to be. As it stalked towards the first wolf, Xalius noted that the dog was bulging with muscle. The bared teeth seemed unusually large too and there was an elemental power and aggression about the thing. It looked like a creature that would not stop until either it or everything it wanted to kill was dead. The eyes were bulging too, mad and unblinking as bloody froth dripped from its jaws.

The second wolf didn't last much longer. Vicious bites to its front legs all but disabled it and then the dog went for the throat once more. Not content with victory, the dog then set about tearing skin off the wolf's flanks.

'Note both the power *and* ferocity,' stated the professor.

'One could hardly miss it.'

'And this is only our fifth subject, sir,' added Ogon. 'The creatures tend to die within days but the initial surge of augmentation is quite remarkable.'

Xalius was both impressed and surprised. It had been obvious that the combination of ancient Ilerian experimentation and the peerless supply of chemical agents stored in Remmar might prove useful. But the ability of Skeltine to synthesise both the learning and the science had accelerated the entire process.

'Very good, very good. Professor, we will continue to provide whatever you need. Please move on to human experimentation as swiftly as possible. The Haar Dari must equip itself with all available weapons of war.'

'Of course.'

That morning, Carli had confided to her master that she had foreseen the arrival of Atavius in Remmar. She could not accurately predict precisely when but she seemed to think it would be within days rather than weeks. Xalius always considered it politic to have something to offer his master.

***

Once they left the peaceful cavern behind, the journey again became a struggle. Elaria remained with Narg, Kryk and Treyda; and the four of them had taken charge of a Militiaman named Olten. His right leg had been horribly mangled by a Wingborne rock but he bore the pain with great fortitude and even cracked the odd joke. He had resigned himself to losing the leg and Elaria just hoped that they would reach a place where a surgeon could perform the operation properly. If they didn't, Narg would take it off with an axe – a stark reality that Olten was fully aware of.

Word came back that there wasn't far to go but none of the terrain had been easy. They were either squeezing through tight crevices and tunnels or crossing caverns that were far less pleasant than the first. The floors were riven by fissures and holes and above were formations that Elaria found as frightening as they were beautiful. According to Narg, the icicle-like structures were formed over many decades by dripping salt and ice. The result was startling: great pointed lumps that threatened to drop at any moment and crush those below.

'Why is there no bloody path?' complained Kryk as they manoeuvred the stretcher over another troublesome fissure.

'How could you make a path through all this?' countered Treyda.

'Someone carved a way through those other sections,' replied Kryk. 'And someone created those windows.'

This and the cavern preceding it were partly illuminated by beams of light admitted through several narrow shafts cut in the roof.

'Someone or *something*,' said Narg.

'No way could dragons do that,' said Kryk.

'Who else then?' asked Treyda.

'Maybe the dragons aren't the only ones to have dwelt here,' said Kryk. 'One of the ancient peoples, perhaps.'

'The Crystal Mountains have belonged to the dragons for as long as anyone can remember,' stated Narg. 'Which is why we should never have come here. If not for your officers, we could have been safe by now.'

Elaria had not heard the Militiaman complain like this before. She didn't like to contradict him but she felt he was being unfair to Sergeant Islorath and Captain Farrow.

'They didn't *choose* to come here. They were following orders.'

'Not all orders are meant to be obeyed, girl. A lot of people are dead just because Blythe thought he could make a deal with these accursed beasts.'

'*King* Blythe,' said Kryk forcefully.

'Let's not argue,' said Elaria. 'We'll be out of here soon.'

***

She had not believed that when she said it but, not long after, word spread that they were close. The main column had taken a break in the largest cavern yet and Rycliff had gone ahead to scout the final section. On the far side of the expanse was a high, narrow fissure and the merest suggestion of daylight beyond. Elaria was standing on a slab of rock and could see that the spy had returned and was now conversing with Captain Farrow.

'Thank the gods,' said Kryk, looking fearfully at the roof. 'We can get out from under these bloody things.' He seemed even more concerned about the pointed formations than Elaria.

'Look at it this way,' she said. 'They've probably taken centuries to form. Why would they fall down now?'

'Because *I'm* here,' Kryk answered forlornly. Given recent events, Elaria couldn't really blame the young man for feeling that fortune had deserted him.

Sergeant Islorath stood alone in the middle of the cavern. He seemed preoccupied; turning this way and that as he examined their surroundings. The cavern was roughly circular in shape, perhaps three hundred feet across at its widest and easily two hundred high. There were several shafts cut into the roof and they cast yellow light onto a flattened area close to where the sergeant was standing. Though the column behind and ahead of him had halted on ground as uneven as any they had crossed, to his left and right the cavern floor was very different. Elaria looked on as Sergeant Norik joined Islorath and pointed first one way then the other.

'What is it, Lari?' asked Treyda, who was squatting beside Olten's stretcher. Now that they were still, the injured soldier had fallen asleep.

'Not sure.' Except that the more she looked at the two sergeants' behaviour and the floor of the cavern, the more certain she became.

From her position, the left side of the cavern was obscured by a cluster of particularly large boulders. To the right, the ground ascended upward to the side of the cavern and there she saw a dark area, like the mouth of a cave. And when she scanned downward to where the sergeants stood, Elaria became certain:

It was a path – a wide, purposefully constructed path that ran perpendicular to their escape route to the fissure. From what she'd heard about the second type of dragons that dwelt in these mountains, they would need plenty of space to move.

Not wishing to add to the tension, she said nothing. Sergeant Islorath, however, ran over to Captain Farrow, while Norik could be seen issuing orders to the column. Elaria and the others didn't need to hear the words. When they saw the soldiers in front of them get to their feet, pull on their packs and lift the stretchers, they did the same. Elaria kept her counsel and took her place at the front of Olten's stretcher with Narg. The Militiaman let out a long sigh, then gave the order to lift.

The effort of transporting their charge was sufficient to occupy Elaria over the next few minutes. By the time they reached the path, it was evident that she was not the only one to arrive at the obvious conclusion.

'Something made that,' said Kryk, breathing hard as they came to a halt only feet from the flattened area.

'Looks that way,' added Treyda.

'What's the hold up?' asked Narg.

He was answered by a man ahead of them. 'Sounds like it narrows up ahead.'

'Course it bloody does,' moaned Narg. 'That's the way out.'

A minute became two; two became five. Even though she was no longer carrying the stretcher, Elaria could feel sweat dripping down her flanks. Again, she had noticed something the others had not. Brannus, the tall, bald Militia Waymaker was gazing to the right, at the dark maw where the path met the cavern wall. Elaria had no idea of the extent of his abilities; all she had seen was him manipulating a camp fire to amuse the other soldiers. But he was standing with one hand on a spear, still staring.

'Are they even moving up ahead?' demanded Narg.

'Yes,' said Treyda. 'Just very slowly.'

The column shuffled forward. The quartet moved Olten a few feet but soon had to set him down again. Elaria found her attention back on Brannus. The Militiaman was now walking purposefully along the road of rock, towards the dark tunnel.

'What's up with him?' enquired Kryk.

Brannus stopped and rested the base of his spear on the ground once more. He was still staring at the tunnel.

'Has he seen something?' asked Kryk.

Brannus suddenly whirled around. 'Captain, get them out! Get them out *now*!'

This drew the attention of everyone within the column and soon Farrow was clambering over boulders then sprinting towards Brannus. Then they all saw it:

At first no more than the suggestion of movement, then the clear sight of something large, moving fast. When it passed under a shaft of light, many cries went up. The Caveking was a great lumbering thing with thick, powerful legs, body and neck. It seemed unlikely that the wings might lift such a weight but they flapped nonetheless as the dragon thundered down the slope at tremendous speed. And with every step, the scale and power of the creature grew more obvious. It was as big as a mammuth, the body easily twenty feet long and ten tall, the elongated tail whirling in the air. And it was not alone; a second Caveking burst from the darkness behind it.

'Bows and spears to me!' yelled Farrow. 'The rest of you, get the injured across.'

'Elaria!' growled Narg. 'Take your side.'

Forcing herself to concentrate on what was in front of her, Elaria reached down for the stretcher pole and lifted it up. To her surprise, those ahead were also moving. But they had only taken a few steps when shouts reached them:

'Back! Back!'

She glimpsed Brannus fling his spear at the Caveking then dive clear. Captain Farrow had his sword drawn but could only dodge the rampaging beast. Others were not so fortunate. Two brave Militiamen fired arrows but the Caveking barely seemed to notice. Its rumbling roar could not have been more different to the piercing screech of the Wingborne. It simply charged straight through the soldiers caught in its path, tossing their bodies aside with casual ease. Once past them, the dragon turned and bellowed. The creature had almost nothing in common with its airborne cousins. The Wingborne had appeared green in colour but the Caveking's hide was an unearthly pale purple. The jaws were less elongated than the flying dragons and the head was topped by two sharp horns. As terrifying as its size was, the expressiveness and intelligence of the large, grey eyes was equally alarming.

By now, several warriors had rushed past Elaria and others had gathered around Farrow upon the road. He and those with him were able to unleash enough arrows and spears to halt the second Caveking. But now the two beasts employed their wings, swinging them downward in lethal arcs. Another soldier was sent flying, his lifeless body landing with a horrible thud.

'No,' ordered Narg, seeing that Kryk was ready to move. 'We get Olten across first. *Then* we fight.'

The four of them set off once more, rounding another Pathfinder who was helping a man with a crutch. Up ahead, Farrow's meagre force had been bolstered by his sergeants and several others. They were between the Cavekings and now formed two lines to face them. Others carried a stretcher through the narrow, precious gap.

Once over a jagged fissure, the quartet didn't have far to go. As the roars of the dragons and the shouts of men filled the cavern, they finally reached the road and the narrow crossing created by the defensive lines. Another blow from a wing sent a man tumbling backwards. He struck Narg on the legs but the Militiaman kept hold of the stretcher. As the man rolled away, groaning with pain, a nearby woman went to help. Elaria had told herself not to watch the ongoing battle but she glimpsed the terror in Olten's eyes as they crossed the road of rock.

The fissure – and the tempting suggestion of light beyond – were no more than a hundred feet away. Gathered between it and the road were a handful of soldiers; those unable to fight.

'Set him down there,' said Narg, nodding towards where two other stretchers had already been placed. Three Pathfinders ran back past them, weapons at the ready.

Once Olten was on the ground, Elaria drew her sword.

'Stay here,' advised Narg. 'Look after them.'

But Kryk was already marching back towards the battle and Treyda was silently pulling an arrow from a quiver.

Narg didn't need to hear Elaria's answer.

'Very well,' said the veteran, 'but at least stay close to me.'

Another group arrived with a stretcher and one of the men had a bundle of spears with him. Narg took two each for he and Elaria. As the man on the crutch hobbled past – refusing the offer of help – they ran back to the road of rock.

Only the speed of the soldiers' response had kept the dragons at bay. To Elaria's left, sergeants Norik and Islorath had around thirty with them. A constant volley of spears and arrows was keeping the dragon occupied but the arrows did not even penetrate the hide and only a single spear had lodged in the creature's neck. The Caveking continued to attack with its wings and one Militiaman narrowly avoided losing his head because Norik yanked him backwards.

Captain Farrow seemed to have less support, so it was to his side that Elaria and Narg went, finding Kryk and Treyda already there. As they arrived, the last stragglers crossed the road. Elaria stood beside Kryk, whose height allowed him to see over those in front. She had to move aside as he pulled back his arm and unleashed the spear. It was a good throw that struck between the beast's horns. The snorting Caveking didn't seem to even notice.

'Here.' Elaria passed one of the spears to Kryk. As he took aim, those in front suddenly surged backwards. The big recruit stumbled and fell, taking Elaria down with him. She looked up in time to see the dragon lash out with one of its great clawed feet. An agonised cry went up and only several arrows aimed at its face deterred the dragon from pressing the attack. As the soldiers recovered themselves, the Caveking backed away. Elaria and Kryk helped each other to their feet and watched the dragon retreat.

Someone gave a cheer but everyone else had seen the true reason for the Caveking's move.

'It will charge,' cried Farrow. 'Get ready!'

The beast rushed forward. With so many in front of her, Elaria could not throw the spear. She made for the side of the road, hoping to be able to strike when the beast passed. Somebody went down behind her and clipped her ankle. She somehow stayed on her feet and – as the noise behind her lessened – turned back.

The dragon was now standing where she had been only seconds before. Scattered at its feet were half a dozen bodies, most of them still. The Caveking unleashed a triumphant roar and stamped down on the nearest fallen soldier. Before she could really register what had happened, Elaria watched a tall figure run towards the beast, a flaming torch in his hand. Sweeping his other hand at the flame, Brannus sent an intense tongue of fire into the dragon's face. Though the flames didn't set it alight, the beast was blinded and didn't see the new danger.

Captain Farrow darted forward and unleashed a powerful swing of his sword. With such power – and at such close range – this was sufficient to slice through the hide. He swung again, chopping at the flesh until blood flowed. Others, Narg amongst them, were not slow to follow. In seconds, ten men were attacking the front legs of the Caveking. A wild sweep of a wing knocked one man out of the fight but the others kept hacking away. Roaring in pain this time, the dragon retreated but now found that its front legs collapsed under it. Light from a shaft above flashed on the soldier's blades as they slashed away. With an anguished groan, the dragon's head came down towards them, Narg picked up a spear and drove it two-handed into the beast's throat. Then came a second spear, and a third. Soon great gouts of dark blood were gushing onto the cavern floor. The pale eyes rolled upward and the Caveking slumped down onto its ruined legs.

'Now the other beast!' yelled Farrow, eyes wild with victory.

Others followed his example and sprang away to help their compatriots. Elaria found herself alone for a moment and as Brannus strode past her, the light of his torch briefly caught the face of a motionless figure lying close by. Blood stained the rock all around. Treyda's eyes were glassy and still.

***

Leaving the others to lead the battle against the remaining Caveking, Malcanoth dropped the spear he was carrying and went to help Norik. The sergeant had been knocked aside by a blow and landed awkwardly between two boulders. Nils Rycliff was already there but could not free him. Norik was firmly wedged, lying on his side and struggling to breathe. Malcanoth and Rycliff put their shoulders to the smaller boulder but could not shift it at all.

'Please,' croaked Norik, his face contorted by pain.

'We'll get you out,' said Malcanoth, with more confidence than he felt.

He was astonished to see that Farrow and his compatriots had downed one of the dragons. When he'd initially seen the power of the beasts, he'd thought it unlikely any of them would escape the cavern alive but once again the captain's leadership and the bravery of the rag-tag column had won out. As Farrow's group streamed past to reinforce the other side, Malcanoth reminded himself to focus on matters at hand.

He squatted beside Norik's feet and tried to push the boulder with his hands. Even before Rycliff joined him, he felt a little movement. And even though he had not called upon the Way, he also felt that rising power within. Before he could even grasp what was happening, the boulder moved – an inch, six inches, a foot.

Rycliff watched in awe. 'How in the name of the gods-'

'-Get me out!' cried Norik.

'Do it,' urged Malcanoth.

Rycliff grabbed the sergeant under the arms and dragged him clear. Malcanoth could feel the Way coursing through him; it was easy to hold the boulder – in fact he was able to roll it away. He could not believe what he had just done.

Then he realised. He'd been so preoccupied that he had missed the obvious answer. The pool in the cavern where they had rested was not just a reservoir of water. Young Elaria had been right; it was no coincidence that the three Waymakers had been drawn there. It was a Waylake. All Waymakers knew that their power fluctuated and one theory held that this was due to the location of the Waylakes. As they were usually underground, the theory was difficult to prove. But Malcanoth had seen the evidence for himself and now knew he temporarily possessed more power than ever before.

'I saw it.' Suddenly the squat figure of Sanzir was beside him. He was part of the second regiment but Malcanoth had heard he was a Waymaker of some skill.

'And I feel it,' added Sanzir. 'The pool. I wasn't sure but I am now.'

Rycliff was close by, helping Sergeant Norik to his feet. 'A Waylake? Here?'

Malcanoth turned back to the battle and saw Captain Farrow bellowing orders. He had spears at the front to keep the Caveking on the defensive and archers still launching bolts at its head. As one struck its snout, the dragon issued a pained shriek. With the soldiers all occupied, there was no one to care for the injured. Several looked beyond help but others were moving.

As Sanzir went to help Farrow, Malcanoth joined Norik and Rycliff.

'Can you go on alone?'

Still grimacing, Norik managed a nod.

'Come, Rycliff, we must help the injured.'

The spy followed him to the closest casualty but could not take his eyes off the bloodied bulk of the dead dragon. 'By all the gods, Farrow killed a Caveking. They'll sing songs about him.'

***

It seemed to Elaria that she could see fear in the creature's eyes. Two spears were lodged in its wings and she was sure it had looked over at its dead companion. For the briefest moment, she almost felt sorry for it. After all, most animals – most people, for that matter – would defend their territory. But all she and the others had wanted to do was escape the Crystal Mountains alive. She didn't know why the Cavekings had attacked without warning but this was now a fight to the death.

When another arrow struck close to the dragon's eye, fear was replaced by rage. The creature stomped forward, knocking several soldiers off their feet and making a hole in the line. But at Farrow's urging, spears struck back immediately. He himself tried to swing at the creature but his sword deflected off the hide and he lost his balance. As if knowing he was the leader, the dragon brought one of its wings down upon him. But the captain already had his blade up and the creature only harmed itself. As blood showered him, Farrow rolled away and jumped back to his feet.

His face now smeared by dark red, the aristocratic officer seemed a man possessed. Snatching a spear from a soldier nearby, he gathered the spear-wielders to him. Elaria felt a chill as she spied the tall figure of Kryk beside the captain. But Farrow wasn't ready to attack again yet. At his orders, several experienced soldiers with swords flanked the spearmen to defend them against the wings. One of them was Narg. Elaria had her own blade at the ready but there were two ranks between her and the captain.

Farrow drove his group onward; spears jabbing at the legs and chest, swords scything at the wings. The first sign of hesitation was enough for the captain and his compatriots were with him as he drove his spear at the dragon's chest. His blow was deflected by the hide but Kryk's struck home. Reaching high, the young Pathfinder held on and pushed again, driving his weapon deep into the flesh. The dragon convulsed with pain and retreated. Kryk lost his spear but those around him thrust their weapons again and once more the dragon backed away.

Bowstrings pinged and another volley hit the head. The great beast at last shied away and began to turn. A victorious cheer went up from the soldiers. Elaria saw Kryk and Narg raise their weapons and soon she too was celebrating.

Something passed through one of the shafts of light. Elaria looked up and saw a shape obscure the other beams, shadowing the cavern floor. Then the shape revealed itself: a third dragon, this one much larger than the others. Yet despite its size, this beast possessed enormous wings sufficient to lift its bulk. And as they flapped, the air shifted, forcing the soldier's cheers back down their throats. Elaria had heard the others talk of the dragon leader – Zikaza. She and everyone around her could do no more than watch as the Caveking descended, wings angling upward as its body neared the ground.

The cavern floor trembled as it landed. Farrow and the others barely had time to raise their weapons as Zikaza reared up. The captain was one of the few to get his spear away but not a single weapon dented the hide. One of the huge front legs came down on his head, crushing him in an instant.

Silenced once more, the soldiers retreated, many entranced by all they could see of their fallen leader – his shattered legs poking out between the hooked claws of the dragon. As the defenders flooded towards her, Elaria could not drag her eyes from the Caveking. Zikaza raised his head and opened his mouth, revealing rows of jagged teeth each as big as an axe-head.

'Enemies.' Spoken as a thunderous growl, the single word reverberated around the cavern.

'Enemies mine.'

Zikaza spread himself, each vast purple wing ribbed with sinew and bone.

'All ... will ... die.'

With Captain Farrow gone, the will of the soldiers broke. As they rushed past her, Elaria found she could not move. The dragon swung its head at the slowest of its foes and sent two figures careening almost as far as the cavern wall. Elaria knew Kryk had been very close to Farrow and now she could not see him at all.

Only when Narg grabbed her arm was she able to move her feet and scramble away. She could hear the dragon behind her and reckoned she and Narg might be the closest to it. Dropping her sword, she leaped over a boulder and followed him away from the road.

Up ahead, most of the fleeing soldiers were already inside the fissure and clear of the cavern. There was no way that the huge Caveking could get through: if they could reach it, they were safe. Knowing the dragon might struggle to cross the uneven ground, Elaria shut out the noise of it and ran with all her might.

By the time they reached the fissure, the last of the soldiers were squeezing through.

Only three men were not trying to escape. They stood twenty feet in front of the crevice, eyes on Zikaza. Elaria could not understand why they weren't moving until she saw four injured figures laid on stretchers behind them. Most of the terrified soldiers had not stopped to help them but these three had.

As Narg grabbed her hand and dragged her onwards, she realised that one of the trio was Sergeant Islorath.

***

At the first sight of the giant dragon, he had found Brannus and Sanzir. The power of the beast made its victory inevitable and though it had defeated the soldiers in moments, the three Waymakers had at least had time to prepare themselves.

Now Malcanoth reached out and held the hands of his fellow mages. None of the three watched the dragon as it plodded towards them, wings outstretched once more.

'Fools,' growled Zikaza. '*Little* fools.'

Malcanoth had never felt such energy but he still did not know if it would be enough.

The three Waymakers raised their arms. Malcanoth locked his eyes on his target then closed his eyes. This too was a battle now; between the power of the Way and the strength of the world. He felt the ground shaking. The dragon was close.

Then it happened. He knew it before he saw it and when he opened his eyes, the formation was already falling. The combined power of the three Waymakers had wrenched a single, colossal shard of rock out of the cavern roof.

Sanzir was the first to see the danger. They had stood too close; it was falling towards *them*. The trio fled but Malcanoth had taken only three steps towards the fissure when a colossal impact and deafening crash sent him sprawling. He cracked his head as he went down and saw no more.

CHAPTER 20

Xalius sat alone in the castle garden, shaded by a tree of pale green leaves streaked with yellow. Another day had passed and he'd still heard nothing from Siad. He allowed himself a smirk. Despite the marshal's posturing and bluster, he clearly didn't want to face him. Perhaps he was aware that Xalius now knew of what he had done to Lisahra. Perhaps he was ashamed; embarrassed. But even provocation had not drawn him into a confrontation.

Xalius had been determined to register his disapproval – even if indirectly – and it hadn't taken long to find a way to make his point. Three days earlier, Darian had passed on the message to the Beastkin chiefs – they were free to return to the woods. Apparently, the creatures were at first wary of some deceit or trap but when the Remmari Captain Yaridian pointed them towards the best hunting grounds, the Beastkin began to return. It was only a matter of time before there was another incident with Siad's officers and it had occurred the previous day. No one seemed sure exactly what had unfolded within the woods but over a dozen Beastkin had been slain along with two of Siad's Ironhands.

The news had reached the city hours ago but the marshal had not yet reacted. Xalius was pleased but also slightly disappointed; a part of him wanted to confront the brute, even though he could not admit the true reason for his ire.

Hearing footsteps, he sighed. A quarter-hour of solitude had not been enough. Still, there would be some pleasure to be taken from this encounter. Xalius remained on the bench as Darian and Vikter Aggor approached.

Aggor's obsequious bow was as predictable as the words that followed. 'Your Excellency, it is truly a joy to see you. I must admit I was beginning to wonder if I might have the pleasure of your company again. I trust you received my letter? Please allow me to apologise once again in person. If I had known that that awful thug would-'

Xalius picked up his walking stick and aimed it at Aggor. 'Enough. What's done is done and the situation has actually worked out rather well.'

Hope radiated from the man's eyes and a little colour returned to his pallid face. 'Indeed, sir – and it does seem that the Beastkin can perform a crucial function for the Haar Dari. I have greatly enjoyed working with your linguists and I must say some of them are coming on very well.'

The six translators were hand-picked and highly gifted. The Imperator had stressed the importance of such specialists from early on; communication would be crucial for the Haar Dari conquest. All six were already fluent in several languages. Two hailed from the Madlands, two from Shya, two from Remmar. Xalius knew for a fact that at least three of them had already surpassed Aggor. The man had clearly made a bold step in learning the basics of the Beastkin tongue but had progressed no further. According to Darian, though the number of words was small, pronunciation and precise communication was very difficult.

'I ... I am aware of what occurred in the woods yesterday,' added Aggor gravely. 'A tragedy. Of course, we do not mourn the deaths of the Beastkin but to lose noble officers of your armed forces…If I can be of any service in ensuring there are no more such incidents-'

'-We are looking into it,' replied Xalius. 'But do not concern yourself with this matter. I have something different in mind for you.'

Aggor seemed wary but straightened up and put his hands behind his back, as if reporting for duty. 'Your Excellency?'

'Ever since our first meeting, you struck me as a very ambitious man; eager to make a mark in the world. Am I correct?'

'Oh, very much, sir. Very much.'

'An opportunity has presented itself. We need a few enthusiastic individuals keen to contribute to the cause. Bearing in mind the…unfortunate incident with Mawraze, this is also a chance for you to demonstrate your loyalty. Sound appealing?'

'It does indeed, sir.'

'Excellent. Well, Darian here will take you to your new superior. He is a man of great talent and vision. You will, I'm sure, consider it an honour to contribute to his work. His name is Professor Skeltine.'

***

The largest Ceremony of Acceptance yet was scheduled for the following week. Having just concluded a meeting regarding the logistical aspects of the event with Mayor Brayber, Xalius was on his way to his quarters for a much-needed nap. He took a short cut through a particular section of the castle he'd become rather fond of.

It was a square, enclosed courtyard covered with lush, well-tended grass and populated by bronze statues of the Skornish kings. They were all approximately to scale, each mounted on a circular stone plinth. According to the staff, the oldest of them had been constructed five centuries earlier. None of the kings wore a crown but most carried iterations of the fabled Sceptre of Bruj. The original sceptre was always kept in the capital and Xalius looked forward to seeing it in the near future. It was said that the globe mounted at the peak of the sceptre was made of purest godglass – if that was true, it might come in exceptionally useful.

The statues were generally well maintained but several had been afflicted by corrosion. The decay seemed to lift the top layer of the metal, as if unpeeling the clothing and skin of the ancient monarchs. Xalius supposed he should have them torn down before the Imperator arrived but there was something about the statues that he found appealing. It would not do to question the will of either the Imperator nor Rael himself but he could not help questioning the wisdom of destroying everything that came before. After all, some old things were of great use – himself, for example.

He had almost reached the far side of the courtyard when he heard a door fly open. Planting his stick on the grass, he turned around and was met by the sight of Marshal Siad Borshan marching towards him. The Gragg's brutish face was frozen in a snarl and sweat gleamed upon his hairless head. Worse, his double-bladed axe was hanging from his shoulder. Much worse, he had three men with him. And when they got closer, Xalius could see that they were his bannermen – his most trusted advisers and bodyguards.

Xalius glanced back through the nearby doorway but could not see even a servant. Ogon was working on the tomes in this wing but was some distance away. At that particular moment, Xalius would have liked to have the young warlock with him; or any of his Waymakers for that matter.

Borshan came to a halt beside the closest of the statues, breathing like some enraged bull.

'The truth, Xalius – did you know the accursed vermin had been set loose in the woods again. *Did you?*'

Xalius brought his stick in front of him and placed both hands upon it. He split his mind in two and told the second part to begin to focus, prepare to cast if it became necessary. He had rarely seen Siad so angry.

'Has something happened?'

'Answer the question,' demanded the Gragg.

'I shall answer however I see fit. Perhaps if you can enlighten me-'

'This is a bloody-' These words came from one of the bannermen, a man as tall as Siad, whose expression was somehow even more angry. When the marshal's hand went up, he elected not to finish his sentence.

'Two dead,' stated Siad. 'One a respected officer. The other Reud.'

'My brother,' added the bannerman. Siad didn't object to this contribution.

Xalius now remembered that the two were siblings and understood why only three of the usual four bannermen were present. It would have been helpful if someone had told him such a senior figure was one of the two killed by the Beastkin. Still, he couldn't deny the satisfaction of hearing that Siad's honour had been so violated. Now the brutish swine knew how it felt.

The bannerman spoke in an enraged whisper. 'They dragged him away, ravaged and mauled him while he still breathed.'

Xalius turned to the brother, whose name he now recalled. 'My condolences, Tuek. It is clear that the assurances given by the Beastkin chiefs were worthless. This is an outrage. I will investigate at once.'

'Investigate?' scoffed Siad.

'I want blood,' hissed Tuek, who had apparently forgotten both his own status and that of the man he was addressing. '*Rat* blood. I'll carve my way through so many of them that the rest will run for the hills.'

Xalius kept his tone calm. 'Marshal Borshan, if your compatriot cannot control himself, I suggest you do so.'

Siad simply looked at him, fingers flexing. Though comparatively measured for a Gragg, Borshan had lost his temper a few times and the results were never pretty.

'The truth, Xalius. Do not lie to me. Did you know? Did you give the order?'

'I do not answer to you, marshal.'

'You do today. If I learn that Reud's blood is on your hands-'

Tuek reeled back under the force of Xalius' strike. It was no more than a middling mind-stun but enough to send the Gragg to his knees, hands gripping his brow.

'If you threaten me again, marshal, the next attack will be directed at *your* head – and it is no small target. I suggest you and your men leave; and return only when you are in a more amenable mood.'

Siad's right hand reached back for the handle of the axe that hung from his shoulder. The blade was as usual covered with leather.

'Really?' said Xalius. 'Surely you're not that stupid.'

Now Borshan spoke with a calculating calm. 'Clearly that is precisely what you believe me to be. We both know that Reud is dead because of you. You have dishonoured and insulted me. And all because a decrepit sorcerer has become obsessed with a girl too young even to be his granddaughter.'

Xalius felt his anger rising. In the right circumstances, rage could augment the Way and this increasingly felt like the right circumstance. Killing Siad would not be so very different to killing Mawraze. He was a legend among the armies of the Haar Dari and anyone who bested him would surely face resistance only from diehards like his bannermen.

And yet…the Imperator. Siad had not fought alongside Atavius as long as Xalius but killing him was still a huge risk. The situation, the relationship, could be salvaged. If he stayed calm.

But Siad now seemed to want the fight. 'People are talking about you and her, Xalius. People are laughing.'

Where is everyone? Where are my bloody warlocks?

Xalius would not have been overly concerned to face Siad alone, but there were four of them; all experienced men who knew the extent – and limit – of his abilities.

'I shall give you one last chance to leave.'

'I – we – are not going anywhere.' Siad took a step forward, his fingers closing around the shaft of the great axe.

'You dishonour *me*!' cried Xalius, mainly to call for help. 'Striking a girl you know to be under my care.'

'Your *care*? Is that what you call it, you dirty…old…man.' Siad slipped the axe from his shoulder and shook off the cover. Tuek had recovered himself. He and the other two Graggs had drawn their swords and now advanced alongside their general.

Xalius estimated that he was five paces from the door. With his aged bones, the soldiers would cut him down before he even got close.

'How often I have wished that Rael would take you in the night,' growled Siad. 'It is unnatural for anyone to live so long. You will die here, sorcerer – alone.'

'He is not alone,' said a young voice.

The air grew suddenly hot, the courtyard darkened and Xalius was sent tottering backwards by the concussive power of Wayforce. He struck the wall but did not fall. In front of him, the three bannermen lay on the ground, not one still in possession of his sword.

Ogon was staring at his master, hands still raised. 'Sir, what–'

His attention was taken by the fast-moving shape of Siad, who had lost his axe but recovered from the attack with remarkable speed. Seeing Siad charge at him, Ogon backed up to give himself time and swept his arm once more. The Wayforce tore a statue off its plinth and into Siad's path.

Xalius' attention was momentarily taken by the bannermen, two of whom were struggling to their feet. One was Tuek, who had just retrieved his sword.

Xalius glimpsed a flash of movement and was astonished to see Siad grab the statue then fling it at Ogon. The huge piece of bronze took the young mage high in the chest, knocking him clean off his feet and into another plinth behind him. His head struck the stone with a hollow thump and he slumped to the floor, the statue lying across his body.

Xalius had no more time to concern himself with the young man's fate. He allowed Tuek's first swing to knock his stick away then focused on the sword itself. This he pulled from the bannerman's grip before spinning it in the air and aiming it at his throat. With another sweep of his hand, he sent the tip straight into Tuek's windpipe. As blood bubbled from the wound, the bannerman collapsed head first into the grass.

His demise was enough to halt the other two but not Siad. With a bestial howl, the marshal picked up his axe and threw it two-handed at Xalius.

It wasn't the Waymaking. Xalius was as powerful as he had ever been and he could deal with the burning pain in his hands.

It was his age. He was old and slow and he knew with an overwhelming finality that the huge spinning weapon would cut him in half. Not a good way to die.

What he did not expect was for the axe to stop in mid-air then drop harmlessly onto the grass with a dull thud.

Siad evidently thought this was Xalius' doing because he was the last to notice the hooded figure floating gently to the ground in a corner of the courtyard. When he did notice, his expression became very similar to the two remaining bannermen, who swiftly dropped to their knees and threw their swords aside.

The Imperator landed and began walking in one smooth movement, robes trailing behind him. He glanced curiously at a nearby statue, then at his two subordinates. Despite the anger evident upon his ruined face, his tone was curious.

'Have I missed something?'

***

Malcanoth was awoken by a pulsing pain. He put a hand against the right side of his head and felt dried blood. The skin had been broken but the cut didn't feel too severe. The rest of his body simply ached. All around him was bright light.

'Move it away,' he murmured. 'Move that lamp away.'

'It's no lamp.' A hand gripped his shoulder and a fair, familiar face came into view. Malcanoth felt relief wash over him because there was no other face he would have preferred to see. Elaria was kneeling beside him and gradually his vision cleared enough for him to also see the soldiers sitting and lying on the grassy slope. Then he saw rocky walls and the glow of a high, hazy sun.

'I'm glad you're awake. Would you like some water?'

Malcanoth nodded and enjoyed every drop; his throat was incredibly dry.

'Are we…where…'

'This is the Low Gorge. Rycliff got us here. Not far from the cavern but it took a while.'

'What happened?'

'I didn't see it but Sanzir told us – the three of you brought a rock down and barred the dragon's path. Brannus was killed but you and Sanzir managed to get out of the way, even though you were knocked out. The men on the stretchers were all right too. We pulled you all out and then set off for here. Narg carried you most of the way.'

Malcanoth could see Sanzir, who was treating one of the injured. Narg was sitting alone, staring blankly at the ground.

'We have to keep moving.' He tried to get up but Elaria gripped his arm.

'We're leaving soon. Rycliff knows the way. He says we can be out of the mountains by sundown.'

Malcanoth's memory of the cavern was foggy; even the sequence of events was not clear in his mind. So much had happened in such a short span of time.

'Captain Farrow?'

'The dragon king killed him. Sergeant Norik is here though. He's hurt but he can walk.'

Malcanoth had not seen that and he found it hard to believe the captain was dead. He realised now that Captain Farrow had reminded him of Shai Kano. Both the officers had been so decisive and fearless. They had led from the front; and paid the price.

'Can I have some more water?'

Elaria gave him the flask and he drank it all.

'Can you help me up?'

Once on his feet, Malcanoth actually felt better than he'd expected. He could see Kals Rycliff walking up the slope towards him. Once sure he was steady, Elaria let go.

'Thank you for looking after me.'

When she answered only with a nod, he realised she was biting her lip, trying not to cry. Malcanoth didn't know what to say. Perhaps it was the intensity of such moments after battle but he realised now that she meant something to him: beyond admiration of her bravery, beyond appreciation of her beauty, he really did have feelings for her.

But she was young and a recruit and this was not the time. Malcanoth was more determined than ever that Elaria reach safety and get a chance to recover from the punishment she had endured since the Battle of Remmar. He wanted to say something but the words simply wouldn't come. He had never been articulate at the best of times and this was far from that.

'The worst is over. We'll make it to Laketon.'

She avoided his gaze but nodded again.

'We'll make it, Elaria. I promise you.'

He doubted she believed him and he couldn't blame her for that. He felt like embracing her, and he reckoned that would make them both feel a lot better. But it wasn't the right thing to do. Perhaps the time would come, but this wasn't it.

With a brief touch upon her arm, he headed down the slope.

***

Elaria wanted to embrace him, hold him close. And not only because she thought him attractive. She was glad Malcanoth was alive for all their sakes. With Farrow dead and Norik injured, the column would need him to lead them the rest of the way. And after so many had been lost, it was simply reassuring to see the modest, resourceful sergeant up on his feet.

As she stood there, alone, Elaria looked at every person sitting or standing upon the steep slope, just to be sure. And when she was done, she repeated the process, even though she knew the truth of it. After Dawin and all those killed at Remmar; after Captain Farrow and all those lost in these terrible mountains; now Treyda and Kryk were gone too. Treyda – who had always been there with a kind word and always put others before herself. Kryk – who had wanted nothing more than to serve his king and protect his kingdom. At least his death had been an honourable one. Elaria would make sure people knew of it; how he had sacrificed his young life for others.

Since joining the Pathfinders, she had seen tremendous courage and tenacity and unity. But she had also seen pain, ruin, suffering and death. And they had achieved nothing but survival.

This was a bloody, pointless business and she wanted nothing more to do with it. She could not simply watch while good people fell and wait for her turn to come. For years she had been the one hearing tales of this exciting life from Tamia and others; now she had plenty of tales of her own. She had been fortunate to make it this far but this was not the Pathfinder life she had dreamed of. All the good things about it seemed meaningless now. It had become a black nightmare and she longed for peace. Elaria wasn't even sure if she would stay with the column or go as far as Laketon.

She would be a Pathfinder no more.

***

Xalius had spent the last few days overseeing the formation of the baggage train. It made sense to gather the vehicles and supplies where there was space, and Darian had chosen the open meadows north of the city. Xalius sat under a canopy close to the road, surrounded by more than a hundred carts containing food, water, weaponry and equipment. It was almost midday and they were now awaiting the main column, which would be led out of Remmar by the Imperator himself.

Atavius had been in the city for eight days and had acted with typical decisiveness and speed. After listening briefly to the complaints of his deputies, he made Xalius and Siad swear by Rael that they would forget their differences. Considering that both had lost valued subordinates, the Imperator reckoned they had suffered equally and should therefore proceed without further rancour. There was of course no question of arguing with him and both complied. Xalius intended to honour that oath but keep further dealings with Siad to a minimum; communicate via their respective deputies wherever possible.

Barely an hour after arriving in Remmar, the Imperator had announced his intention to move against his next target with absolute haste. Xalius thought they were perhaps reaching too far too fast but – other than the incident with the Pathfinder patrol – the Haar Dari had encountered little resistance. The experimental Beastkin raid had been a resounding success and the Imperator clearly approved of how Xalius had handled them. He was also impressed by the progress of the experiments and had given his blessing for Skeltine's work to continue apace.

Atavius seemed quite proud of his own recent contribution; an agreement with the dragons of the Crystal Mountains. A potentially difficult complication had been avoided, leaving the Haar Dari free to focus on their human foes. Even so, Xalius suspected that the Imperator harboured ambitions of one day bending even those ancient, powerful creatures to his will.

He would have been quite happy to remain in Remmar but – if he had to travel – he wished to do so with as much comfort and safety as possible.

So, he had taken ownership of the largest and most luxurious carriage in all of Remmar, which was drawn by four strapping horses. He knew Atavius would not begrudge him this luxury; the Imperator had made his own choice when it came to transportation.

Xalius had also formed a new personal bodyguard of four. Among its members was Lisahra, who – though inexperienced – had already proved herself loyal and capable. The fact that her presence at his side would annoy Siad was an added benefit. Ogon was difficult to replace but Xalius had brought in another of his warlocks: Fyrex had honed an ability to sense the intentions of others, particularly hostiles – which made him exceptionally useful. Completing the team were two Irregulars that the spy Izilis had hand-picked for his master. The pair were brothers – hunters from the island of Takatari – who had killed dozens of foes for the Haar Dari. Xalius had trebled their wages and instructed them to never be more than twenty feet from his side. They were currently leaning against the carriage, sharpening knives. Fyrex was sitting beside one of the carriage's wheels, reading. Lisahra was also close by, juggling five apples with ease.

Xalius couldn't help feeling a bit sorry for poor old Darian as he picked his way through piles of horse shit. 'Sir, a flag from the sentries. The column is on its way.'

***

First came the vanguard: Siad and his two hundred Ironhands upon their huge steeds. Xalius had moved to the roadside to greet the column but the pair studiously ignored each other. Then came the Sand Lions: eight hundred of the black-skinned skirmishers. Then a thousand Irregulars, the rest left behind in Remmar to ensure the city's obedience. Next came the Haar Dari's newest recruits: seven hundred spearmen formerly under the command of King Flint. These ruthless fellows were being very well paid and their families back in Remmar were receiving preferential treatment. It was only a matter of time before others saw the wisdom of following their example. Next came two and a half thousand Wildfolk. For once, they did not constitute the most bizarre contingent of the Haar Dari force – this was provided by the one thousand Beastkin who formed the rearguard.

Accompanying the brood-chiefs was the Imperator himself; an honour he had bestowed upon these recent recruits to his army. As if the host behind him wasn't outlandish enough, Atavius had somehow tamed a huge desert dog and now sat atop the beast, one hand casually holding the chain around the creature's neck.

As he approached, the Haar Dari dropped to their knees, Xalius included. Atavius raised a hand in acknowledgement. The others kept their eyes on the ground but Xalius watched his master. Though he was hooded, his scarred features in shadow, Xalius was fairly sure he noted a smile.

As he stood, Lisahra came to stand beside him, scarcely able to hide her excitement as she watched the Imperator ride on. During the last few days, she had barraged her master with endless questions about what the leader of the Haar Dari had done, could do and would do. Xalius had enjoyed recounting tales of past glories though it annoyed him to see how much she admired Atavius.

'He likes all this, doesn't he?' she said. 'War. Conquest.'

Now Xalius smiled. 'Quite so. In fact, I would venture to say that he likes nothing more.'

Printed in Great Britain
by Amazon